A THOUSAND FACES

A THOUSAND FACES

JANCI PATTERSON

GARDEN
NINJ
BOOKS

Edited by Kristina Kugler
Cover Design by Melody Fender
Cover photograph from istockphoto.com/Johnnyhetfield
Author photo by Michelle D. Argyle

Published by Garden Ninja Books

JanciPatterson.com

First Edition: September 2015

0 9 8 7 6 5 4 3 2 1

For Brandon,
who writes about heroes
and is one.

ONE

When I stepped out of the parking garage in downtown San Jose, I looked exactly like Emmeline Sinclair. As I walked down the street toward Emmeline's engineering firm, I concentrated on keeping my face thinned, my nose pointed, and my eyes lightened. The comb Mom had bought at Emmeline's favorite jewelry store dug into the back of my skull, holding up my hair, which I'd faded to blonde to match Emmeline's subtle highlights. I glided down the street in three inch stilettos, a giant teal scarf wrapped around my neck—bought at the flea market where Emmeline liked to go on weekends. I was grateful for it, because the cut of the blouse was lower than I liked, and Emmeline's breasts were a full two cup sizes bigger than mine to emphasize it.

Emmeline might have had better fashion sense than me, but at least I had the intelligence not to walk three blocks every day in shoes with no arch support and no grip. This outfit was ridiculous; Emmeline was an engineer, not a movie star. But today I would wear it, because that's what Emmeline always did, and my job was to be exactly like Emmeline.

My parents were counting on it.

As I approached the building, I pulled the lanyard bearing Emmeline's name tag out from under my scarf. It doubled as a key card—a method of security as common as it was easy to duplicate.

The lobby was open, so I didn't need to scan the card to get in.

The real test wasn't the door. It was one thing to look like Emmeline, and another to act the part so her co-workers wouldn't notice anything amiss. As I moved through the revolving doors, I tossed my scarf over my shoulder with a flick of my wrist, like I'd seen her do in the security footage.

My shoulder twinged. Mom had made me practice that little maneuver a few too many times. Between that and the stilettos, I was going to need a chiropractor after this.

I strode across a lobby filled with large fake ficus. A security guard—Frank—stood behind a counter looking down at his workstation. He sipped coffee from an extra-large Styrofoam cup. Even if he'd been a useful mark, I couldn't have impersonated him; Frank had a jagged scar over his left eyebrow—something that even my parents couldn't duplicate.

"Morning, Em," Frank said.

"Good morning," I said. I'd practiced this interaction from security recordings. I wanted to say his name, to prove I knew it, but Emmeline never did that. Frank probably wouldn't have noticed the difference, but lots of little inconsistencies would gather his attention, even if Frank couldn't put his finger on why. When it came to impressions, trying too hard was the easiest way to fail.

Don't be nervous, I told myself. I was Emmeline, confident engineer today, not Jory, frightened girl on her very first solo job. I'd been doing impressions since I was a child, but impersonating my best self was always the hardest one.

I headed down the hall to the elevator, resisting the urge to tug at the front of my shirt. These weren't my breasts; they were Emmeline's. But that didn't make me feel less exposed.

The doors opened just as I got to them; Frank had called the car from the front desk. He was good at his job, and I was glad it wasn't him I was here to embarrass.

I forced myself not to wince. Even that was a sign that I was soft. My parents wouldn't have thought twice about getting him fired, if the price was right.

Once in the elevator, I scanned Emmeline's name tag, which would give me access to the fourteenth floor: the research and development department.

When I stepped out of the elevator I found myself in a small sub-lobby with nothing but a padded bench, an emergency phone, and an identity verification machine. My heart beat faster. This was what professionals called a man trap. I'd come through one set of security measures, with more still in front of me. If Frank suspected anything, he could lock down the machines on either side while he called for backup. My hand went to my face. There was Emmeline's long nose, her sharp cheeks. There was no reason for him to doubt my impression.

The only thing standing between me and Emmeline's office was my nemesis: the eye scanner. I stepped up to the biometric machine, concentrating on breathing normally. Frank could see me through the security cameras, and there was no reason for Emmeline to be afraid of an eye scan she passed every day.

I, on the other hand, had studied for this test for hours, and I still wasn't sure I could do it. An iris or a fingerprint required too much concentration to hold on to for a long period of time—it was too intricate, so I couldn't bring it with me like I did the rest of the persona. I had to be able to summon it from memory. Mine was sharp—a good memory was a survival skill for a shifter.

But the number of variables in an iris scan stretched it to its limits.

I put my hand on the palm pad first. Emmeline always did both the eye and hand scanner together, but if I tried to do both at once, I'd be twice as likely to fail. I'd chance one tiny inconsistency if it meant improving my odds of getting through. I'd matched each detail of the fingerprints at home, practicing over and over until I could do the whole thing in seconds. Now the scanner lit up, reviewing each wrinkle and crease. A green light flashed.

I relaxed my shoulder muscles, loosening the knots forming in my neck.

I'd passed.

Now the eyes.

We talk about eye color like it's simple. Mine are brown; yours are blue. But the truth is that irises are colored in complex patterns—much more complicated than the sheen of highlighted hair, or the tilt of a nose. Those things could be faked to create a general impression that would fool the human eye.

But the scanner? If I was even a millimeter off of Emmeline's iris pattern, it would know. I adjusted my irises, pushing them into the scattered star pattern of Emmeline's blue eyes. I sharpened the ring of brown around the outside of them, making sure I had the ripples of its edges just right. The center of the star I tightened last.

Unlike a fingerprint, the lines of the pattern didn't follow one from another, which made it harder to ensure I'd gotten every bit right. But I couldn't stand here forever fiddling with it. Frank was watching.

I pushed my face against the forehead rest and stared into the light ahead. The machine made a low beep, and the light inside it turned off. I looked down at the palm pad. The light now glowed red.

The knots in my neck reformed. I squeezed my tear ducts, narrowing them to avoid all danger of crying on the job. I'd done this at home. I should be able to do it now.

Of course, when I failed at home I was able to try again with no consequences. If only I could stop thinking about those now.

I took a deep breath, reshaped the iris stars, and pressed the palm pad again, but the machine just made the same low beep noise. The tiny room seemed to close in tight around me.

Failure number two. Either our practice scanner wasn't as sharp as this one was, or, more likely, I'd failed to match the exact details of the pattern.

Was it the center of the iris that was off, or the edges? If it were a fingerprint I'd be able to trace it through and find the problem.

10

With eyes? No such luck. And I'd gotten it right so many times at home.

I straightened up to Emmeline's full height, shifting my spine fully erect. I'd wanted to do this job perfectly, to prove to Dad that I could. But now it was time for a different kind of test.

The door opened behind me, and a security guard walked in—Leonard this time, not Frank, who wasn't supposed to leave the lobby. "Morning, Emmeline," Leonard said.

I tried to be aware of my body, holding Emmeline's neck and arms still and confident, so Leonard wouldn't perceive I was upset. The real Emmeline would be annoyed, but she wouldn't take a malfunction personally. Projecting that emotion at Leonard would draw undue attention.

"Morning," I said. I kept my voice as light as I could manage, and tilted my chin to the side, the way I'd seen Emmeline do when she spoke. "Scanner's being picky."

Leonard looked at me and at the scanner. He jabbed a ballpoint pen into the reset button on the side. "Try it again?"

The walls pressed in further. This time he might notice if I did the pieces separately. I hadn't let go of the handprint, though, so I put my palm back on the reader, and looked into the eye scanner. Perhaps I'd made the center of the eye too tight. I loosened the pattern a little and hit the button again.

The machine made the low beep a third time. I let my brow furrow, both for Emmeline and for me.

Failure number three.

I let my neck muscles wind tighter. Mom always said that if we had to let the frustration go somewhere, at least work it out internally, where it wouldn't show.

Outwardly, I spoke slowly in Emmeline's cool, gliding voice. "It worked yesterday," I said.

Leonard pressed his own palm and forehead to the machine. The light glowed green, and I heard the door snap open. "Huh," he said. "It's not the machine."

Oh, crap. I clamped down on my lungs, controlling my

breathing. Excuses raced through my mind.

I heard my Dad's voice in my mind. *Stay calm*, he always said. *Don't make excuses. You'll just sound guilty. Let them find their own explanations.*

And, after a moment, Leonard did. "Maybe your data is corrupted." He gave the machine a dirty look. "I'll make a report."

I forced a smile. "Thanks," I said. I gathered myself up to Emmeline's full height, and moved toward the exit to the man trap.

Leonard held the door open as I passed.

I kept that smile pasted on my face as I walked down the hall. Leonard was also good at his job—he'd come to check that I was actually Emmeline, instead of just bypassing the eye scan portal remotely, like a lazy guard might have. Dad said not to judge security guards just because we foiled them. Odds were slim that either Frank or Leonard had ever heard of a shifter.

Good thing, because if he had, I'd have been screwed.

I walked down the hall to Emmeline's office and sat down in her chair. The seat back stretched up over my head, and the swivel glided so smoothly that I wanted to kick my legs out and twirl around. But Emmeline wasn't the twirling type.

Time to get the job done, before Emmeline's co-workers stopped by to ask her questions I couldn't answer. I plugged my flash drive into Emmeline's computer and restarted it, using the keyboard commands Kalif had given me to enter on startup.

For me, this job was a test, but not for Kalif. He was only six months older than me, but he worked for my parents all the time, and had been working for his for years. The program he'd installed on the flash drive bypassed Emmeline's computer security and let me onto her desktop. I opened her computer files and found the information on the new tablet prototype she was overseeing. I set the files to download while I was working.

I took a deep breath. The data theft was just a side project. It might help Mom and Dad or Kalif's parents with assignments for other companies, or they might just sell the information. When it came to new tech development, there was always a buyer.

Now for the real job, and then to get out of the building as quickly as I could. I opened the web browser and typed in the string of commands I'd memorized—a protocol to upload Kalif's files to their server via FTP. They'd break down the internal firewalls that kept one department from looking at the work of the others. Kalif had designed the program himself. He was brilliant like that.

The breach would be discovered immediately, by design. The client was the company's systems manager, who was also the son of the owner. He'd been telling his dad for years that their network security had all sorts of holes in it—that anyone running an inside job could easily compromise it. But his father wouldn't listen, so he hired my parents to create a problem his father couldn't ignore. He'd be monitoring the system. The servers would be shut down within minutes, and he'd be the hero who discovered the problem. After that, his father would have to raise the network security budget.

I watched the download progress on Emmeline's computer screen. As soon as it finished, I could make my exit. The progress bar was at ninety percent when a knock came at the door.

I froze. *Stay calm*, I told myself. These people might not be expecting a shifter, but if they thought Emmeline had just tampered with their network security, they might detain me. It wouldn't take long for anyone who knew Emmeline to determine that I wasn't her, and the situation would deteriorate from there. This was why my parents rarely let me out on field missions, and never alone like this before. If I screwed up, I might not get another job until I was twenty.

I switched off the computer screen, and waited until I was sure I could speak casually in Emmeline's voice.

"Yes?" I asked.

The door opened. A woman with a pixie cut stood there, wearing a flowing brown blouse, a pair of slacks, and brown flats. She was one of Emmeline's co-workers, another engineer.

13

I wished we could have picked her as our target, but she had braces. Our bodies couldn't shift into anything unnatural, and dental installations were out of the budget for this particular job, even if it had been safe for us to wear them. Which, since we couldn't shift them, it wasn't.

"Hey, Em," she said.

I forced a smile. "Hi, Brooke."

It took all my effort not to cringe. There I went, throwing out names just to prove that I knew them.

"Did you get the email about the meeting this morning?"

Thanks to Kalif's AM hack, I had. "Pushed back an hour," I said.

"Right. I was thinking we could use that time to go over the presentation again."

I chewed the inside of my cheek, where Brooke wouldn't be able to see. Now? I knew nothing about Emmeline's presentation. I could put her off, but the more things I committed to, the more pieces of evidence there would be that I'd been here instead of Emmeline.

I put my hand on the phone and gave Brooke an apologetic look. "I've got someone on hold," I said. "Sorry, my head's a bit full at the moment. Ask me again in twenty minutes?" I tried to casually cover the hold lights with my fingers, so she wouldn't see that they were all dark.

Then the phone rang.

I gave her a flustered smile, letting some of my real feelings show through. "Seriously," I said. "I've been here five minutes, and it just won't stop."

Brooke nodded. "Big day. I get it. I'll be back."

She shut the door on her way out, and I melted back into my chair. I needed to get out of here, stat.

But first I answered the phone. "Hello?" I said, in Emmeline's voice.

"Oh, hi," a stranger's voice said. "I just wanted to let you know you forgot your dog's collar."

That was the code, to let me know the real Emmeline had arrived across town to pick up her dog. Even though I was alone in the office, I made my face look concerned. "I'll be right there." The line went dead, and I tapped my nails on Emmeline's desktop calendar while the files finished. Kalif's dad had let the dog out last night when he broke into her house and stole her cell phone. He was supposed to call her on her house line today to tell her he'd found her dog, and then Kalif's mom was supposed to turn off her land line and her internet, so she couldn't call into work to say she was going to be late.

That was the other problem with Brooke. She didn't have a dog.

My data finished downloading, and I pulled the thumb drive from the computer.

The job was done. Time to make my exit.

I stood up and walked back down the hall to the elevator. These heels were beginning to wear on my ankle. I buffed up a callus to protect it.

Getting out was easier than getting in. I didn't need an eye scan to leave, nor a key card to select the lobby. I gave Frank a worried glance on my way back. "I just got a phone call," I said. "My dog escaped from the yard. I need to go pick her up and take her home."

"Glad she's safe," Frank said. "It's strange. The IT department says there's nothing wrong with your data. Leonard told them he saw it fail with his own eyes, but they said there shouldn't be an issue."

I edged toward the door. Getting caught by Frank would only be marginally better here in the open than inside the man trap. "Those IT guys," I said. "They never believe there's a problem."

Frank chuckled. "Ain't that the truth. Leonard'll meet you at the scanner when you get back. We'll find the issue if I have to call them down there myself."

My heart pounded. "That's not necessary," I said. "Let's see if the problem resurfaces before we bother them."

15

"Eh," Frank said. "It's their job to be bothered."

I forced a grateful smile, when really I wanted to beg him to forget about it. "Thanks," I said. And I turned and strode away from him, careful not to look like I was running even though that's exactly what I wanted to do.

Ugh. It would have been a clean job, if I just could have handled the eyes. Now when Emmeline returned she'd be more likely to talk to Frank about her dog problem, and discover that he'd already seen her this morning, even though she hadn't been in. That would raise her suspicions, so she might question Brooke if she implied that she'd asked her the question about the presentation already today.

I walked out through the revolving doors, around the back of the building, and found a car waiting for me by the Dumpster, out of sight of the back door security camera. In the front seat were two people I'd never seen before, a man and a woman. The woman sat behind the wheel. The man had a thick head of unfamiliar black hair, but I recognized his eyebrows. He'd used them before.

I tried not to physically trudge toward the car. Not only was that unprofessional, but someone might be watching. I paused at the driver's side window to take the woman's hand before I got in the car. It grew smooth and cool on the surface as she gripped mine, and I pushed mine to become warmer, just like Mom and I always did. Then I made my hand sweat a little while Mom chilled hers gradually, a degree at a time. This was shifter code—the only way we could make sure that we were really looking at each other and not a copy.

The man on the passenger side reached across, extending me his hand as well. I was pretty sure that this was Dad based on the eyebrows, but we couldn't be too careful, so I took it, checking that his palms grew softer at the edges as our grip tightened, and thinned my own, nearly to the bone. This was definitely my father. No one else knew the code—not even Mom. We had to take care to keep them private and complex, so they wouldn't be given away if we gave the first part of the code to the wrong person.

I climbed into the back seat. "Stop using those eyebrows," I told Dad. "I remember them."

Dad grimaced. "Will do."

I should have been happy that even a professional like him could make a mistake. But there was a big difference between using elements his shifter daughter would recognize and exposing us to security on the job.

As Mom pulled out of the alley and turned onto the busy street, I handed Dad the flash drive.

"You got the data?" he asked.

"Yup. And uploaded the files. Firewall should be dropping any minute now."

"Then it's all in the client's hands," Dad said. "Did you have any trouble?"

I slouched in my seat. "I failed the eye scan," I said. "Three times. But Leonard let me in anyway."

Dad groaned. "You practiced that for hours."

I kicked off Emmeline's punishing heels. I hadn't forgotten. "I must have lost the details. I'm sorry."

"It's okay," Mom said, mostly to him. "All that mattered for this job was that you get through, and you did that."

She didn't sound convinced, and from the look on Dad's face when he twisted around in his seat, I knew he wasn't, either.

"Did you play it off?" he asked.

I cringed. "Yes. He didn't suspect anything. But Frank's going to talk to Emmeline about it when she comes in, so there's basically no way they won't be confused about what happened."

Dad picked at the lint on the back of the seat. He always did that when he was upset, and trying not to take it out on Mom and me.

"How can I fix it?" I asked. "Should I go back in? Be a maintenance worker? Pretend to fix the scanner?"

Mom shook her head. "The client will want to cover our

tracks. He'll make excuses for us. They'll be confused, but that doesn't mean they'll jump to the right conclusions."

Dad nodded, but when he turned around in his seat, he kept his eyes on the side mirror, watching behind us.

Mom put a hand on his arm. "It'll be fine," she said.

"Sure," Dad said. But he didn't relax.

I sat up straight and looked at the traffic behind us. There were lots of cars—the tail end of the morning rush. It was impossible to tell if any of those cars were following us specifically, but I knew that wasn't all Dad was looking for.

He was also searching for black vans.

Eight months ago, Dad had been on a job stealing a prototype from Megaware, and someone followed him home. The next night, a row black vans rolled down our street, slowing down, looking. We moved, of course. Dad wanted to leave the state, but Mom convinced him that one small slip didn't merit giving up all the profiling work and all the job leads they had in the Bay Area. Dad agreed, and they settled on a new apartment one city over, which, combined with our new names and ever changing faces, should have been enough. We'd moved again since then, but as much as Dad tried to cover it, he was still watching.

Mom put a hand on Dad's arm. "It's fine," she said again. "No one's following us."

Dad nodded at Mom and readjusted the side mirror, but then he leaned over to watch behind us out of the rearview.

I closed my eyes. Mom never wanted me to go out on jobs— Dad was the one who said that if they didn't give me a positive outlet for my abilities, I'd find ways to use them on my own. He was the one who'd taken me with him on small missions, working me up to this opportunity to try one on my own. But if working with me made him nervous now, he might agree with Mom that I shouldn't be in the field.

I ran my still-long nails over the seat upholstery. I didn't need them anymore, and no one outside the car could see them, so I let them slide down toward my normal shorter length. Mom was right—if my mistake was going to come down on anyone, it would be Emmeline. Mom and Dad regularly got people fired, or arrested, by pinning jobs on them. The only thing we didn't do was kill people—*ever*—no matter how much easier it might make our work. Legends told of dark, shape-changing assassins in the shadows, but that wasn't us. It was the first rule, and the only rule.

It always made me nervous that we didn't have more. Mom and Dad worked like a well-oiled machine—get in, get the job done, get out. I was too new at this, too green. I couldn't help but think about the people whose lives we were ruining.

Maybe that distraction was part of my problem. Like my parents always said, we were shifters. Fooling people was our life and our business. I hated that I wasn't perfect at it, because little slipups created suspicions, and suspicions caused rumors. If we were lucky, rumors became legends. If not, they grew into beliefs.

I shivered, tugging Emmeline's dress to cover more of my shoulders. At all costs, we had to avoid inspiring belief, because that would be followed by action, and, inevitably, violence.

Mom saw Dad peeking in the rearview and adjusted it so he couldn't see behind us anymore. She gave Dad's shoulder a squeeze, and Dad let out a long sigh, finally relaxing back into his seat.

I tried to relax as well. If I'd screwed this up, they'd fix it. Or, if they couldn't, we'd run, together.

At least I had my parents. Without them, I'd be entirely lost.

TWO

On the way home, Mom pulled through an underground parking garage. When the car was angled lower, blocking us from view of any security, we all shifted back to our home bodies.

Instead of the deliberate flexing that turned me into Emmeline, to shift back I just needed to relax. My home body was the one my body wanted to be—the one that was a reflection of my own self-image. When we drove out of the parking lot, we looked like a family. My hair was a shorter version of Mom's fluffy brown; my forehead a smaller, more feminine version of Dad's wide heart shape. I looked more like my parents than a regular person would, since my subconscious body literally made itself in their image.

The first order of business after any job was to go to the Johnson's townhouse to report. As Mom pulled into their driveway, I sank down in my seat. Telling Aida I messed the job up would be bad; listening to Mel razz me about it would be worse. But I really, really didn't want to fail in front of Kalif. He'd helped me train with the eye scanner; he was so sure I could do this. And then I went and messed it up. "I'll just wait in the car," I said.

Mom turned off the car and reached between the seats to pat me on the knee. "This was your job," she said, "and it's not done until you report."

My body shrank smaller against the seat. Little shifts like that were almost imperceptible—since people's bodies were always changing slightly due to mood, hygiene, and health, normal people wouldn't notice.

But my parents weren't normal. I could tell by the way Dad eyed me through the car window that he noticed. "Come on," he said. "You got the job done. You don't need to be ashamed of one little mistake."

Maybe not, but I'd wanted to excel, not just skate by.

I climbed out of the car, leaving Emmeline's shoes on the floor. I didn't understand why women wore shoes it took so much practice to walk in. In my mind, shoes were for making your feet more comfortable, not less. But since I dressed like other women as much as I dressed like myself, I was out of luck.

Mom knocked on the door, and Aida answered it. Her dark eyes and dark hair were a mirror image of Kalif's, or, I supposed, the reverse.

"Come in," Aida said. She stepped aside and we all wandered into her kitchen. Mel sat at the table, working on a laptop.

We exchanged hands all around, checking for the right palm codes. We all had separate ones for each other person, which could have gotten out of hand, except that our two families represented all five of the shifters I knew: my parents, and the three Johnsons.

Their last name wasn't really Johnson, of course. I would have been surprised to discover that their real names were really Mel and Aida, but that's what they called themselves, so that's what we called them. Mom and Dad had been working with them since Aida and Dad discovered each other while on assignment six months ago. Aida had the opportunity to pin her own job on Dad, but instead she covered for him and invited him to work with her.

Before the problem at Megaware, he would never have taken her up on it, but I think he was worried about what would happen to Mom and me if those black vans ever caught up to him. He and Mom spent a month following Mel and Aida around first, to make sure they were who they said they were. Even then,

I knew Mom and Dad were always ready to bolt. That was the nature of our business. We could never really trust anybody.

When we finished the hand signals, Aida beamed at me. "I just got off the phone with the client. He told me the security glitch showed, and he has his people shutting it down. He had just enough time to gather evidence for his father, but not so much as to create a major security breach. He's thrilled."

Dad clapped me on the shoulder. "That's my girl," he said.

I smiled, shifting my shoulders into a more relaxed posture. Dad had my back. Now that we were standing in front of Aida, all traces of nervousness and disappointment were gone. Dad might be a mess these days, but he was also a fine actor. We all were. The job required it.

But full disclosure was part of the report. I caused a problem, so the whole team needed to be aware of it. Might as well get it over with. "I failed the eye scan," I said to Aida. "The security guard is planning to follow up."

Mel looked up from his computer screen. "I told you we should have sent Kalif."

I forced my body to stay loose. Kalif was awesome behind his computer, but he never did field work. Mel was just trying to get under my skin—and it was working.

Dad laughed. "I've seen Kalif's impression of a woman. He couldn't have gotten past the front door."

I glared at Dad. That was true, but uncalled for. "Hey," I said. "Quit it."

Dad was right, though, and I could tell by the gritted teeth that Mel knew it. His gaze softened as he turned to me. "You should work with him on that," he said. "We all know I've tried."

Finally. An excuse to get out of this conversation. "Is he downstairs?" I asked.

"Of course," Aida said. "Go on down."

I bounced out of that room even faster than I'd left Frank's lobby.

Kalif was almost always downstairs. His bedroom was in the basement, and doubled as the tech room. His parents had been letting him run their personal server for years, maintaining all their internet security and running their online surveillance.

As I headed down, I found the door to the basement open. Kalif sat behind his computer, his eyes glued to the screen. The rest of us looked Caucasian; Dad said it was because we lived in the States, where even in this day and age, white was the color of power. Kalif's skin was a shade darker, and his bone structure looked like he might be of Arab descent. I'd wondered why that was, but hadn't asked. Asking a shifter why he looked the way he did was like poking around in his psyche, and much as I might want to be, Kalif and I weren't that close.

It wasn't genetic, that was for sure. We couldn't truly shift until we were older, but even as babies, our newborn features formed in the likeness of the parent we bonded to at birth— usually our mothers. As we aged, we'd grow to look more like our fathers as well, but we couldn't know what our genetic selves looked like until we were dead.

When Kalif didn't look up, I hesitated. He was no doubt in the middle of hacking some computer to get important information for his parents, or mine. That was the difference between me and Kalif: I got to run errands occasionally, but he did vital work every day.

I walked into the room and took the stool beside him at his desk, waiting quietly for him to look up at me.

When he did, I slouched. "I failed that eye scan," I said. "Repeatedly."

He looked ruefully at his computer screen. "I failed this four gate."

I leaned over to look. His screen was full of images of soldiers destroying buildings with blue explosions.

Okay, so maybe not *everything* he did was vital.

I smacked his arm. "Yes," I said. "Your video game is totally as important as my mission."

"Obviously," Kalif said. "Goes without saying." He grinned at me, and his eyes caught on my clothing. He quickly looked away, and I swear his cheeks grew a little pinker before he corrected them.

It wasn't until then that I became fully aware of myself sitting there in my home body and Emmeline's clothes. My own body might not fill it out like Emmeline's did, but it was still more revealing than anything I usually wore in front of Kalif. Plus Emmeline's bra wasn't exactly offering support.

This time, I did tug at the neckline.

"You look great," he said. But he kept his eyes glued to his keyboard.

I tugged even harder on my blouse, and checked my bra straps. "Shut up," I said. "It's just a costume."

Kalif straightened his mouse pad. "I know. I was just saying you look nice in it. That's all."

He thought I looked nice? In Emmeline's clothes? "Well," I said, "you should have seen me as Emmeline. She's movie-star gorgeous."

Kalif shot me a skeptical look. "Maybe," he said. "But if your subconscious looked like that, you'd be unbearable to talk to."

I smiled, stretching my neck and torso into Emmeline's slender super-model build. "Please," I said. "Tell me this isn't an improvement."

Kalif shook his head. "Cut it out. You looked better before."

The room grew warmer. I snapped back to my home body. He thought I looked better this way?

He thought about how I looked . . . at all?

My pulse picked up, and I focused on keeping my face from flushing. When I dared to look up again, I found Kalif staring at his hands.

If I could have, I would have shifted into the stool I sat on: plain, and unsexy. I should have just dropped it when he looked at me. He'd been embarrassed by the way I was dressed, and my dragging the moment on just embarrassed him further. He probably thought I was fishing—trying to get him to say I was beautiful.

Now, I just wanted to become the office furniture. But, alas. We couldn't turn into anything that wasn't human.

I stayed as myself.

Kalif cleared his throat. "So, did you get caught?"

"No. I covered."

Kalif looked impressed. "So you didn't fail."

I cringed. "Not technically. But I left a mess."

"Meh. I can match an eye scan, but I couldn't talk myself out if I didn't."

I smiled. It was sweet of him to try to make me feel better. "Yeah, well," I said. "The rest of us can run the missions, but none of us can handle the server."

Kalif patted the box on his desk. "I keep her company."

"Please," I said. "You've been keeping her company since you were thirteen. That makes you some kind of prodigy."

Kalif grinned. "It makes me a bored kid with no friends. But if you're going to call me a prodigy, I'm not going to argue."

He had more reason not to argue than he'd admit. Before my parents met the Johnsons, they kept all their records on paper, written in a cipher. It took Kalif's parents quite a while to convince them that keeping the information encrypted on a server was actually much safer and more reliable. I wasn't sure if the Johnsons knew, but my parents hired a guy to hack into the server before they handed Kalif a single one of their files, just to make sure that their information would be safe. The guy had a ton of experience, but he couldn't crack Kalif's security.

"Jory?" Dad called down from the top of the stairs.

I stepped into the basement doorway. "Yeah?"

Dad paused, giving me a strange look.

I shot him one back. "What?"

Kalif leaned into the doorway, and Dad smiled like he'd just heard an amusing joke. "Nothing," he said. "Your mom and I are going home. You coming?"

I nodded. Better go now before I embarrassed myself further.

"Later," I said to Kalif.

He waved goodbye. "If you want to practice eye scans some more later, I'll be around."

"I will," I said. Just as soon as my ego recovered.

I walked out to the car in my bare feet. Mom had barely started the engine before Dad turned around and eyed me.

"You sure look nice," he said.

I ran a hand through my hair, but it felt normal.

Mom glared at him. "Dale."

"What?" he asked. Then he snickered.

Mom smacked his shoulder with the back of her hand.

I glanced down at my neckline, but nothing was showing. Clearly I was missing something. "What?" I asked. "What did I do?"

Mom looked over her shoulder at me. "Your face is thinner."

I put my hands to my cheeks. Crap. They were right. I wasn't intentionally shifting, but my waist had tightened, too, forcing my figure into a true hourglass.

I leaned my head back against the seat, closing my eyes. With shifts this tiny, a normal boy wouldn't have noticed.

But Kalif wasn't exactly normal.

Good job, Jory. Way to be obvious.

Dad kept going. "It's been doing that a lot lately. But it mysteriously only happens when that young man is around."

"Dale," Mom said again. "Stop it."

"I didn't do it on purpose," I said. That, of course, was Dad's point. My body responded to what my subconscious wanted—for Kalif to find me attractive.

My face flushed. This time, I let it burn.

Apparently failing to let embarrassing things drop ran in the family, because Dad charged ahead. "It pains me," he said, "that my own daughter has absorbed the cultural standard that thin is the same as pretty."

"That's not entirely true," Mom said. "Her body is curvier, too."

Now they both snickered.

I clutched the front of my blouse to my chin. "Argh," I said. "Did I really do that?"

Dad broke out in a full laugh. I buried my face in my hands.

"Don't encourage her," Mom said. But she was still stifling a laugh.

"It's okay," I said through my hands. "I'm not exactly feeling encouraged."

"Hmm," Mom said. "Still."

I knew what she meant. Mom had told me a thousand times not to get too attached to Kalif. We were working with his family for now, but shifters could never stay in one place for long. I'd left apartments, houses, neighbors, childhood playmates, even the stuffed tiger I loved as a child. I was used to living my life like the only pieces of it I could keep were my parents. I knew I couldn't be with Kalif. He wasn't interested anyway. I was just parading around like he was, humiliating myself.

I squeezed my eyes shut. "Do you think he noticed?"

The car bumped as Dad pulled into our driveway—just down the street from the Johnson's. We'd moved to their townhouse complex to be closer to them after we started working together. "Did you notice his shifts? I swear that boy's dimples get bigger every time he sees you."

I snapped upright. He liked me?

Oh, no. That was the wrong thing to hope for. If Kalif was interested, I was being unfair to him by leading him on.

"Really?" I asked.

"Don't worry," Mom said. "If he's reciprocating, that probably just means he finds it flattering."

I slouched down in my seat. Great. Now we were back to humiliation.

Dad unbuckled his seatbelt. "Just what that kid needs. An ego boost."

"Oh, come on," I said. "He's not like that. It's just his dad."

Dad climbed out of the car and walked into the house. I

27

could see him still chuckling all the way to the door. Mom turned around in her seat, giving me an apologetic smile.

I rubbed my forehead. "I didn't mean to be so obvious."

Mom draped her arms around the headrest. "But you do like him."

I rolled my eyes. "What do you expect?" I asked. "He's the only shifter guy I've ever met." Being both brilliant and sweet was also a winning combination.

Mom shook her head. "Don't feel like he's the only guy in the world. You'll meet others."

I raised an eyebrow at her. "Other shifters?"

She shrugged. "You don't have to date shifters."

"I know," I said. Relationships were complicated for us, though. It took a lot of trust to be with someone who could literally change their face and do whatever they wanted when you weren't looking. It was one thing to have that trust between two shifters, but for a normal person to trust a shifter that much . . . I just didn't see a relationship like that lasting very long. Plus, they always had to begin with deception, since we couldn't go around telling the full truth to everyone we were interested in.

I picked at a tear in the seat upholstery, digging out strands of white fluff with my nail. I knew I couldn't be with Kalif, but I wouldn't have minded finding him again in a few years, when we were older and more ready to be on our own. I squinted at Mom. "Did you embarrass yourself like this when you first met Dad?"

Mom's eyebrows shot up.

"Not that I'm thinking about marrying him," I said quickly. "I know we won't be around forever."

Mom gave me a wary look. "But it's on your mind."

I squirmed. "You guys brought this up. Not me."

Mom's face softened, and as she looked out the car window, it seemed to shift younger, so she looked more like me. "I was embarrassed that your dad found me," she said. "He was running a job at the company I'd been conning for months. I was a beginner then—anyone might have caught me. I was lucky that your dad was the one who did. He took me—or my persona, I suppose—out to dinner and told me he knew what I was. I was about to break for the door when he shifted his hands under his napkin, showing me he was the same." She looked at me dreamily. "He was the first other shifter I ever met. He taught me everything. I don't know what I would have done if I hadn't met him when I did."

I melted into my seat. If Mom meant to make me less attracted to Kalif, this wasn't helping. "And did you change yourself to impress him?"

Mom nodded. "It took several months before I showed him my home face. But the personas I picked in the meantime were all conventionally beautiful. Like I said, I was a beginner. It took years for me to catch up to his skill."

I smiled. I'd never heard that story in so much detail before. Dad's parents were both shifters, but Mom's weren't, so it made sense that he'd been more experienced than her. Dad said shifters were literally one in a million—there was only one of us for every million people on earth. But being born to normal parents made Mom more like one in a hundred million. She'd had it rougher than most of us.

"So did you know right away?" I asked. "That you loved him?"

Mom rested her chin on the back of the seat. "I'm not trying to encourage you, you know."

My cheeks burned some more, but I planted my palms on the edge of the seat. "Please? I just want to hear the rest of the story."

Mom smiled. "He says he knew. But I think I was caught up in the thrill of being saved, and I let that convince me for a while. Love came later."

"Before you were a team? Or after?"

"During," Mom said. "I think it's the way we worked together that made me really convinced that I couldn't live without your father."

"That's why I don't want to date normal guys," I said. "I want that."

29

"Well," Mom said. "Be careful with Kalif."

I picked up one of Emmeline's shoes, toying with the buckle. "You're right, though. He probably doesn't even like me."

Mom gave me a look.

"What?" I asked. "It's not like he's putting moves on me. If he knows, he's probably just flattered, like you said." Those sounded like excuses, even to me. Ugh. "Next time I see him, I'll try not to send any more embarrassing signals."

Mom gave me a knowing look. "Come in the house," she said. "I'll try to make sure your dad lets this go. You try to forget about it, too. It's good for you to have friends your age. Just enjoy it."

Sure. Enjoy just-friendship with the sweetheart shifter genius who just happened to live practically next door.

No problem, Mom.

As I walked into the house, Mom put a hand on my shoulder. "Your dad and I are set to go at three AM, so we'll probably be asleep when you go to bed. We'll be home by breakfast."

I nodded. They'd been running late night missions without me since I was nine. "Be careful," I said.

"Always," Mom said.

As she walked upstairs, I was aware that my face had shifted even younger than normal. Tonight they'd be doing real work, the kind they'd prepared for over months. And I'd stay home, like I was still a child.

I drew myself up to my full height, short though that was. They'd sent me out on one mission. If I could just get some more practice, maybe I could get good enough to be a regular part of the team.

For that, though, I'd need more than better eye scanner skills. The rest of our team moved through missions with confidence, certain of their goals, certain they would succeed.

I hoped that part came with practice, too.

THREE

When I woke up the next morning, I rolled out of bed and looked at myself in my full-length mirror. My subconscious controlled my body in my sleep, reverting to my home body whether I liked it or not. Whatever I was feeling, it was bound to show up in my first-thing reflection, before I started making subtle changes. Today my face was rounder and puffier than normal, making me look younger than I was.

Like the kid who always got left at home. Ugh. I needed to find something useful to do, stat.

Maybe Mom would have something for me, now that they'd finished their job.

I walked down the hall to Mom and Dad's room. I expected the door to be closed, since they'd probably come home in the early hours of the morning. But instead I found the door open, and their bed made.

I headed downstairs. Sometimes they were so wound up after missions that they didn't go to sleep at all, electing instead to drink coffee and use the leftover buzz to plot their next mission. But the living room was empty; so was the kitchen.

Had they not come home? I pulled my home body in to be leaner, stronger. They'd probably just gone out already.

I peeked out the window. Their car was in the driveway, but they often took a cab or a bus to jobs, to reduce the amount of turnover we needed to do on our cars. They also each had a car

31

for the personas they'd been using at Eravision, parked in pay lots downtown.

But they wouldn't have taken the bus on an errand this morning, would they? Not without leaving me a note. I checked the kitchen table, the counters, and the front door. No note. I checked my phone. No messages.

I could feel my muscles hardening, not for strength, but out of fear. This never happened. Mom and Dad were late sometimes, but they always let me know when that was a possibility. They always texted. They always made sure I knew they were safe. If they thought a job was going to be dangerous, they always went in one at a time, so that I'd still have a parent at home if something went wrong. I had never, never woken up to find them gone with no explanation.

A pit formed in my stomach as I thought about Dad watching behind us yesterday as we left the job. I'd made a mistake, sure, but a tiny one. How would they have traced that back to us?

They couldn't have. Could they?

The corner of my eye twitched. I couldn't just sit here wondering. I needed to talk to Aida. Checking in with her was always the first order of business after any mission, so Aida knew what to say when the clients contacted her. She'd know what was going on. She should have texted me by now, but since I wasn't an official part of the mission, she must have forgotten.

I ran upstairs to get dressed. I'd just pulled on my jeans when I heard a knock on the front door. I threw on a t-shirt and ran downstairs, then peered through the peep hole. I could see Aida standing there, in her home body.

I opened the door and we shook hands, giving our signals. "My parents aren't home yet," I said.

Aida leaned against the doorframe. "They haven't checked in, either."

My stomach dropped. It was one thing for them not to contact me, but if there was trouble, they should have called Aida. Unless it was the kind of trouble that meant they couldn't call anyone. "Was this a difficult job?"

Aida frowned. "It wasn't supposed to be."

I put my hand on my cell phone in my pocket. "They always let me know when they're going to be late."

Aida took a deep breath, and nodded. "I'll send Mel to investigate. If they suspected someone followed them, they may have decided to lie low for a while."

Now Aida was spinning theories. Hers didn't sound any more plausible than mine.

I took a step closer to her. "Tell me what I can do to help."

Aida put a hand on my arm. "Just stay safe," she said. "That's what your parents would want."

I cringed. She made it sound like they were dead. And though I hated to admit it, she was right that they'd want me safe.

I was afraid Aida was going to tell me to stay home, but instead she said, "Why don't you bring your work down to our place?"

I bit my lip. "Okay." It was better than sitting home alone, wondering.

Aida squeezed my wrist. "Don't worry," Aida said. "Your parents are capable. They'll figure it out and be back soon, I'm sure. Mel was just making breakfast. You can eat with us."

"Thanks," I said. I shut the door and deflated against it. Aida sounded confident, but it was her job to be a good liar.

My parents had been gone for hours. By now they could literally be anyone, anywhere.

So why hadn't they texted to let me know what happened? Maybe they'd had to ditch their phones, and also couldn't come home. I checked the clock. If that was the case, they'd buy new disposables and contact me soon. Stores were just now opening for the day.

I trucked a stack of security catalogues down to Kalif's place. Dad and I had a game where whenever we walked into a building, we'd name all the locks we passed by type and manufacturer. Last week he'd stumped me on a set of solid core metal doors with an electrified lock. I'd gotten the type, but not the manufacturer. That wouldn't happen again. Plus, it was intense work. I needed that, if I wasn't going to obsess about my parents.

Even so, I checked three times on the way over to make sure my phone was on, and that the volume was all the way up.

When I got to the Johnsons' place, Mel met me at the door. He took my hand for a moment, giving me his code.

I was pretty sure Aida had been intentionally remaining calm for my sake, but Mel didn't seem to think that was necessary. His palms were sweaty, and that wasn't part of the code. His hands kept reaching into his pockets and then back out again, like he meant to grab something but kept forgetting what.

My fingers went cold, and I intentionally warmed them. It was one thing to hear that Mom and Dad were missing, and another to watch an unflappable spy worry about it.

Mel scrutinized me. "You've checked your phone? You're sure your parents haven't called?"

Obviously. "I'm sure. You?"

Mel rubbed his forehead. "Nothing here. I'm going to go poke around the company," he said. "I knew we shouldn't have sent them in there alone."

Please. I was a novice, but my parents were professionals. "Aida said the mission wasn't dangerous," I said. "They've done tougher jobs alone."

"Sure," Mel said. "But we should have had trackers on them, at least. Now we have no idea where they've gone."

I narrowed my eyes at him. Trackers? My parents didn't even send *me* out with one. Too much risk that someone else would use it to track me, as well.

Aida stepped out of the kitchen and gave Mel a look. "Stop scaring her. I'm sure they're fine."

I wasn't. "Do you think someone caught them?" I asked Mel.

Mel rubbed his chin, leaning toward me. "Do you know anything I don't?"

A cold wave washed over me. There were the people in the

34

black vans, who followed Dad home. But why would they have found him now, after all this time? Not because I'd failed one eye scan at an unrelated company. "All my ideas are completely paranoid."

Mel studied me for a moment, and then his face softened. "Just sit tight," he said. "I've got this covered." He pulled on a ball cap and walked out the door.

I drew a breath from the bottom of my diaphragm. I wished I could believe that he did, but he wasn't exactly projecting confidence. Instead, I exchanged hand signals with Aida again.

Aida was right that my parents would want me safe, but they weren't always right about everything. The question was how to convince Aida of that.

"Isn't there something I can do?" I asked.

"You can sit down and have breakfast," Aida said.

Over her shoulder I could see Kalif sitting at the table with a book open in front of him. He gave me a sympathetic glance, and I half-smiled back.

I looked Aida in the eyes. "If it were Mel who disappeared, wouldn't you use every resource to find him?"

Aida closed her eyes. "Hard as it would be, I'd trust him to find his way out of whatever situation he found himself in."

I raised my eyebrows. *Really?* I looked sideways at Kalif. He stared at his book, but his eyes didn't move across the words.

Aida put a hand on my arm. "Give them time. Your parents will work this thing out." She hesitated there, waiting for me to agree.

I sighed. Playing into her expectations would give me some freedom to do what I needed to without her watching me too closely. "Okay," I said. "But let me know as soon as Mel finds something."

Aida gave me a sad smile. "Your parents will probably beat him back here. You'll see."

I wished I could be as certain, but doubt gnawed at me, like a little dog tugging on a rope.

35

I followed Aida into the kitchen, and she handed me a plate with sausage and scrambled eggs and half a peach on it. At our house, we usually had cold cereal for breakfast.

Kalif munched on a link of sausage. He looked even more like his mom this morning, which was something that usually happened when his dad was around. He wiped his fingers on a napkin before offering me his hand. As he gave me his signal, he held on a moment longer than he strictly needed to. My hand tingled, and I rubbed it against my jeans.

He was just trying to be comforting. There was no use assigning meaning to it.

Still, I double-checked my face, to make sure I hadn't thinned out my cheeks, or narrowed my chin. My face was naturally a bit round, just like Mom's. I padded it just a little, to make up for whatever my subconscious had been doing to it around Kalif. I hoped it hadn't already given him any unfair ideas.

Kalif pulled out the chair next to him. I sat down, paying special attention to my body, to make sure I wasn't filling it out, or sitting with my posture open toward him. I didn't want to shun him, either, so I settled for sitting with my shoulders squared to the table, neither leaning toward him, nor away.

It was especially bad now, if something had gone wrong with this job. Trouble always meant a change in our cover, and that would mean moving, leaving everything behind.

Relationships included.

"Thanks for breakfast," I said.

Aida waved a hand dismissively. "It's the least we can do."

Kalif looked me over with concern. "You okay?"

I tried to relax into the chair, but even that motion came out stiff. *Please*, I thought. *Let him attribute that to worry about my parents.*

I really needed to do some drills at home for acting normal around hot boys. That wasn't something my parents had trained me to do, and clearly my education was lacking.

Kalif looked at me expectantly, his worry obviously increasing.

Oh. Right. He was waiting for me to answer his question aloud. "Not really," I said. "My parents never do this."

Kalif's eyes flicked toward his mom. Out of the corner of mine, I could see her sipping her coffee, watching us. I'd offered to help twice. She didn't believe I'd give it up, just because she said I should.

She was right. If just Mom or Dad had gone on this job, the other one would be out looking right now. Once, Dad got arrested and it took him two days to slip out. That was particularly dangerous, because we can't hold onto personas in our sleep; the subconscious takes over whether we want it to or not. So Dad had to break out of jail after being awake for fifty-plus hours. I was only ten years old, but Mom was out every minute, looking for him, sending me messages about exactly where she was and exactly how she was keeping herself safe, so I wouldn't lose two parents just because she couldn't sit at home and wait for Dad.

Back then, I couldn't help much. Shifters are born with the ability to form our own faces, but we can't look like adults until after puberty, and we don't have control of our powers immediately. Since babies don't have a self concept, our brains model ourselves after our mothers from the moment we're born. We keep our biological anatomy through our first decade of life— long enough for most of us to develop a gendered self-image. We continue to form ourselves after our parents as we grow, gaining powers little by little as our psychology becomes more complex. I was first able to control some shifts at six years old, but I couldn't do a full impression of an adult until I was twelve.

Now that I could shift at will, things were different. There had to be something I could be doing.

I waited for Aida to finish her coffee, and turn to rinse her mug in the sink. Kalif looked up from his book at that moment, as if he'd been waiting, too.

I jerked my head toward the door to the basement, and he gave a sharp nod.

"I need to do some server maintenance," he said. When he

stood up to go downstairs, I followed. Aida didn't stop me, though I could feel her watching us go.

At least we'd get a minute of peace. That would be enough for me to ask Kalif for help.

Kalif sat down at his desk. I paced the floor behind him. "I'm nervous."

Kalif turned around on his stool, watching me pace. "Do you have any way of finding them?"

I squeezed my hands together. "We have a meeting place," I said. If we were ever permanently separated from each other, we'd agreed to meet at an apartment complex we'd picked out in San Mateo. We'd rent an apartment and hang a sign outside that said "Happy Spring!" no matter what time of the year it was. "But if they can't get to a phone to call me, do you really think they're waiting there?"

Kalif looked down at my hands as he shook his head.

I looked at my hands myself. Was he worrying about the way I held them? I was as bad as Mel, fidgeting instead of acting, but for the life of me, I couldn't remember how to hold them normally.

This was stupid. I knew better than this. I needed to pull it together, so I stopped pacing and turned to face him. "I can't just sit here. I need to do something."

Kalif hesitated. "I get that, but you heard my mom."

I groaned. "Did she really mean that? Would she abandon your dad?"

Kalif nodded frankly. "He disappeared for six months, once. She didn't look for him then."

The room seemed to tilt, and I sank onto the stool next to Kalif. Six months? I'd just discovered Mom and Dad were missing. If hours turned into days, or weeks, or *months*, what would that mean? "Jeez," I said. "I shouldn't be whining then, should I?"

Kalif looked up at me in alarm. He shook his head. "That's not what I meant. It's not the same situation."

I looked sideways at him. He was still staring at my hands,

and I swear I saw his own fingers twitch on his knee. "No?"

His hand moved slightly, and I thought for a moment he was going to grab mine, but he folded his arms across his chest instead. "No," he said. "We knew when he went on the job that it might be a long time. And it was just him who disappeared, not both of them."

I put my hands on my knees. "So you didn't spend every minute wondering who'd caught him, and if he was being tortured, or tested in some lab?"

Kalif cringed. "Maybe we should talk about something else."

My leg bounced up and down on the floor, so hard it was actually shaking the stool. Jeez. Way to bring up bad memories. "Sorry," I said. "I didn't mean to pry."

Kalif reached a hand toward my knee, but stopped just short of touching me. "I meant for your sake. You're shaking."

I planted my feet on the rung of the stool. "Technically," I said, "I'm jittering."

Kalif smiled. "My point stands."

It did, but being quiet wasn't going to help. "I'm going to think about this stuff whether we talk about it or not."

Kalif sighed. "I was scared. I thought at the time that this must be what families feel like when men go off to war, and you don't know if you'll ever see them again. But Mom always said he'd come back, and he did."

I looked over at him. Our stools sat a foot apart, but our bodies leaned toward each other, our arms and knees nearly touching. So much for avoiding my unconscious signals. I knew I should pull away, but he smelled clean, like Ivory soap, and everything in me wanted to lean into him, rest my face against his flannel shirt, and let him wrap his long arms around me.

Jeez. If my mom wanted to keep us apart, causing me stress was *not* the way to go. I hadn't realized how much harder staying away from him would be.

Maybe we'd been better off upstairs.

Kalif met my eyes, looking from one to the other.

39

I coughed. "Do you know what your dad was doing when he disappeared?"

Kalif turned away from me slightly, and I locked my own body down, forbidding it to follow him. "Mom wouldn't give me the details," he said, "but I'm pretty sure he was seducing someone's wife."

My stomach dropped. Mom and Dad didn't take jobs like that. Mom said there was a fine line between cheating on each other and just doing their jobs, and they tried to keep out of situations that blurred that line. "Your mom was okay with that?"

Kalif shook his head. "Not really. Things were tense for a long while after Dad came back—almost worse than while he was gone."

I looked toward Kalif's open doorway. I hadn't heard any noise from the kitchen, or on the stairs. I hoped his mother couldn't hear us, for more reasons than one. "Things got better eventually, though, right?"

Kalif shrugged. "I was never sure if things actually got better, or if they just got better at faking it, for each other and for me."

My heart ached, and I realized too late I'd been leaning toward him again. Our sleeves just barely brushed.

Kalif sat up straighter, and I corrected my posture as well. I was such a spaz.

He looked at me sideways. "I try not to think about it, you know? You're the first person I've told."

"Really?" Oh, man. I bit my tongue, wishing I could go back and clip the eagerness from my voice.

But Kalif didn't seem to notice. He just shrugged. "Yeah. I mean, who would I tell?"

Oh, right. It wasn't about me, just about his isolation. "You could tell anyone you want. They don't have to know who you are."

This time, I was pretty sure that Kalif did notice my defensiveness, because he smiled, his lips parting slightly. "Well, maybe I never wanted to talk about it before."

My heart beat in my throat. I made him want to talk about his family? His past? Things he didn't want to think about? Dad said this was how you groomed a source—you told them personal things, to develop a close relationship.

Could Kalif be grooming me for something?

Or—I swallowed—was he trying to get closer to me for real?

Kalif shifted uncomfortably. He's just said this totally personal thing, and then I'd been quiet for too long, again.

"Oh," I said. "Oh." I closed my eyes, mentally clocking my head against the desk. What was *wrong* with me?

When I opened my eyes again, one corner of Kalif's mouth crooked up in a smile. "Look, I wasn't trying to one up you."

I forced myself to sit upright. "I know. I asked."

Kalif resettled himself on his stool. "Yeah, but it's okay that you're nervous for your parents. I'm not trying to shut you up."

"Have I shut up?" I asked.

He looked me up and down. "Kind of."

Ugh. The closed posture was *also* the wrong answer. I needed to stop studying eye scans and start studying clear interpersonal signals.

If only I could decide which signals I was trying to send.

"So, my parents," I said.

For a split second, I thought he looked sad. Then he nodded. "Your parents. You want to do something to help, but you probably shouldn't."

I turned around to face his computer. "We don't have to do anything big. Can't you hack into their security and see their video?" Kalif sometimes got remote pictures of areas our parents were going to infiltrate by breaking into the servers of the companies in question.

"Not at Eravision," Kalif said. "Their security cameras are on old machines. They aren't connected to the network."

"But they must store the video somewhere."

Kalif nodded. "On hard disks, routed by cable. I tried to get into it before your parents took jobs there, but I couldn't do it. Their security is pretty low-budget, which in this case gives them an advantage. Dad's going in person, though. He'll probably find something."

I tapped my nails on the edge of the desk. If just Mom were missing, Dad wouldn't depend on Mel to do the looking. "But if your mom didn't even go looking for your dad after he disappeared, how hard do you think they're going to look now?"

"You make a good point," he said. Kalif's program beeped, and he punched some keys.

I looked at the clock. "It's almost eleven. They've been gone for eight hours. Everyone at Eravision is at work by now. Something is seriously wrong."

"You're probably right, but that doesn't mean you should put yourself in danger."

"I'm not going to do anything stupid," I said. "Not yet."

Kalif ran a hand through his hair. "Great. That makes me feel lots better."

I wanted to ask why he was so worried about me, but if I was trying to be fair to him, fishing around to know why he cared was definitely off limits. "Let's just go over the mission parameters, and see if we can find anything your parents missed."

Kalif considered me for a moment. Finally, he sighed. "We can look at it. I can't see what the harm would be in that."

Kalif pulled up the mission profile for me. It looked simple enough. The client had hired us to steal some data on their competitor's new software, and then frame two of the competitor's employees for the breach. The people we were to frame were both former employees of the client, who took classified information with them when they left. Eravision stole information and engineers from Circom, and now Circom was coming back at Eravision to ruin the traitors' careers and steal data in return.

Backstabbing was a way of life for big-time tech firms, and we were the ones who benefited the most. More often than not, Mom and Dad played both sides, stealing from one firm in one set of personas, and then adopting another to offer revenge. We couldn't enjoy flashy spoils, like a big house or other permanent things, and I knew that my parents lived extra modestly because they were worried if they spoiled me I'd turn into a brat. But the jobs were challenging, and netted us more than enough money to run and start a new life anywhere in the world whenever we wanted to.

We never quit working, though. Mom and Dad enjoyed their jobs too much for that. Mom always said our talents made us good at one thing—fooling people. It did no good for us to pretend to be straightforward, or upstanding, because that wasn't something we could ever be. "So what was the plan, exactly?" I asked.

"Your parents were taking on the personas of the people they were framing," Kalif said. "Going in with their door codes and key cards and everything, downloading the information from their boss's secure computer, and then leaving and pretending to botch the cover-up on the way out."

"Sounds easy," I said. "Like it should have taken less than an hour."

"Right," Kalif said. "And they've both been working at the company part time under different personas, so they had complete profiles on the people they were framing."

I looked at the case file over Kalif's shoulder. "The easiest way for that to go wrong is for them to get caught by the people they were impersonating. Who were they?"

Kalif pulled up the profiles in question, complete with photos, personal information, and daily schedules. I looked at the profiles over Kalif's shoulder, careful not to get close enough to give him the wrong idea.

Mom had spent the last month profiling Art Cambrian and Nick Delacruz—following them home, chatting them up at the office, tagging them with trackers and tapping their phones. Art was a wiry man with a thick black goatee, and Nick had his head shaved, revealing a skull the shape of a potato. Their images stared up at me, complete with three-sixty rotations of

43

Mom and Dad, dressed up in Art and Nick's bodies and clothes.

I put my elbows on Kalif's desk, leaning toward his computer. "Where were these guys supposed to be last night?"

"Art left the office at five o'clock to go home. There was a Giants game on, which he never misses, so he was supposed to be home all night watching that. Nick Delacruz has a weekly date night with his wife. They have little kids and are too paranoid to get a babysitter, so they order in a pizza and watch a movie. He told your mom this week was his wife's turn to pick, so he was going to have to watch a chick flick."

I blew my hair out of my face, then thickened it to make it stay put. Sometimes I didn't know how Mom did it. She got right into the details of these people's lives, chatted them up, pretended to be friends, and then turned around and got them fired, or even arrested. I had to learn to be like her, if I didn't want to feel guilty for the rest of my life. "So that's why they chose last night, then," I said. "Because both subjects had places to be, but they shouldn't have had solid alibis."

Kalif nodded. "Right."

"So it couldn't hurt to check on Art and Nick," I said. "See if they went in to work today, or if they've been fired, or what."

Kalif closed the files and turned on his stool to face me. Our knees were a hair's breadth apart; goose bumps broke out down my legs. "My dad thought the first thing to do," Kalif said, "was to check the site and see if the job's been done."

I tried not to let my emotions show on my face. I shifted my knee away from his, just slightly. *Come on, Jory*, I thought. *Get a grip.* "Sure," I said. "But your dad has that covered, right?"

"Probably. So we should wait for him to come back."

I rubbed my temples. "That could be hours." I needed to check on Cambrian and Delacruz now.

Kalif sighed. "If you really have to start looking, it seems like the first thing to do would be to check your parents' email. It's right here on the server. I can do that without putting anyone in danger."

Kalif could do that without me. "Okay," I said. "That sounds like a good idea, too."

Kalif narrowed his eyes at me. "You told me you weren't going to do anything stupid."

I held my hands in the air. "I'm just going to make some phone calls. Where's the harm?"

Kalif crossed his arms again. His elbow barely brushed mine, and the goosebumps spread up my arms. "What would your parents say if they knew you were going to do that?"

I flattened my skin, trying to focus on the question. How *would* my parents react? "Dad would be proud of me. Mom would be pissed, but she wouldn't have a leg to stand on. In my situation, she'd do the same."

Kalif rolled his eyes. "I should stop you. But I'm not going to."

I smiled. "You're the best. I'll be back in half an hour."

Kalif nodded, but he didn't look happy. It was harder than I wanted it to be to drag myself away from him, but I did it, walking purposefully up the stairs. I wished I could take him with me—make the phone calls with him right there. But I couldn't afford to be distracted while I was interviewing Art and Nick, and I certainly couldn't call them where Aida might overhear.

I ran into Aida on my way to the door. I checked my posture as I stopped to talk to her. It was one thing to send unintended messages about my feelings for Kalif, and quite another to put my parents in more danger by alerting her to what I was doing. "I'm going to walk down to the gas station and buy a soda," I said.

Aida hesitated. "I'm sure Kalif would go with you."

I shrugged. "It's okay. I just want to clear my head. I'll be back soon."

"Okay," Aida said. "But come back quickly. I want to be able to tell you as soon as I hear from your Mom and Dad."

And if she suspected that I was working behind her back, like any good spy, she didn't let it show.

FOUR

Instead of going to the gas station, I rushed home. From the computer in Mom and Dad's bedroom, I accessed the Art and Nick profiles again, pulling up their phone numbers.

I started with Art Cambrian. Last night he was supposed to have spent time watching a baseball game, which should make for a difficult alibi. I marked a black slash on one of our disposable phones, then dialed his cell.

I held my breath while the phone rang, but Mr. Cambrian didn't answer. If Mom and Dad didn't even make it to the job, he was probably at work, going about his normal day. If they had, he might be in the process of being fired, and therefore screening his calls.

Nick Delacruz didn't answer his cell phone either, but I had a second phone number for him—a home phone. That one rang three times, and then a woman answered.

"Hello?" she said.

I checked over the profile. This would probably be his wife, Roseanne, lover of chick flicks. Since I was starting with a woman, I kept my female voice, but made it a bit deeper and smoother, to sound older and more sophisticated.

"Hello," I said. I let my insecurity bleed into my voice, to put her at ease. "I'm not sure if I have the right number. I'm looking for the Nick Delacruz who's under investigation for data theft?"

I closed my eyes, waiting through the long pause. It was only eleven AM. Even if my parents had succeeded in framing Nick, she might not even know yet.

She paused for long enough that I could tell she knew something. "Who is this?" she asked finally.

I shifted my voice a little deeper, rattling off the next part like I'd said it a million times. "This is Eva Long. I'm a lawyer with Goodman and Finch." I jotted down the names on the back of an envelope as I made them up. I didn't want to put them in the digital file, where Mel or Aida might look and see that I'd been poking around.

Roseanne sounded reserved, like she was bracing for bad news. "Maybe I should let you talk to Nick."

"I'd love to talk to him," I said. "Is he home?"

"Hang on."

I stood up, pacing at the foot of my parents' bed. He was home in the middle of the day. Unless he was ill, something must have happened.

A moment later, Nick's voice was on the line. "Who is this?"

"This is Eva Long with Goodman and Finch," I said again. "I'm not sure if I'm talking to the right Nick Delacruz, but if I am, I was told you might need representation."

Nick sounded defensive. "Where'd you get this number?"

I let my own voice sound unsure again, to undermine his defenses. "The phone book," I said. "Hence the uncertainty." I was glad I wasn't having this conversation in person. Mom or Dad would have phrased all of this better.

Nick paused. "Where'd you get my name?"

I was clearly going to have to give some information before I got any in return. "A friend who works at Eravision gave me the tip. You understand I can't tell you who—he took a chance even telling me, but he was concerned. Have you been contacted today about an investigation for data theft?"

"Is that what's going on over there?" Nick asked. "They think I stole something?"

I paused, grinding my heels into the carpet. I couldn't answer that question without knowing exactly what my parents had done. "Why don't you start from the beginning? Tell me what's happened." That was a gamble. Nick had no reason to trust me, but sometimes when people are scared or angry, they'll spill things they shouldn't.

Nick hesitated, and I closed my eyes, sure I was going to lose him. When he spoke, his voice was low. "My boss called this morning and wanted to know if I was okay."

My hands went clammy. I sank onto the end of Mom and Dad's bed. "Why would he do that?" I asked.

"You tell me," he said. "That's not the first question I'd ask if I thought someone stole from me."

I had to keep tight control over my vocal cords, to keep my fear from seeping into my voice. "That does seem odd," I said. "Did he say anything else?"

"He asked me what happened at work last night. I told him I was home all night, and he just kept asking if I was sure. He asked me three times, and finally I asked him what the hell was going on."

"And?"

"And then he told me to just stay put, and he'd be in touch. And now you call me, telling me I'm under suspicion for data theft. What the hell is going on?"

Whatever Nick's boss knew, it was enough to make him worry about Nick's safety. He wouldn't have called if he thought he had Nick in custody, which meant he was probably looking at video evidence. If he had video of something happening to Nick, but Nick was fine and said he wasn't there, the boss would have to explain that to himself. Someone might have come in dressed as Nick, or wearing makeup, or used CG on the video. In the digital age, people didn't recognize the supernatural, even when it was staring them in the face.

But none of that explained why my parents hadn't come home. "I wasn't told much," I said. "Just that you might be facing legal troubles, and could use someone good on your side. Do you have a lawyer?"

"No," he said. "I didn't know I needed one."

"If there's anything else you can tell me—"

"That's all I know," he said. "You're a lawyer. Aren't *you* supposed to be helping *me*?"

I bit my lip. Nick was starting to get defensive again, which meant it was time to make my exit. "There's not a lot I can do for you until your work contacts you again. Why don't you call me if they ask to interview you, or if they decide to pursue disciplinary action. I can sit with you for questioning, or help you put together your wrongful termination suit."

Now Nick got sarcastic. "For a fee, of course."

I had no idea what lawyers charged. "We can talk about a retainer if you find you need me. Can I give you my number?"

He sighed. "Why not? Let me get something to write on."

I gave Nick the number of the disposable, and made a note of it in the file. As soon as I got off the phone, I changed the voicemail message on that phone to Goodman and Finch. Nick would probably check the internet and discover that the firm didn't—as far as I knew—exist. If I wanted to keep up the charade, I could have Kalif set up a dummy website, but I didn't think I would need this contact again. Still, it didn't hurt to have a contingency set up, in case it became useful later.

My hands shook as I hung up the phone. I sat there, waiting to stand until my head stopped spinning. Unless there was some large coincidence at play, Mom and Dad must have shown up for the job last night as planned. But Nick's boss had seen something—probably in the security footage—that made him call Nick in a panic, asking if he was okay. But whatever he'd seen had happened not to Nick, but to someone who looked exactly like him.

My mother.

I sat on the end of my parents' bed, wishing I could ask them what to do. They'd see things I'd overlooked, and I trusted them to be more thorough than Mel or Aida.

I looked down at the cell phone. I couldn't ask them. I was on my own.

I shifted my jaw and forehead to look older, more determined, then I walked over to look in the bathroom mirror.

See it, then be it. That was our motto. I wasn't really alone in this. Mom and Dad would be fighting as hard as they could to get back to me.

I hoped it was them that we were all relying on, and not me.

Aida met me at the door when I returned, and checked my hand. "I heard from Mel," she said. "The security department at Eravision is running around like the sky is falling."

My knees went weak. "Something bad happened."

"Not necessarily," Aida said, slowly. "If your parents finished the job successfully, this is exactly what we'd expect to see."

Crap. Of course it was. If I wanted to work in secret, I had to anticipate things like that.

Aida went on. "Mel says they definitely started the job, but he can't tell if they successfully finished it. If someone did intercept your parents, it's possible they've already discovered that there are shifters involved, so he needs to be extra careful."

What I'd done certainly didn't qualify as *extra* careful. "So he'll go in tonight, then?" I asked. "After everyone leaves?"

Aida shook her head. "We agreed he's going to hang back for now. Keep an eye on things from a distance."

Great. *That* was sure to turn up nothing. Mel was so worried about being caught himself, he would leave my parents completely out to dry. "Let me know what you find," I said. And then I walked slowly down the stairs, trying not to carry myself like a girl with a plan.

I found Kalif in the same place I'd left him, sitting in front of his computer. I shut the door behind me.

"Did you find anything in the emails?" I asked.

Kalif shook his head. "I got in. Your parents hadn't added any encryption beyond what I set up. But there's nothing unusual, and nothing since last night. Did you have any luck?"

"Not exactly," I said. "But Nick Delacruz told me that his boss called him in a panic, wanting to know if he was okay."

Kalif's eyes widened. "Really?"

I sank onto the stool next to him. For some reason, watching Kalif be alarmed made the situation feel more real. "Yeah. And then his boss asked him three times if he was sure he wasn't in the building last night, and ended by telling him not to come in to work."

"How'd you get Nick to tell you all that?"

"I pretended to be a lawyer offering to represent him."

Kalif looked impressed. "Clever. I hope my dad doesn't think of the same thing."

"If he does, he'll just be the second ambulance chaser. Also, unoriginal."

Kalif smiled.

"I just saw your mom. Your dad found out that my parents started the job, but he isn't looking any deeper because he claims it'll be too dangerous."

"They do have a point," Kalif said. "Since we don't know what form your parents will be in, it's hard for us to know how to help them while being sure we won't make their situation more complicated."

I let my face twitch, to show my annoyance. "Sure, but are they worried about protecting my parents, or themselves?"

Kalif stared at his hands.

Ouch. These were his parents I was talking about. If I wanted to send negative signals his way, this was one way to do it. But I needed Kalif's help. Insulting his family wasn't a good way to get it.

Instead, I put a hand on his knee, trying to keep it casual and light. "I need your help," I said. "I need to get in there and see whatever Nick's boss saw."

Kalif stared down at my hand, but he didn't physically react. I wondered if he had his own body locked down as hard as I had mine. To avoid betraying, what? Annoyance? Embarrassment? Disgust?

51

"You can't go in there now," Kalif said. "Even if we could get away from my mom, my Dad is there, watching everyone. One slip and he'd catch you. Besides, everyone at Eravision will be on high alert as well, since there's been a security event. It's not safe."

I hated to admit it, but he was right. That was the ironic part of security; everyone was most vigilant right *after* something went wrong. I leaned toward him. "I'll go in tonight, then," I said. "Once everyone's left the office."

Kalif gave me a look, and I withdrew my hand from his knee. If he wanted to, he could tell his mother what I was planning. I had to keep him on my side. "It'll drive me crazy not to know," I said. "Will you help me, please?"

Kalif rolled his eyes. "You don't have to use those tricks on me."

I straightened. "What?"

He waved a hand at my body. "That thing you're doing. You don't need to. You were already gorgeous."

All the blood drained from my face, and I corrected my skin quickly to its natural color. I could feel my stomach letting out a little from where I'd tightened it in, my body relaxing out of the exaggerated hourglass shape. My eyes contracted, my lips drained a little of color. I hadn't realized I'd been using my body against him, but now that he called me on it, I stammered a little.

He thought I was gorgeous? I had no idea what I was supposed to say to that, but in this case I figured it wasn't "thank you."

"Sorry," I said, when I finally got full words out. "Too much training, I guess."

Kalif looked like he was covering a laugh.

I wanted to disappear. "Don't make fun of me. I'm really scared."

He gave me a half smile, his one cheek dimpling. "I know. But just talk to me straight, okay?"

I leaned back, careful to keep my body from contorting suggestively. It was harder than I'd imagined to curb that impulse. Even regular people changed themselves—their posture, their expression, their stance—to manipulate the people around them without even realizing they were doing it. The changes in my body were subtle, but the overall effect made me much more adept at the rhetoric of appearance than a normal person could be. Dad would have been proud that my training was so well ingrained, but he would also agree that this was so not the time. "Okay. So will you help me?"

"Yeah," he said. "It's impossible to say no to you."

I couldn't breathe. "Since when?"

"Um," he said, "since it's obvious you're going to do this whether I help you or not."

My whole body shrunk. No. *Now* I wanted to disappear. "Oh," I mumbled. "Well, thanks."

He gave me an exasperated smile. "Don't thank me yet. Let's hear your plan."

FIVE

he important thing when presenting the plan to Kalif—
besides controlling my subconscious wiles—was not to
sound like I was making it up on the fly. "I can go in
as Mom's employee persona," I said. "Her name was Andrea."
She'd been working there for weeks, and we had key cards for
her identity. "Mom was wearing Nick Delacruz's body when she
went in. She didn't have Andrea's clothes with her, so the odds
of her using that one at this moment are slim."

"That could work," Kalif said. "What'll you do once you're
inside?"

My mind raced. "I'll look at the security recordings, and
leave. It's just in and out. I can do this. And it'll be safer if I have
you to watch my back."

Kalif ignored the implication that he should come with
me. "Okay," he said. "Let's see how well you can fit into your
mother's clothes."

He switched his monitor back on. Over his shoulder, I could
see he'd been looking at a message board for shifter conspiracies.

"What's that?" I asked. "Something to do with my parents?"

"No," Kalif said. "I finished with the email before you got
back. I was just baiting the nuts. They're hilarious."

I leaned in to read the posts over his shoulder. Even if there
was only one of us for every million people on earth, that still
added up to several thousand shifters in total. That meant that
some normal people knew about us, and some of those people

thought the best way to tell the world about it was to use the internet. Those people always looked crazy, so they weren't a threat to us.

Eravision, on the other hand—if they'd caught themselves a pair of shifters, and knew what they had, they might turn my parents over to any number of scary government organizations. Considering what the NSA did to regular people, I didn't think they'd hesitate to torture and dissect a shifter.

Kalif looked up at me. "What's wrong?"

"Nothing," I said quietly. "I'm just running scenarios." But as I became aware of my body, I knew the lie was obvious. My muscles were all tightening, becoming more wiry. My eyes had enlarged, preparing to take in more of my surroundings. This wasn't training. My body was preparing for primal fight-or-flight.

Kalif leaned closer. "If you're going to do this job, you need to calm down and concentrate."

His face was just inches from mine, and even as I relaxed my muscles, trying to get control over my body, I saw his eyes drop down to my lips.

I stood up straight, rolling my shoulders. I couldn't remember the last time I'd been such a mess. "Sorry," I said. "Let's get to work."

Kalif pulled up the files with my mom's persona record—the pictures and voice recordings she made to practice her new employee cover until she could do it flawlessly every time. Now I had to do it just as perfectly, without as much practice.

I studied the record. Andrea Lyman had frizzy brown hair cut in a sort of mushroom over her head. The idea of the persona was to blend in, so she wasn't pretty, and wore thick glasses. I could retrieve those later from Mom's closet. Since Mom had been working twenty-five hours a week at Eravision, she had Andrea's wardrobe handy, instead of stashed with our other costumes.

Kalif set the three-sixty view of the persona spinning, and I

55

began to change, starting with the face. I slimmed down my nose and narrowed my cheeks a bit, then raised my forehead and hairline until my face looked long and gaunt. My chin I widened, and then stretched my spine so that my neck and head would make up a slightly larger proportion of my total height.

I turned my head back and forth, making adjustments to my bone structure near the temples, and the cartilage on the bridge of my nose. My home nose was small and stout, but Andrea's was something of a beak. It would be an effort to remember all the changes there.

Kalif switched on his web cam and opened a window for it, so I could see Mom's image and mine side by side. I added a deposit of fat on the sides of my jaw, evening out Andrea's angular face. Other than that, I'd done well on the first try.

"What do you think?" I asked.

"She's five-nine," Kalif said, looking from the computer to me.

My home body was five-six, just like Mom, so I had a couple more inches to go. The face was the most important part, but details like relative height might make a co-worker sense that something was wrong, even if they couldn't pinpoint why. "What do you think of the face?"

He squinted at me. "It's hard for me to tell when you haven't done the hair."

I stared at myself in the mirror. I was used to doing this part with Mom or Dad, who would have been able to pick out the most nuanced details and tell me exactly what I'd done wrong, before I had completely finished. But I had to work with what I had, so I frizzed out my hair and lengthened it a little. The cone cut Mom had chosen for Andrea was truly terrible on her, but that was the point—plain women are invisible.

"That looks right," Kalif said.

"Good." I knew it wasn't perfect, but hopefully it was close enough.

The rest of the body was easier, since people are mostly

identified by their face. I still had to string out my frame a little, lengthening my legs and widening my shoulders. I sucked in my spine at the waist, so that my proportions of leg to torso were more exaggerated. As a result, the jeans I was wearing became an inch too short, and my shirt hung longer over my hips.

"Is that right?" I asked.

Kalif looked me up and down, like he was hardcore checking me out. I tried not to squirm. I didn't even look like myself; he was just checking my metrics.

"I think you've got it," Kalif said. "Back up against the wall so I can measure your height."

Kalif had pencil marks on his wall to show various heights—at home we had one of those in practically every room. I stepped up against it.

He stood closer than was strictly necessary, and squinted at the top of my head. "You overdid it by half an inch."

When he looked down at my eyes, I was at a sudden loss for what to do with my hands. "Okay," I said quickly. I stepped around him and shortened my thighs just slightly, where I was pretty sure I'd exaggerated the proportions. It was unlikely that anyone would have noticed so small a discrepancy, but if I got all the details we noticed right, hopefully no one would catch the things we overlooked.

"All right," I said. "Play the video for me."

I paced back and forth in Kalif's room, trying to get Andrea's stance and gait right, which wasn't easy with his floor being so covered in cords and cases. He cleaned up around me as I worked, shoving everything under his corner desk.

"All that's left is the voice," I said finally.

I was decent at vocal impressions, so I always left them for last. After a long session of endless parental corrections, it was always nice to watch Mom or Dad smile when I hit the voice right after the first few tries.

Andrea's voice was low for a woman, and a bit soft spoken. Voice is a combination of anatomy and mannerism, and I listened carefully for both as Kalif played the audio file. I repeated the phrases Mom recorded several times—"How was your weekend? Can I help you with something?"—feeling out the cadence as much as the tone and volume.

"Well, how am I doing?" I asked Kalif in Andrea's voice.

"That's great," Kalif said.

I looked down at the total package. "I doubt that, but it'll do."

Now for the last step, the on/off switch. I closed my eyes and ran my mind over my entire body, memorizing the bend of the face, the feel of each bone, the hang of the flesh. Then I relaxed, as if releasing tension from every part of me, and became myself again. As soon as the transformation was complete, I tensed up again, getting back into Andrea's form before I forgot it. I checked myself in the webcam to make sure I'd gotten it right again, and then repeated the process. Relax, flex, relax, flex. I couldn't hold on to minutiae like fingerprints and irises without concentrating, but I needed to be able to become all the visible parts of Andrea at a single moment's notice. If I could make Andrea almost as natural as my own self was, then I could maintain her by muscle memory, without having to concentrate.

When I could turn Andrea on and off like a light bulb, I shifted back into me and stayed there. "Your turn," I said.

Kalif looked terrified. "What?"

I put a hand on my hip. "My dad was working at the company, too, so there's a persona for you."

Kalif sighed. "I'm not as good at all that as you are."

"Do you think I should go alone?" I asked. "I can do that, if you think you can back me up better remotely."

Kalif waffled. "You're looking to break into the security footage. You don't have any experience with that, do you?"

I sat down on the edge of his bed. "I don't."

"So it would be ideal if I were there."

It would, as long as I could keep my head screwed on straight. "You'll have to get Dad's persona right. Can you do it?"

He pulled up a three-sixty composite picture of Dad in his

Eravision employee persona. "Let me try."

Kalif changed slower than I did, and more deliberately. He zoomed in on the face and took a ruler to the screen, counting out the proportions of the nose and the eyes in increments. "This would be easier," he said, "if I could just get that stupid program working."

Kalif and Mel had been working on a program that could scan faces and tell us how well we were matching, but getting the program to find solid reference points was complicated. Mel had been pushing Kalif pretty hard on it the last few months. Kalif didn't seem to mind, but I was pretty sure Mel was only forcing it because he wanted Kalif to get better at shifting than me.

"You can't use computers for everything," I said. "You can't reduce shifting to pure numbers."

"It works for irises. And fingerprints. And retina."

I shook my head. "That's just for biometrics. When you're interacting with people, you have to seem like the person, not just look like them."

Kalif gave me another of those half-smiles that made my heart do a Riverdance. "You don't think I can make a program to do that? I thought I was a prodigy."

Calm down, Jory. I put on my best, unflappable shifter smile. "If you do, I'll buy you dinner. For now, we do things the old way." I sat on the stool next to him and watched as his face grew longer and squarer.

"Is that right?" he asked.

"A little thicker in the chin," I said.

Kalif messed with the bone structure, filling out his face too much, and then scaling it back, trying to find the right shape.

"There?" he asked.

"Better," I said. "But your skin is still too dark."

Kalif adjusted the tone.

"Do you know why you make your skin darker than your parents'?" I asked.

Kalif rolled his eyes. "Dad says it's because I've been raised

59

hearing about my heritage, but I think it's because of my name."

Mel believed that we were all descended from the assassins of Hassan-i-Sabbah, which would make us all of Arab descent. Dad said that was just wishful thinking—trying to look back and fit ourselves into history. We could have had our DNA analyzed to determine our heritage, of course, but Dad wasn't brave enough to do that, even to prove Mel wrong. The fear that scientists might discover something bizarre in our DNA and send the government after us was too overwhelming.

The name thing made sense, though. His subconscious formed his body to match the cultural assumptions about the label his parents had given him.

"Is the heritage thing important to you?" I asked.

He grimaced. "It's important to my dad. I'm not even sure if it's real, but I wouldn't say that to him. My skin makes him proud, like he's raising me right, or something."

I'd never heard him talk about his dad with so much scorn. "You think he's wrong about our ancestry?"

Kalif shrugged. "I don't believe anything until I see evidence." He pointed to his face. "Is it still too dark?"

"Yes," I said.

He lightened the skin around his eyes.

"Too far," I said. "Now you look like a cancer patient."

Kalif grinned at me, his own dimples showing through John's blanched face. "Maybe this guy got really sick overnight. You don't know."

I laughed. "Yes, let's go confess cancer to his coworkers. That won't draw any attention."

Kalif leaned closer to the webcam, examining his eyes on the screen, and trying to get the color just right.

"Almost there?" Kalif asked.

Almost was an overstatement. "You haven't done the freckles."

"I hate those," Kalif said. "Why did your dad have to use them?"

"Because they're hard and he's good at remembering them."

60

It was one of the things I would look for, if I ever had to go looking for my dad when he was in persona. That wouldn't be easy, though. I hoped this situation wouldn't come to that.

When Kalif turned to me again, he did almost have it. "Well?" he asked.

"Your jaw is still off."

Kalif turned back to the camera and started adjusting, but he was lengthening the lower mandible instead of the upper.

"No," I said. "Here." I reached out and ran my hand from his ear to the curve in his jaw bone. His face was rough, like he had a five o'clock shadow. I had to give him props for that—John probably wouldn't have shaved in a while.

Kalif turned slightly, his lower lip barely brushing my thumb. My insides tingled. When he nodded against my hand, I realized I'd left it there longer than I needed to. I pulled away and focused on the picture in the computer. *Idiot*, I thought. I should have pointed there, instead.

If Mom were here, I'd have asked her for help with my just-friends signals. I was sure she'd love to coach me in that. Except I wouldn't need that coaching once I found her. She and Dad would want to split, immediately. If all went well, tonight would be the last night I'd spend with Kalif. And since I'd have my parents back, that should feel like good news.

So why did I feel this crushing weight in my chest?

"Better?" Kalif asked.

I turned to his image on the screen, instead of to him. "You need to adjust the hairline." I pointed at the computer image this time. "Here."

"You're really good at this," Kalif said. "Thank you."

"No problem," I said. "I mean, you're doing this for me, after all."

His image in the computer monitor smiled at me, and even that took my breath. "I should have been practicing with you all along," he said. "You're way more patient about it than my parents."

I braced my arms on his desk. "Well, now we know."

"Yeah," Kalif said. "I just hope it's not too late. I don't want to mess up this mission."

No kidding. That was my job. "You'll do fine," I said. "Do the rest of the body, and then we'll try the voice."

That was where we ran into real trouble. Kalif reached for the voice and came up sounding too young, then too deep. He tried to lighten the tone and sounded like Michael Jackson. I smothered a laugh.

"Come on," Kalif said. "Mock, but help."

I held up my palms. "I don't know what to tell you. It comes naturally to me."

Kalif grit his teeth at himself in the webcam. "To my mother, too. It's a shame I didn't inherit her talent."

"Try it again."

But when he did, he sounded effeminate.

"Just give him a cold," I said. "Then you'll have an excuse for not showing up to work today." Hopefully the bosses would be out of the office, and we wouldn't need excuses, but it couldn't hurt to have them, just in case.

"That I can do," Kalif said. I waited while he narrowed his nasal passages and inflamed his throat. "How's that?" he asked in a stuffy voice.

"More scratchy," I said.

"Who's the genius now?" he asked. His voice was so hoarse that everyone would notice, but no one would suspect anything was amiss.

"I don't know," I said. "But let's just hope you don't need to get through a voice recognition portal."

Kalif shook his head. "They don't have any. I have the security schematics." Though his voice remained scratchy, he sounded more confident once he could talk about things he was prepared for.

"Okay," I said. "Practice turning it on and off, and we can stop torturing you."

Kalif had almost mastered the instant change when we heard footsteps on the stairs coming down to the basement. Kalif shifted back into himself and sat down at his computer, closing the image program and pulling up the server thing he'd been working on before.

His mom opened the door without knocking, and found us sitting on stools at Kalif's desk. "Any word?" I asked.

"No," she said, taking each of our hands. I don't know who we would have been but ourselves, unless we decided to swap identities just to mess with her, but the habit ran deep.

"Jory was giving me pointers on voice changes," Kalif said. "She's a good teacher."

That was smart of him to say. If she'd heard any of what we were doing, now she'd have an easy explanation, and maybe she wouldn't suspect that I'd lied to her.

Aida looked surprised. "If she can coach you in voices, she must be."

I wanted to defend him, but Kalif didn't look insulted—probably because Aida was right, about his skill level at least.

"Do you need help with lunch?" Kalif asked.

"It's already done," Aida said. "I was just coming to tell you two to come up and eat."

Kalif nodded. "We'll come now."

As I followed Kalif and Aida up the stairs, I wished I was a better teacher. I was going to have to depend on Kalif to keep up his persona during the stress of the mission.

When it came to breaking in to Eravision, we could both use all the help we could get.

63

SIX

We agreed that his parents might suspect something if we stayed in his room all day, so I declined Aida's invitation to dinner and went home in the mid afternoon to go over Andrea's profile and to pack the essentials: flashlight, lock picks, disposable cell phones, and a change of casual clothes. I did fine until it got dark, and then I paced the downstairs hallway, looking at the pictures on our walls—sunsets, weeping willows, an oversized canvas of the Golden Gate bridge cutting through fog. Nothing personal, nothing that would identify us. Nothing that we wouldn't very shortly be leaving behind.

I stood in front of the Golden Gate picture. My father had bought it at IKEA along with most of our furniture. We could get another one just like it in the next place we landed, if we cared to. So I knew when my eyes teared up that it wasn't the picture I was torn up about leaving behind.

It was past midnight when Kalif finally knocked on my door; I must have stared at the photo for an hour, but I hadn't let the tears slide farther than the corners of my eyes.

I opened the door to find Kalif standing there barefoot in sweats and a t-shirt. I stuck out my hand and we pressed our palms together, his shifted temperature as usual, and my eyes threatened me again. I tightened my tear ducts, sucking them dry.

Kalif looked down at his clothes. "I thought it might convince my parents I was going to bed," he said. "Too much?"

"No," I said. "It was probably a good idea."

He grinned. "But my feet are freezing."

I swung the door open wider. "Come in."

I'd already changed into Andrea's clothes, and practiced shifting in and out of the persona to make sure I had it. It had taken me a minute to adjust the warp of my corneas to see properly through her glasses, but holding onto that was much easier than an iris pattern, especially since if I lost concentration on it, the world blurred.

In both my home body and in hers, Andrea's clothing hung loosely from my frame, just like it did in the pictures of Mom. I appreciated that—it meant my anatomy could be less exact.

While Kalif changed in the bathroom, I slipped on Andrea's shoes; I wasn't sure what it said about me, but her plain, brown, round-toed flats were much more my style than Emmeline's flashy heels. I wondered which ones Kalif liked better, but I didn't want to ask, for fear it was the heels.

Not that it matters, I reminded myself.

When Kalif stepped out of the bathroom, he was in full persona. He might have been Dad standing there, all ready for work. I walked up to him and offered him my hand again. Andrea and John's hands shifted from cool to warm to cool, just the way ours had a few minutes ago. Even though Kalif didn't look like himself, the signal alone sent tingles up my arm.

It felt like home.

I pulled my hand away.

Damn. I was in so much trouble.

"I read that Andrea's car is parked in a garage downtown," Kalif said.

He'd gone over the profiles, too. I nodded, trying to focus. "And John takes the bus."

"The bus sounds impractical," Kalif said, "so we should drive to the garage and get the car."

"We can take my parents' car to the garage. We need a cover story. Andrea might go in to get something she left in the office.

65

John was sick, of course." I paused. "Maybe they both were, and they just failed to call in. But I'm not sure why they would go in together."

Kalif looked in our living room mirror. This was the real tell that shifters lived here: full length mirrors in every room. "We could change the personas a bit," he said. "Decide that they're dating, which is against office policy. I checked the employment materials your parents collected."

My stomach fluttered. It was a good idea, and he said it without interest. But if dating was the first excuse on Kalif's mind, I was in exactly as much trouble as I thought I was.

I should have told him no, should have come up with another story, but even as I tried to conjure one, my mind blanked.

"Okay," I said finally. "That way we could act caught if we run into anybody." Which we might do anyway, at the rate we were going.

Kalif motioned to the door. "Should we go?" he asked. If my embarrassment was showing in my face, Kalif didn't react to it. Maybe I was just imagining his intentions.

"Yes," I said. "I'll drive." I charged out the door before I could make things more awkward than they were.

I took the long way out of the townhome complex so we wouldn't drive by Kalif's place. Not that I expected his parents to be sitting by the front door, watching, but we couldn't be too careful. We could evade them by shifting, but they'd recognize the car.

Kalif guided me through the city to the correct parking garage—Mom had paid for a permanent spot, so she could leave it there whenever Andrea wasn't at work. I pulled out John and Andrea's lanyards with their employee name tags, and we both looped them over our heads. Those we hadn't even had to duplicate—since John and Andrea were employees, the company had handed them over freely.

We switched over to the second car. "You better drive again," Kalif said.

"Will do," I said. I steeled my nerves and locked in my physical form before I brought up the details of the plan. If we were going with this dating thing, we need to iron it out before we tried it on. "So how long have we been dating?"

"A week," Kalif said. "Keep things recent."

"Sounds right. Sometimes new relationships make people flaky." Or batty, in my case. Not that Kalif and I were headed for a relationship. I needed to get that idea out of my head quick, or I was going to botch everything.

Kalif just went on talking like we were discussing the weather. "And we're back to the office because you left your phone there."

"If we're together, that also explains why we're both sick."

Kalif smiled.

My cheeks burned. "I just meant . . . I mean . . ."

"I got it," Kalif said. "Calm down. Don't forget we have to hide the relationship. Company policy."

I took a deep, slow breath. "Hopefully we won't run into anyone. No story would be the best story." And given where this conversation kept going, it was the story I clearly should have suggested.

"Turn left here," Kalif said. "Eravision will be on your right."

I turned. I'd driven past the building before, when Dad was doing his initial reconnaissance. We'd passed by at night, studying the building.

"What is it trying to tell you?" Dad had asked.

The building had huge glass windows, and a revolving glass door. "It's modern," I said. "Up to date."

"That's what it's trying to tell its customers and employees," Dad said. "But you're here to threaten it. What's it trying to tell *you*?"

The front of the building rose from the sidewalk like a sheer cliff face. Since the front was glass, I could see into the lobby, which was lit with dim, recessed light even though the building was officially closed. Inside, a wide counter horseshoed around the room. There was no easy way to walk in the front without going right by it.

"They're paying attention," I said. "The glass makes the building seem transparent, like they'll be able to see everything I do. I don't want to break in the front door, because the open area makes me feel exposed."

"Is that all?"

"It also makes it seem like they aren't afraid of people breaking in. Like their electronic security is so good, they hardly need physical security."

"What do you think about that?" Dad asked.

"It's bull," I said. "No guards have come by. They have cameras, but the ones at the corners of the building aren't wired to anything I can see, so they're either transmitting picture to the mainframe wirelessly, or not at all. How's their security budget?"

"Low," Dad said.

"So, they're not spending money on bandwidth to keep them on."

"According to the schematics your mom got, they're triggered by alarms inside."

"So they'd record a get away, but not an approach. They're not recording us now."

"Fortunate for us," Dad had said, pulling down the street again. "Makes our job much, much easier."

Tonight, though, Kalif and I weren't casing the system—that work was done. My eyes were on the road in front of us, and the sidewalks on the side. Kalif turned halfway around in his seat, watching behind us. Tonight, we were looking for police.

"I didn't see anyone," I said as I drove around the block to make another pass.

"Me neither," Kalif said. "Maybe Nick's boss didn't call the cops."

I didn't know what I was hoping for. If Mom and Dad got captured, they were in trouble, which I didn't want. But if they didn't, where were they now?

We made one more pass around the block, but still the place

looked deserted. The lobby of the building was empty, and with good reason. The employee entrance was in the parking garage. Anyone who had reason to be here this late at night would come in from that side.

I turned into the alley that ran behind the row of buildings from the cross street. The Eravision parking lot was underground, directly below the building. The driveway descended from the alley and snaked around the perimeter, ending in an unmanned checkpoint with a vehicle barrier and a badge scanner.

I rolled down the window and scanned Andrea's keycard. The garage was mostly empty—only five cars on the first floor. I drove down to the second level to get a feel for exactly how many people were in the building, and found four more cars there—some of them parked far from the entrance, indicating that they'd been here since at least mid-afternoon, when the lot would have been full.

I parked right next to the elevator, and we both got out. Kalif walked a bit stiffly, like he was trying too hard to get the movement right in his larger frame. "Relax," I said.

Kalif smiled at me, but even his smile looked scared.

To get into the elevator, I scanned my keycard again. Kalif punched the button for the third floor. Andrea's office was on the opposite side of the building from the security office, but at least they were on the same floor. John worked in a cubicle on the floor above, so we'd chosen our excuse well.

We stepped out of the elevator on the third floor and walked down the hall to an open room full of cubicles. A light was on in the cubicle against the farthest wall, shining a ring of gold on the ceiling above it. Beyond that I didn't see any signs of life as we crossed the room and came to another hall and a row of offices. Andrea's cube was second on the left.

"Got the phone?" Kalif whispered. His voice was scratchy again now, taking on John's chest cold.

I touched Andrea's cell in my pocket. We usually used disposables, but whenever Mom and Dad took on a long term persona, they got a real cell phone to go with it.

"Right here," I breathed at him.

We paused at Andrea's cubicle, where I opened and closed a desk drawer, as if to remove the phone. I stood on my tiptoes, peering over the top of the cubicle, looking for anyone who might notice us, but aside from a few lights, I saw nothing.

Silently, we moved toward the security office. The big glass windows made me feel every bit as exposed as I'd told Dad that they would, but I tried to walk confidently. Andrea worked here. She was allowed to come in late at night.

We came to the security room, and I tried the door. The handle clicked, and refused to turn.

The easiest way to get in would have been to find someone with a key and lift it, but that would require a more complex operation. We'd have to use mundane skills to do this job. Luckily we had plenty of those. Mom always said it was a sloppy shifter who relied on that talent in every circumstance, when practice and training were often all that was necessary to get the job done. Since I could practice lock picking in a controlled situation, I'd done a lot of it.

I sized up the door. It was made of hollow metal, and the lock was a simple cylinder lock—not electrified or magnetic. The make had a reputation for quality. It was also a deadbolt, so getting in wouldn't be as simple as sliding my ID card between the door and the frame.

Kalif scanned the hall behind us for other employees while I checked the door and frame for signs of alarm switches—the kind that would trigger on the opening of the door, or at least record it, but there were none. Out of habit, I checked the hallway for cameras. There was one behind us pointing back toward the elevator, but not one pointing in this direction.

In the movies, every space of every building seemed to be under constant surveillance, but in real life, security systems were held back by two things: the size of the budget and the ingenuity of the maintenance and design staff. Eravision seemed to be lacking in both.

I turned my attention back to the door. No light escaped around it, no sound came from underneath. I pulled a piece of paper from a printer in a nearby cubicle, sliding it under the door to make sure there wasn't any weather proofing applied to it that would block the light. The paper slipped in easily, which meant either the office was empty, or whoever was in there liked to spend office time in total darkness.

"We're clear," I said.

"Here, too," Kalif said. "What's our cover if someone happens by?"

I pointed past the office. "The break room is back there."

Kalif nodded. "Let's get some coffee. Then we won't have to explain."

That was a good instinct. With the shape we were in, the fewer words we had to say, the better.

The coffee pot was already full of hot water—someone who'd stayed late had the same idea we did, though certainly for different reasons. Kalif poured a packet of instant into two Styrofoam cups, and topped them with water. He carried both as we walked back to the security office. So far, so good.

When we reached the security office again, I pulled a tension wrench out of my pocket, slipped it into the keyhole, and turned. Then I knelt beside the door with my cheek pressed against it.

Kalif sipped from the cup. "This coffee is disgusting," he said.

Mel was a connoisseur of gourmet coffees, so the Johnsons didn't drink instant at home. "It's the free break room stuff," I said. "What did you expect?"

"People drink this? Don't they know any better?"

"You sound like your dad."

Kalif glared at the offending cup, but I was pretty sure he meant to be glaring at me.

"Sorry," I said. "But hush now. You can complain later."

I maneuvered my lock pick so it could flip the tiny pins inside the cylinder up and down. With my ear pressed to the door, I waited for the tiny click that would tell me the pin was engaged in the right position, so I could move on to the next one. As I listened I picked up on every tiny sound—the ticking of a clock, the slurp of Kalif's mouth on his cup, and the hum of the army of computers and printers and other electronic devices throughout the offices. On my sixth try with the pick, I heard a click. First pin was in position.

A floorboard creaked around the corner, and I nearly jerked the pick from the lock, ruining my work. I hesitated with my hand still on the lock. If I pulled out the pick, I'd lose my work, but if I left it in place, someone might see it.

The floor creaked again, closer this time. I left the pick in the lock and stood in front of it, running a hand through Andrea's bushy hair to tame it.

Kalif thrust my coffee cup at me, and I took a long sip as an overweight man in a shirt and tie came around the corner, carrying a plastic thermos.

Kalif was right. This coffee was terrible.

The man's tie hung loose around his neck, and his shirt was wrinkled around the arms and collar, like he'd been leaning back in a chair in it all day.

Kalif gave a nervous wave, which looked more like a teenage move than a professional one. I took a tiny step forward, making sure to stay between the man and the door, and glanced down at the badge hanging from his lanyard.

"Hey, Devin," I said. "How's it going?" I remembered Mom mentioning Devin in her persona reports. They were acquaintances.

Of course, that didn't mean I had to go spouting off his name like a rookie.

Devin, for his part, didn't seem to notice. "Fine," he said. "I heard you didn't come in today." He peered over my shoulder. "Hey, John."

"Hi," Kalif said. He sounded uncomfortable, and I hoped

72

that was well-acted discomfort because we were supposed to be secretly dating, and not a slip.

Devin looked at me expectantly. He was waiting for me to explain why I hadn't shown up for work. The pause was already getting suspicious. I needed to pull it together—fast. "We're both sick," I said. "And we . . . forgot to call in."

Devin looked from John to me and smirked. I was glad I hadn't talked Kalif out of the dating excuse. It gave us an easy cover for my awkward execution.

"Did you hear about the break in?" Devin asked.

"Uh," I said. My stutter sounded nervous, so I took a long swig of my coffee and coughed, as if I had a dry throat. *Pull it together*, I thought. I handled this better at Emmeline's office. "What happened? I haven't heard a thing."

Devin nodded knowingly. "The alarm got set off last night. Security locked all of our workstations today and sent us home early so they could figure out what happened. No one knows who did it, but rumor is someone from HR is going to get fired."

My heart thudded. Nick Delacruz worked for HR. "What did they have to do with it?"

Devin shook his head. "I don't know. I just came in to get some things ready for the meeting tomorrow, since I couldn't do it today. I'm sure we'll know more by tomorrow. You are coming in tomorrow, right? Allan was pissed when you both no-showed."

"Yeah, of course," I said. Since I'd already made an innuendo out of my last excuse, I figured I might as well keep lumping us both together, like we were one person. That was also a new-relationship thing. "We're both feeling better, now."

Devin gave Kalif a half-smile. He seemed to have gotten the message. "Have a good night," he said.

I was pretty sure he intended that as an innuendo, as well.

I kept my voice light and cheery. "Night," I said.

We watched as Devin disappeared into the break room,

presumably for more crap coffee.

"He'll have to come back this way," Kalif said. "We better not be standing here when he does."

Our options were to skulk around and wait for him to go back to his office, or get into the security room before he came back. I knelt down, ear to the door, and went back to work on the lock.

I was on my last pin when I heard a flutter of paper. It could have been the turning of a page, or the slip of a sheet into a recycle bin. It could also have been Devin returning to poke his nose into what we were doing. I held my breath as I waited for the final click. If I pulled the tension wrench out now I'd have to start all over.

Another flutter, then the final click. I stood up, turning the tension wrench like a key, and the bolt snapped in the lock. The handle bent down as I pressed on it, and I held the lock open, with the door still closed.

I shifted my spine straighter. Done.

"See anyone?" I whispered.

"No," Kalif said. "But I heard something."

So I wasn't forming ghost sounds from the white noise. It might be Devin coming back from the break room, or it might be someone else working late. I didn't want to wait around to find out.

"Come on," I said. I turned the door handle and slipped into the security office.

The room was tiny—almost a closet. The hall light dimly illuminated a desk and shelves jumbled with cords.

I turned around as Kalif slid in behind me and shut the door.

"Don't turn on the light," I said. "Wait for Devin to pass again, or he might notice we're in here."

We stood practically on each other's toes, right inside the dark room. The only light came from the buttons on the computer tower and monitor. They caught in Kalif's eyes, and I became aware of him, standing facing me, just inches away, with not a

74

single part of him touching me.

I moved my hand slowly through the dark space behind me, feeling the edge of a desk. Slowly the shadows of the rest of the room took form. I leaned back against the desk, and cringed as a pen rolled across the top of the desk surface and stopped when it hit something—the keyboard perhaps.

Kalif and I both breathed for a moment, and as I looked down, I could make out the shape of his hand, hanging at his side just inches from mine. His fingers flexed.

I looked up into his face, and my body leaned into him. Though he looked like John, he still smelled like Kalif.

I swayed back against the desk, and Kalif put out a hand, steadying me with two fingers, like he was trying to minimize touch. I felt drawn to him, like a ball rolling down a hill, but I pushed against the feeling, restraining myself.

The floor creaked again, and I shook myself. Footsteps thumped down the hall from the break room—probably Devin.

I sank onto the edge of the desk, and when I was steady, Kalif dropped his arm. I could hear him sigh in the darkness, as the floor fell quiet outside.

I squeezed my eyes shut. It was just as well. This wasn't the time or the place to start something.

But moments from now, we'd find the security footage. I'd know what happened to my parents—and hopefully have a lead to find them. And when I found them, Kalif would go home. That had always been what would happen; we were too young and too untrained to leave home. Even if he did want to make a move, he had to know that our moment had passed, not just now in this office, but weeks ago.

We were both too early, and too late.

Kalif took a breath that seemed to come from the bottom of his toes. "Okay," Kalif said. "Let's get this over with."

I reached for the light, but Kalif held up his arm. Instead of grabbing my hand, he held his up in warning, not an inch away. "We don't need it," he said. He sat down in the chair at the desk and jiggled the mouse. As the computer woke up, a sign in screen appeared, brightening the room with blue light.

"Time to work your magic," I said. In the brighter light, I could see why the room felt so cramped. It was crammed with two filing cabinets, a desk with a computer, and a humming mass of hardware I couldn't identify—servers, maybe, or backup drives for their security video. Cords ran everywhere. Whoever worked in here was not very organized.

Kalif didn't take his eyes from the screen. "Do you want to keep watch?"

"Are you trying to get rid of me?" I asked.

"No," Kalif said. "But if someone wants to come in here, I'd like to have some warning."

I sighed. I wanted to stand right behind him, to see immediately what he found about my parents. But he had a point.

I took the full cup of coffee and slipped back into the hall. Leaning against the wall, I sipped my coffee slowly, trying not to twitch like a frightened sparrow. I waited for what seemed like forever, trying to quiet the voices that hissed in my ears. What if Kalif found nothing? What would we do then? He was used to hacking from the safety of his own room, but I'd hoped he could get through this one a bit faster. Finally, I cracked the door.

"Almost done?" I asked. Kalif stuck out his hand to check my identity, and I reciprocated.

"Yes," Kalif said. I waited for an explanation to follow, but it didn't.

I gave one last glance at the empty halls and ducked back into the office with him. "What did you find?"

He watched the numbers on his file transfer, refusing to meet my eyes. "Security footage. I'll show you at home."

My throat went dry. I couldn't wait that long. Not all the way out of the office, all the way home in the car. Not when there might be more we could do while we were here. "Show me now."

Kalif still didn't look at me. His data transfer neared

completion. When he spoke, his voice was clipped. "Let's talk later, okay?"

My hands gripped the back of his chair. "You can't do that to me," I said. "I'm going to imagine it's much worse than it is."

The file finished transferring, and Kalif ejected the drive and pocketed it. "I really think it would be better—"

"No," I said. My voice was getting louder than it ought to. I lowered it again. "Now."

Kalif looked up at me, registering the fear on my face. I saw something in his eyes, a flicker of feeling.

Oh, no, I thought. *It's pity.*

What had he seen that inspired *that*?

"I need to see," I said.

Damn. I sounded like I was begging.

Kalif nodded slowly. He turned back to the computer, moved the cursor over a file, and clicked.

Then he reached for my hand.

A video opened, showing the empty hallway between the cubicles. It was footage from the camera I'd just noticed in the hallway. The time stamp showed it was sometime in the early morning, about twenty hours before.

The hall was empty.

"There's no one there," I said. "I thought the cameras didn't monitor all the time."

"They don't," Kalif said. "This one triggered when the front door was breached."

I shook my head. "My parents wouldn't go in the front door."

Kalif squeezed my hand. I was so riveted to the screen that I barely felt it.

"Wait," he said.

Nick Delacruz's head appeared at the bottom of the screen. As he walked down the hall, the rest of his body came into view.

I held my breath. That had to be Mom.

"She came from the break room area," I said. "The elevator is the other way, so it wasn't her who tripped the door."

Kalif's thumb rubbed the side of my wrist. The way his eyes stayed riveted to the screen told me this wasn't romantic. He was bracing me for something.

The elevator doors opened on the far side of the camera's view. Still in Nick's persona, Mom stopped and casually leaned against a cubicle wall, checking her phone. It was a good pose—one that wouldn't draw suspicion from a passing co-worker.

But out of the elevator came two figures dressed all in black, ski masks over their faces. They ran at Mom, who looked up in surprise and then turned to run. One of them grabbed her arms and twisted them behind her back, applying pressure to the back of her knees to force her to the floor. Another stretched a ski mask over her head, but with the eye holes in the back so she couldn't see.

I bit my tongue to keep from crying out. I wanted to run out into the hall to save her—to find her where we'd just been. But this footage was from last night. I couldn't save her. All I could do now was watch as the men bound her at the wrists, and forced her to her feet. They grappled her into the elevator. The doors closed behind them, and the screen was still again.

SEVEN

I couldn't rip my eyes from the screen. "Where's Dad? Why didn't he save her?" Maybe that's what he was doing now—trying to find her, trying to get her out. Maybe that's why he hadn't had time to call.

Or text.

"There's more," Kalif said. "From the camera on the street." He closed the video and pulled up a second file, all without letting go of my hand.

My throat closed up. This one showed an image of a large vehicle, parked along the curb, as four people disappeared into the front door.

An unmarked, black van.

Only Kalif's hand kept me anchored to the floor. Without it, I would have spun right off the earth and into oblivion. "No," I said. "No way."

Kalif stood out of his chair, bracing me by the shoulders.

"That van," I said. They'd parked so I couldn't see the license plate. The face of the driver was obscured by a ski mask. But I'd seen one of those once, cruising down our street, hiding the faces of those inside behind tinted glass.

"Lots of people use them," Kalif said.

I barely heard him over the blood rushing in my ears. Not a lot of people had the cause or know-how to kidnap my parents in the middle of a job. "Why would they go in the front? That's stupid."

Kalif's arm tightened around me. "Maybe they weren't afraid of being caught?"

I stared at the van, still parked in front of the Eravision building, waiting. "You're always supposed to be afraid of being caught. Why are they just sitting there?"

Kalif hit a button and the video fast-forwarded. Two black-clad figures emerged from the building, dragging along another man with a ski mask stretched backward over his head. I didn't have to ask who it was—I recognized Art Cambrian's clothes. I'd helped Dad pick them out.

I held my breath, waiting for Dad to break loose, to knock his assailants out, to run around the building, shift, and escape. But though Dad fought, twisting against his captors using the same moves he'd taught me, they kept hold of him and shoved him into the back of the van.

Moments later the other team dragged Mom—still dressed as Nick Delacruz—out through the glass doors and into the van as well. The masked people slammed the back doors and boarded through the front, and the unmarked van disappeared down the street.

I watched the rear of the van, searching for the license plate numbers, but the license plate was covered with tape. It didn't matter if we could zoom in on the footage, we weren't going to get an ID from that.

The image of the empty road was still on the screen—the space where my parents had once been, the last place that I might ever see them. My head spun, and I leaned back against the wall and closed my eyes. My parents had been kidnapped by the people who'd been following my dad for months. The ones we thought we'd lost. The ones who scared him so bad he didn't feel comfortable working alone.

Kalif closed the file and shut down the computer. He faced me, placing one hand on each of my shoulders. I no longer felt like curling into him—all my joints felt stiff. I wasn't sure I would ever move again.

"Stay with me," Kalif said. He cracked the door, checking the hall.

I double checked Andrea's persona, to make sure I'd held onto it. I had, but I'd lost half an inch of her height—a small enough amount that an average person would chalk it up to posture, but sloppy all the same. I restored it, trying to steady myself.

Kalif turned back to me. "It's clear. Let's get back to the car."

I nodded. Finding my thoughts was like groping through fog. He was right; we had what we came for, now it was time to make our exit. But my limbs felt sluggish. I couldn't possibly move fast enough to escape. "That's all the footage from last night?"

Kalif shook his head, his face close to mine. "There were other cameras. But I didn't even have to dig into the raw footage. Someone had already flagged and isolated these files."

My mouth felt like sandpaper. "Nick's boss saw it this morning."

"Office security must have alerted him. Who knows what they think of it. Nick and Art are still walking around, denying everything."

Images flashed through my head of my parents, kneeling in the back of the van, black clad figures pointing guns at their heads execution-style. My breath caught in my throat. Mom might kill to get out if she had to; she said self-defense was a human right. Dad wouldn't, though. *Maybe if we were innocent,* he always said. *But in our line of work, we forfeit the right to self-defense.*

At that moment, I wished I could count on him to beat his way out of that van at any cost.

"They're gone," I said. If Mom and Dad hadn't made it out in the first twenty hours, that was a bad sign. They both had self-defense training, but judging by how quickly those teams took them down, they were outmatched.

My head throbbed. Like an idiot, I hadn't thought anyone could outmatch my parents. Like an idiot, I'd thought breaking in here would lead me right to them.

Kalif anchored me in place. "We need to get you out of here."

I knew we should make a plan first. Always have a strategy, that's what Mom said. What were we going to wish we'd done while we were here?

My mind had turned to taffy. I had the questions, but not the answers. So I followed Kalif down the hall to the elevator, past the same spot where I'd seen Mom dragged away. Kalif pressed the button to call the elevator, and I tensed. There was no one here to hurt us, I told myself. That was last night. They were long gone.

The image of the gag being jammed into Mom's mouth played over in my mind. They'd been dragged to the van still in persona. Mom and Dad had been up for almost thirty hours by now. How long could they stay awake, if they had to? Maybe three days, but not longer. Especially not without stimulants. They'd fall asleep and revert to their subconscious bodies. If their kidnappers didn't know they had shifters before, they sure would then.

Kalif took hold of my hand as we rode the elevator down. I felt detached, like someone else was controlling Andrea's body with strings. Kalif kept giving me worried looks. He nudged me as the elevator doors opened, and I realized I'd been staring into space, my eyes fixed on events we were far too late to change.

Kalif had to let go of my hand to get in the car. I went to climb into the driver's seat, but Kalif steered me around the other side. "I'll drive," he said. "You are in no shape." I sat down on the passenger seat, pulled off my glasses, and hugged my knees to my chest. Andrea's legs were gawkier than mine, and her knees knobbier, but I held them tight.

Kalif climbed in the driver's side and put a hand on my arm. Now that we were in the car, he dropped John's stuffy voice for his own. "You're shaking."

"Let's just go," I said. We needed to get out of here before I lost concentration on Andrea. In the rearview mirror, I could already see that her face was looking younger and rounder, an outward manifestation of my utter uselessness.

As we drove back to the parking garage to return Andrea's car, Kalif kept glancing at the rearview to make sure no one was following. "It's clear," he said. "Whoever took your parents, I don't think they're still watching."

Mom didn't think they were watching anymore, either. She'd told Dad over and over we were safe.

And look what happened to her.

Kalif drove through the streets, toward the garage where we'd swapped cars. "This is progress, right?" he said. "Now we know we should be looking for them."

Logically, he was right. Knowing they were kidnapped didn't actually make them more kidnapped than they had been before. But this felt like a thing that had happened just now, before my very eyes.

"We've got some leads," Kalif went on. "I can try to ID the van."

My tone came out flat, like a machine. "It's from Megaware," I said. "They were following my dad before we met you."

Kalif paused. "Megaware. I read about them in your dad's files."

"They probably know he's a shifter," I said. "Otherwise they wouldn't have been able to track him so far." My eyes burned. Twenty-four hours was enough time to sell my parents to the government, hook them up to lab machines, and begin to dissect them. There were stories—no, legends—that we didn't even have genetic faces, just gaping pits where our features should be.

Even if we could find them, I couldn't identify my own dead parents.

I could feel my body shrinking in my seat, and I struggled to hold on to Andrea's form. "Have you ever seen a dead shifter?" I asked.

Kalif put a hand on my shoulder, keeping the other one on the wheel. "Don't. Your parents are fine. We're going to find them."

My voice sounded small, like a child. "But have you?"

"No," he said. "I haven't."

My hands shook. "Me neither. I asked my mother once if she

had, but she wouldn't tell me."

Kalif spoke slowly and quietly, like he was trying to coax a frightened deer. "You can't think like this. We've got a lead. We'll keep looking."

I stared at the dashboard. He was right. We could look. But my whole body felt cold, and I couldn't drum up the will to warm it artificially. I just sat there, frozen.

Kalif pulled the car into the garage and parked Andrea's car in the spot where we'd found it. Instead of hopping out of the car, he squeezed my arm.

"Jory," Kalif said. "Talk to me." He leaned closer, his arm stretching around my shoulders. Even his nearness wasn't enough to thaw me.

I wasn't like a regular girl, with neighbors and family and school friends. We'd moved so much, fled so often, that my parents were the only people who really knew me. If we didn't find my parents, what would happen to me? Would I just disappear?

"Jory?" Kalif said. I turned to look at him, and his face was closer than I'd anticipated, only inches from mine. I'd been so caught up in the idea of leaving him that I hadn't even stopped to consider it was my parents I might never see again. Kalif ducked his head a little so it was even with mine, looking me straight in the eye.

"Really," Kalif said. "Don't panic. We'll find them."

My voice wouldn't rise above a whisper. "They could already be dead."

Kalif held my gaze with his, though his eyes were John's icy blue instead of his own deep brown. "If these people wanted them dead, they could have killed them in the office."

I squeezed my eyes shut. "Not if they didn't want to leave a mess."

"Hey," Kalif said, gripping my shoulder. "Don't think like that. They're okay."

My words came out as a wail. "You don't *know*."

Dread passed over his face like a shadow. "No," he admitted.

"I don't. But these are the thoughts that are going to get you through this, so you need to think them, okay? Will you try?"

I straightened in my seat, stretching Andrea back to her full height. He was right. I did no good to anyone paralyzed. If Mom and Dad were already dead, I couldn't make a difference, but if they weren't, I shouldn't be wasting time lamenting what might have happened. I had to stay focused, until we knew for sure.

I shifted my voice to sound confident. "They're probably fine," I said. "We'll find them."

Kalif squeezed me, drawing my face even closer to his, his eyes still trained on mine. "That's right. We're going to look until we do."

I took a deep breath. Even though Kalif still looked like John, I could feel his breath on my face, warm and soft, and my body still felt cold and frozen, like I might never move fluidly again.

"Thank you," I said.

"Hey," Kalif said. "That's what I'm here for."

He hesitated, his eyes leaving mine. And again, I could swear that he looked directly down at my mouth. He bit his lip, as if steeling himself for a decision, and then slowly retreated, widening the space between us.

Panic choked up in my throat, rushing in to take the place where he'd been.

"Wait," I said. I sat forward, drawing him close again. I put a hand on his arm, and I swear I could hear his sharp intake of breath. His eyes searched mine. I reached for all the reasons this was wrong—the fear, the inevitability of loss—and my thoughts came up empty.

I had nothing left to lose.

So I closed the inches between us, and let my mouth find his.

The gear shift dug into my hip. Despite the long moments of hesitation, Kalif's lips were soft with surprise.

And then his arms wrapped around my waist, and he pulled me in. The heat from Kalif's mouth raced through me, melting my frozen paralysis. I wanted to climb over the gear shift and into his chair and melt away into him, but I settled for sliding my arm around his side, and pressing our foreheads together.

When he broke away, I was so startled to see John's face looking into mine that I actually jumped.

Kalif laughed, his smile lighting up his whole face. And though I should have made him fix them, his version of John still had Kalif's dimples. He whispered into my ear, "you might have waited to do that until we were ourselves again."

"If I had," I whispered back, "I would have backed out."

Kalif's smile didn't fade. "Am I that ugly?"

And, in spite of everything, I laughed. "Hideous."

Kalif pushed Andrea's hair behind my ear. Then he gave me a long look, like he was trying to decide something.

"What?" I asked.

He looked regretful, like he hated himself for saying it. "We should get you home."

I shivered. "I don't want to be alone."

He smiled, his thumb grazing the corner of my mouth. "Let's at least get out of here and back to ourselves, okay?"

"Okay," I said.

I barely remembered the drive home. My mind overloaded, like when Kalif ran too many programs at once on his computer, and its processing slowed to a crawl. When we arrived, we sat in the driveway for a moment, both of us quiet. I looked up at the empty house.

I was aware of Kalif giving me sideways looks, like he was trying to decide what to say. But he stayed quiet—maybe because he couldn't think of anything that was better than the silence.

When we got out of the car, Kalif came in and changed. Then he hovered by the door, like he wasn't sure what to do. I wanted to clamp my hands around his arm, to hold him there so I wouldn't be alone in the empty townhouse, with no hope that my parents would be home on their own.

"Do you want to stay for a while?" I asked.

Kalif ran his hands up and down his arms. "Do you think it's safe?" he asked. "I don't want my parents to notice I'm gone."

I could tell that there was more, and for a painful moment, I wondered if I'd ruined everything. Did he regret kissing me? I couldn't afford tension between us now—not when I needed his help to find my parents.

My parents. They were the point, and they had to be my single focus.

"We need to keep looking," I said. "They can't stay awake forever."

Kalif looked me over. "You need sleep."

My hands shook. "I can't sleep now."

Kalif gave me a long look, appraising me. And then he closed the distance between us and gathered my hand in his. "You're no use to them if you work without rest."

I let my head fall against his shoulder. Why did he have to be right? If I tried to work in this state, I'd miss important things, or worse, make mistakes that would expose my parents to even more danger.

"Fine," I said, my voice muffled against his sleeve. "Then we should tell your parents. They can start working on Megaware."

Kalif hesitated.

I looked up at him. "What?" I asked. "They have to help us once we show them the footage."

"Do you think so?" he asked. "Because what my mom said before still makes sense. They've been kidnapped, but the cleanest way to get them out is for them to do it themselves, from the inside."

I took a step back. "But you saw what happened. They were tied up and gagged. How would they get out of that?"

"Your parents are shifters, and they have lots of experience. My parents will trust that implicitly, even though you don't."

I tried not to take offense to that. "So you don't think we should tell them."

He sighed. "I think we should find a lead, first."

I squared my feet to face him. "So we should start working on that. We begin with Megaware."

Kalif nodded slowly, like he was afraid to make sudden movements. "After you sleep."

I crossed my arms over my chest, Andrea's sleeves draping at my elbows. "I know what you're saying makes sense. But I hate it."

Kalif smiled. "Your parents aren't helpless. They're better at this than us. If they've been caught by someone who doesn't know they're shifters, they'll get out on their own."

"If that were the case," I said, "they'd be out by now, wouldn't they?"

"And maybe they are. They might have called my mom after we left. You don't know."

I pulled out my phone and checked it. No messages.

"If you need me to stay," Kalif said, "I will."

But he was right. He should get home before his parents figured out he was gone—of, if they'd already discovered that, before they figured out where he went.

"No," I said. "That's okay."

As he walked to the door, I chewed my lower lip. I shouldn't blame him for what he was saying. The fact that I wanted to was a testament that he was right; I needed sleep.

No doubt my parents did, too. I could see them, now, locked in a closet, whispering to each other to stay awake, even in the darkness. I could go upstairs and go to sleep, clearing my mind to search smarter in the morning. But they couldn't do the same, so they would be functioning at lower and lower capacity the longer it took me to find them.

And I'd wasted almost a whole day, debating.

"Text me if you need me," he said. "I'm not far away."

Then he slipped out, and as he did, an alternate image intruded—my parents slumped in that same closet, their bodies twisted with a stranger's dead and staring features.

I shut the door behind him and leaned against it.

Kalif was right. I had to believe that they were alive. I had to let that be real enough to me that it fueled my search efforts, until I found them. Until I knew, one way or the other, what had happened to them.

At least then, I'd know the truth.

EIGHT

M y body must have been stretched to the point of exhaustion, because I did fall asleep that night, almost as soon as I turned out my light. But I woke up early in the morning, before Kalif texted or knocked on my door.

I glanced at the clock. If yesterday was an indication, it would probably be another hour before Aida came to get me. I couldn't wait that long. Kalif and I needed to get to work.

Now.

I dressed quickly in jeans and a t-shirt and ran down to Kalif's. When I knocked on the door, Mel answered in his bare feet, and he took my hand.

After we exchanged signals, he raised his eyebrows at me. "Have you heard anything?"

Time to get my lie on. "No," I said. "Have you?"

He shook his head regretfully. "The situation at Eravision is too hot."

I stepped into the house, relaxing my face and evening out the tone of my voice, even though I badly wanted to rub it in his face that Kalif and I had done better than he had. With the risks we'd taken, he wouldn't have been impressed. "You must have learned something."

"We've found out they did the job," Mel said. "But, unfortunately, they botched it."

I kept my cheeks the same color, even as blood rushed toward them. I hardly thought kidnapping constituted a botched job.

Mel kept going. "Art Cambrian was supposed to go home and watch a baseball game. Instead, he met some friends at a sports bar. There are a dozen witnesses. I haven't been able to see the tape they're all buzzing about, but the security at Eravision is sure that the break-in was faked."

They would be, since Art and Nick had clearly not been kidnapped. "So if my parents finished the job, what happened to them?"

"I don't know," Mel said. "But we're cutting loose from the client, just in case. Aida's already gotten rid of the phones she was using to talk to him. The best scenario now is that your parents decided not to come back because they didn't want to tell us what happened."

It was a good thing I'd slept, because if I'd been up all night, I might have slapped Mel right across the face. Was he completely incompetent?

No. Mel and my parents had been working together for six months. If he wasn't a capable spy, we wouldn't have stuck around half that long. Mel might be wrong about how difficult the Eravision situation was—Kalif and I got in easily enough—but he was right about the general circumstances. If someone grabbed my parents, they probably knew they were shifters. And that made things perilous for all of us.

I needed to convince him to get on the same page. "Maybe you'd learn something more if you saw the security tapes," I said.

Mel nodded. "Aida's out seeing what she can glean from one of the security guards who's off duty today. I'm going to join her in an hour. But I don't think we'll be able to get into Eravision today. We want to give things some time to calm down."

I stared at him. I couldn't imagine that Mel would be this frightened to go in if he hadn't seen what I'd seen. He probably *had* seen it, but was hiding it from me. Made sense, if he didn't want me panicking, running off, and getting myself caught. "I understand," I said. I wondered how long he was planning to keep the whole truth from me. He had to know that I'd do my own poking around eventually. "Is Kalif up yet?"

Mel nodded. "He grabbed a waffle already. Something about having a lot of server maintenance to do."

I nodded. We were going to have to work on that excuse—I didn't know anything about servers, but if they needed as much maintenance as Kalif supposedly gave his, they'd be prohibitively expensive to run.

It was only after I started downstairs that I realized I should have argued more with Mel. I was being too calm about this whole thing, and the only reason I was able to manage that was because I had a lead to work on. Hopefully Mel didn't know me well enough to pick up on that.

Kalif's door was closed. I paused on the last step, staring at the handle.

I'd *kissed* him last night. In a moment of desperation and panic, I'd broken all my rules and kissed the boy I needed to help me find my parents. On my list of all-time greatest decisions, that ranked pretty low. What if he didn't want to see me today? What if he *did*, but he just wanted to make out? What if he didn't even bring it up, and our friendship devolved into chronic awkwardness?

Ugh. Living the awkwardness couldn't be that much worse than thinking about it. Could it? I took a deep breath and knocked on the door.

"Come in," Kalif said. I closed my eyes, hoping he didn't think I was one of his parents, half-afraid he'd be sitting on his bed in nothing but his underwear. But when I opened the door, I found him dressed in jeans and a hoodie, sitting on one of the stools in front of his desk. Like a guy who might be doing server maintenance.

"Hey," I said.

He looked up at me. "Hey," he said back. "My mom already left, but there's waffles on the counter upstairs, if you want some."

I fidgeted with the top seam of my pockets. Was he trying to get rid of me? No. Sending me up for waffles would only buy him a few minutes, so that couldn't be the master plan.

Please, I thought. *Get a grip.* "I'll eat later," I said. And I walked around and sat down on the stool next to him. The program up on his screen was something I didn't recognize. We checked hands, and then he released mine right away, like he didn't want to hold onto it.

I tried not to read anything into that, but I failed. Hard.

"Are you sure?" he asked. "You should probably eat."

I took a deep breath. According to the clock on Kalif's monitor, it had been twenty-eight hours since Mom and Dad left, which meant that they might still be awake, but they wouldn't be able to keep it up forever.

"No," I said. "We need to get to work."

Kalif looked down at my hands, which were shaking, though more from nerves than from lack of food.

I rested my elbows on his desk. "Really. I'm fine."

Kalif watched me, like he was trying to figure me out.

"What?" I asked.

"Nothing." He turned away, opening the mission files on his computer. "I'll pull up everything we have on Megaware."

His face shifted slightly, his eyes sinking millimeters back into his head, their shine dulling.

I closed my own eyes. Clearly this was not about waffles. I *had* screwed everything up, but I didn't know what I was supposed to do to make it better. "I'm sorry," I said.

He held up a hand. "Don't. It's fine."

"It's not," I said. "Obviously it's not."

He sighed, and took his hands off the keyboard, turning toward me. "You were a mess last night. Let's just forget about it and find your parents."

I could feel my own face shifting in ways similar to his—my features sinking and deflating. I might not be able to identify the emotion in him, but I could identify it in myself.

Disappointment.

Kalif watched me. He was waiting for me to agree with him. "Is that really what you want?" I asked. "To forget about it?"

He turned back to the computer. I could sense a question hanging unanswered between us. Did I want him? Or was I just using him to deal with the stress of my parents?

If he didn't want me, I couldn't fathom what he was upset about. I watched his mouth, his lips parted just slightly as he searched the files for references to Megaware.

We needed to work. But I had to clear the air before we did, or I'd never be able to focus. I put a hand on his arm. "Hey," I said.

He sighed and turned back to me. "Really. You don't have to—"

But I kissed him before he could finish. His mouth hesitated on mine, but only for a moment before he leaned in.

I wasn't ready for how different it was to kiss Kalif in his own body. It shouldn't have mattered. He was the same person. But his skin felt softer against my face, and our noses touched like they were made to fit together. I kept my eyes open, staying aware of the curve of his forehead, the length of his eyelashes. Kalif's arms tightened around me, pulling me in. When we broke apart, I lay my head back on his shoulder, and he held me close.

His breath blew warm against my ear. "I thought you were going to blame this on temporary insanity."

I laughed, burrowing into him. "If it's insanity, I haven't come to my senses yet."

He stiffened and pulled back slightly.

Crap. That was *exactly* what he was worried about. "I'm just joking."

"Are you? Because the timing's suspicious."

"Oh, please. You had to know I liked you before."

"Mmm," he said, burying his nose in my neck. "The kissing is new."

"Maybe I was scared."

"So now I'm ugly *and* scary."

I giggled despite myself. "Terrifying. But come on. There's no way you didn't know."

"Ha," he said, his lips barely grazing my jaw, "you underestimate how hard you are to read."

I leaned away. "*I'm* hard to read? Please. My mom said I was totally obvious."

His eyes widened, and I wished I could snatch the words back. His face curved up in a smile. "So, wait. You were talking to your *mom* about me?"

I pointed to the computer. "So about Megaware—"

Kalif's hands curled around my waist. "You're not getting out of this that easily."

I groaned, plopping my head on his shoulder. "If we don't get to work, I really am going to go insane. And then who knows what I'll do with you."

Kalif glanced over at the computer, and then down at me. "Wait, was that supposed to convince me?"

I smacked him in the arm, and he laughed.

"At least you haven't lost your sense of humor," he said.

I turned back to the computer, shifting my stool closer so our legs rested against each other from hip to knee. "We need to work fast."

"I know. But we can't rush."

I sighed. Our parents didn't do rush jobs. They always figured out what needed to happen and proceeded forward at a careful, calculated pace. We would be wise to do the same.

Kalif brushed my hair back over my ear. "You know I'm right."

My resolve crumbled. "Okay," I said. "I'll go slow. But let's work the problem."

The first thing Kalif pulled up was Dad's report about getting caught at Megaware. Dad had impersonated one of their employees, but then the mark showed up halfway through Dad's job. Dad had thought he made it out of the building okay, but the cameras caught the employee in two places at once. Dad got into his car in persona and shifted on the way home, ditching the car at a junkyard later that day.

People had wild imaginations; they should have blamed the incident on make up, or prosthetics. They shouldn't have been able to trace it back to Dad. But those slow black vans passed the house twice a day after that, until we skipped town.

"There's nothing here to work with," I said. "If we're going to trace them this way, we're going to need to get into the company communications."

Kalif nodded. "If we can get through their network security, I could search through their company emails, billing, you name it. If there's any suspicious funding or communication, we'd be able to find it."

I rubbed my temples. That wasn't a job I could do. "How long will that take?"

"Depends on their security." Kalif pulled up the workup Dad did before he ran the original job. I put my palms on the desk and studied it. The first thing I gathered was that Megaware had spent a truckload of money on their original security system.

"This is intense," I said. "If their network security is half as good as this, I gather it's going to take forever to hack them."

Kalif held up a finger. "If that's the only way in, almost certainly. But if we had someone inside, they could let me on the network from one of their work stations."

I perked up. "Breaking in is something I can do."

Kalif smiled. "I thought you'd like that part."

I took a look over the security schematics again. "Looks like they only have biometric scanners for the sensitive areas. I should be able to get in and use a computer with just a persona and a door code."

"We don't want to use your dad's profiles," Kalif said. "Since his work was compromised, they might be looking for those personas."

I nodded. "I'll need to pick a persona close to my own size."

We didn't actually change mass when we shifted—our bodies could look like a person in every detail, but our weight would be our own. Dad had told me that the few people who knew about shifters sometimes had fancy detection systems that analyzed a person's likely weight based on their body type and triggered alarms if there was a large discrepancy, like there might be if a two-hundred pound man decided to take on the persona of a fifteen-year-old girl. This was one reason our secret was important. If everyone knew about shifters, that kind of security would be everywhere.

Kalif scrolled through Dad's workup on Megaware. "How do you want to go about building a profile?"

I tapped my fingers on the desk. "Let's start with the internet."

Megaware was a publicly traded software company, which meant finding the details of their company hierarchy only required a simple search.

Kalif typed some keywords into the search engine, and scanned over the results. "There's the CEO," Kalif said. "A man, so probably not him."

High level officials would draw more attention anyway. "Right."

Kalif opened a page with profiles of some department heads. "There are three senior engineers, two men and a woman."

The fewer variables I had to reach for, the better off I'd be on short notice. "Tell me about the woman."

"Susan Aftland," Kalif said. He pulled up a picture from a social media account. She wore the barest of makeup, and had teased up her blond hair to cover its thinning. She looked close enough to my weight to be a safe candidate, and she didn't have obvious scars, braces, unnatural hair dye or tattoos in visible places. "Forty-seven years old. Husband, two kids. Address out in Tracy, so she must commute to the city."

Tracy to San Jose was a long commute, but people did it, as evidenced by the morning traffic. I squinted at her company bio. "You'd think with a job like that, she'd be able to afford to move closer."

Kalif ran another search. "It's been eight months. Maybe she has. But the White Pages still has her listed there."

I shrugged. "That means that once she leaves for the day, she won't be dropping back in."

Another quick search yielded a social media account with a few public pictures of Susan, and a video of a press conference where she announced a new product. As she spoke, I practiced her voice and mannerisms.

"We can't count on her driving the same car she was eight months ago," I said. "And we don't have access to the security footage, either, correct?"

"Right," Kalif said. "Not without hacking through their firewall, which I can do . . ."

"But not quickly," I said. "That's fine. But it means the fastest way to figure out if she's at work would be to get into the garage and run license plates. Then we can tag her car so we know when she leaves work."

Kalif nodded. "Garage security shouldn't be that bad. We can walk up the driveway if we need to. But what's our cover?"

I wavered for a moment. "Loiterers," I said. "I think we can pull that off."

Kalif's knee pressed harder against mine. "Loiterers in love. It'll be adorable."

I tried to look serious, but the muscles of my mouth bent sharply upward into a grin. "We have a job to do."

Kalif leaned toward me and kissed my neck, directly under my jawline. "I know," he said in my ear. "I'll pay attention, I promise."

I could keep the goose bumps from appearing on my arms, but I couldn't stop the tingling. Another day, I would have wrapped my arms around his neck and kept him there as long as I could. But today I stood up, clearing my head. "Let's go."

He followed, but that didn't stop him from grinning at me. I gave him a warning look, but I let him take my hand as we walked up the stairs.

Loiterers in love might be the only cover we were capable of today.

Mel left the house shortly before we did, so it wasn't hard to slip out. I grabbed a tracker in a magnetic casing from my place; we could have used one of Kalif's, but Aida and Mel might have noticed it missing.

We took Mom and Dad's car again. If Dad were doing this job, he'd have bought a crappy used car just for the occasion. A few hundred bucks could often buy a car that would run for a night or two, at least. But buying and selling cars would involve a lot more time, and time wasn't something we could spare.

When we arrived, we parked in a pay-by-the-hour garage across the street from the Megaware building—the kind that wound up for floors and floors. We got out of the car and moved into the concrete stairwell. The cameras in this garage were concentrated on the entrances and exits, not the stairs. When we were sure we were out of sight of all cameras and windows, we shifted.

I chose a persona I'd worked on with Mom a couple of months ago. Her hair was longer and blonder than mine, her face more elfin. She wore her hair down and wispy, with bangs cut evenly across the forehead of her heart-shaped face. She was adorable, to match Kalif's plan.

Kalif chose a young-looking guy about his same height, but with shorter hair and lighter skin. That was a good choice. Racist though it was, an Arab teenager loitering by corporate offices would draw attention. To remain inconspicuous, white was the way to go. Sometimes I felt guilty thinking things like that, but Mom always reminded me that it was our job to use other people's prejudices to our benefit, so we had to be constantly aware of them.

We walked around the garage so we could come to the Megaware building from up the block. Mom used to tell me that the key to acting was to find something inside you that fit the part and just be that, letting all the other parts of you melt away. I quieted all the voices that told me that Kalif and I would never last, that I should hold him at a distance or we'd both get hurt. I linked my arm through his, and leaned over to kiss him as we walked. We lumbered awkwardly together, throwing each other off balance.

My heart fluttered as we pulled back. Even in persona, Kalif's smile radiated so brightly that I couldn't help but echo it with my own.

We're working, I told myself. *It's not real.*

But unless Kalif had suddenly developed extraordinary acting skills, it had to be. Under different circumstances I might have taken notes on his expression, the way both his eyes and his mouth crinkled at the corners in mirror images of each other.

Today, though, it was all I could do to stay focused on our surroundings, to keep from being swallowed up in him entirely. Walking close together, I was acutely aware of the way that his body had filled out under his clothing, his shoulders broader, his muscles more defined. Obviously that was supposed to impress me, whether consciously or subconsciously. His body could have been anything; the physical shape wasn't a particular turn on. But the idea that he wanted to impress me . . . *that* made me tingle all over.

We approached the parking garage, both of us grinning. I caught sight of the rear corner of a black car through one of the doorways, and an image passed through my mind: my mother's body, bound and gagged and dragged into the back of the van. Ice shot through me, and it was all I could do to maintain my smile. Kalif must have seen me falter, because his arm tightened around me, bearing me up.

I leaned against him. Wise or not, we were in this together. Pulling away from him would only distract me more.

When we arrived at the edge of the parking garage, Kalif peered down the driveway. He was obviously looking for guards, which wasn't suave but was totally in character. We found an unmanned card booth instead of a guard station, so I giggled and grabbed Kalif by the arm, pulling him down the ramp. We skittered like teenagers afraid to get caught. It felt odd to behave like such fools in a situation where I'd normally be suppressing my fear and acting cool, but Mom always told me to use what assets I had. Today, these were ours.

The garage was small—only two levels. As I'd suspected, many of the employees probably paid to park across the street. I looked around eagerly, trying to appear like a young girl taking in a moment, when really I was searching for cameras.

Kalif pulled out his phone. Through his remote link to his computer he could access the programs our parents used to do background checks and run license plates. He started dialing in the numbers on the few cars on this level.

We really needed to scope the place, first. "Come on," I said, pulling him in for a kiss. His mouth crashed into mine, and we made out all the way up the driveway to the second level.

On the second floor we stumbled across our prize—a row of reserved parking spaces labeled with names. A wine colored station wagon was parked in the spot labeled Susan Aftland. The bumper sticker announced Susan as a proud parent whose kid was on the honor roll at Kimball High. Kalif already had his phone in his hand.

"Is that in Tracy?" I asked.

He nodded.

"And without running the plates," I said, hanging on Kalif's arm. "I win this one."

I spun Kalif around to kiss him again, all the while checking over his shoulder for cameras. His hands dug at the back of my shirt. I tipped my head to the side, looking around Kalif to the ceiling support beams. Kalif followed my lead, wrapping his arms around me and burying his face in my neck. Goosebumps prickled all over my body, as much from his breath on my skin as from the knowledge that parking garages were almost always monitored.

Kalif kissed my neck gently, just above my shoulder. I took in a sharp breath, and that's when I found it. A camera recessed into the concrete, about twenty feet away, positioned to take in this section of the garage.

We were being watched.

But not stopped. Not yet.

I tucked my nose toward Kalif's ear, letting my hair fall over my face to shield it from the camera. "They're watching," I said. "Push me up against the car."

Our heads rose together, our mouths locked. And either this boy was an acting god, or he'd been thinking about kissing me long, long before last night. His hips pressed against mine, backing me up slowly, one step at a time.

My heart pounded, and I forced myself to stay focused, to shift so my hip was concealed from the camera by Kalif's, and to pull the magnetic tracker out of my pocket, covering it with my hand.

My heel hit the back tire of Susan's car, and Kalif pushed me against the trunk with the weight of his body. My head spun. I kissed him back, wishing we'd done this last week, last month, sometime when we could have given our parents the slip and made out for hours, just him and me, somewhere where security guards wouldn't peep at us.

But here we were, in the middle of a job. I rubbed the heel of my shoe against the back of the tire, kicking it off.

I threw my head back and shrieked, holding Kalif near me with one arm while I reached down to get it. I didn't dare steal a glance at the camera, but I did make sure to position my hand behind Kalif's leg as I snapped the magnetic tag underneath the bumper of the car.

I laughed, and put one hand on Kalif's shoulder, using his body to steady me as I hopped on one foot, tugging the heel of my shoe back on with the other hand.

We were both entangled in each other, hopping and laughing, when the door to the elevator opened.

"Hey," the security guard yelled. "This is a private facility. No trespassing."

My heart was already hammering double time, but I made myself spin around and shriek again. Then, I did what I figured any lovesick sixteen-year-old girl would have done. I hauled Kalif by the arm and ran back down the driveway. Kalif grasped my hand and we raced together across the first floor, and out to the street.

I glanced behind us. The guard didn't seem to be following. I was glad for that. We could have knocked him out; we had the training. But we were also trained to only use violence as a last resort, because no matter what you see in the movies, anything that causes unconsciousness will sometimes kill a person. Besides, if these guys were on the lookout for shifters, the last thing I wanted to do was put them on high alert.

When we were three buildings down, we ran into an alley and leaned against the wall together, panting.

Kalif leaned over, wrapping his arms around my shoulders and kissing me hard on the cheek. I smiled. We were out of range of Megaware cameras by now, so this was no longer for show.

Kalif's heavy breath in my ear sent shivers over my whole body. He caught his breath enough to speak, though his voice still came out thick. "You," he said, "are so much *fun.*"

Fun? What the hell was I doing? My parents had been kidnapped and I was having *fun?*

My breath wasn't slowing. I gasped for air. And as I leaned against Kalif to steady myself, I could see the end coming, like the lights on a train at the far end of a tunnel. The better things were now, the harder it was going to be when I had to leave him. The events that would allow us to stay together were too terrible to consider seriously. We'd find my parents. Of course we would. It was Kalif who'd convinced me of that.

I squeezed my eyes shut, shifting my chest muscles to be larger, bearing them down on my lungs to get control of my breathing. "Focus," I said, more to myself than Kalif. "We need to figure out how I'm going to get into the building."

He studied me quietly. I could sense there was something he wanted to say, but he must have thought better of it.

He took my hand. "Come on," he said. And he pulled me into a back alley, where we could approach Megaware from the opposite side. The back door had a digital keypad, the kind where the numbers appeared in a random order each time, so a bystander couldn't discern the code by watching someone type it in from afar. In this case, that bystander was us.

"Figures," Kalif said. "Points for them."

"We need to get out of here," I said, pulling Kalif down the alley toward the main street. "If we look any more, that guard might notice that we're casing the place. Let's check the local restaurants. There's got to be a few places that deliver." That was the first rule of casing: even though it's always against company policy, the pizza guy knows the door code.

We walked the long way around the block, so we wouldn't be in line of sight of the Megaware building. Kalif held my hand even after we'd changed back into ourselves in the stairwell. My heart still pounded, and I felt like a helium balloon tied by a string. If he'd let go of my hand, I might have floated away.

I closed my eyes, leaning against the concrete wall and taking deep breaths, while Kalif did some searching on his phone. "There's a Chinese place around the corner," he said. "Their network security probably isn't spectacular, but it'd still be easier to get the information in person."

My body was finally beginning to calm. "We should use different personas, though. Less cute this time." *And no more making out on the job. Ever.*

Kalif nodded. "Still teenagers? We're dressed for it."

He had a point. "Okay," I said. We shifted as we passed through the narrow driveway that led to the street. This time he chose a blond, and I went with a brunette who was a bit taller and more muscular than the last, long in the legs, with a runner's build to match. I'd be fine as long as no one asked me to run a marathon; changing our physiology could give us the muscles of an athlete, but there was much more to athletic ability than simple muscle mass. I wouldn't have the pacing and form know-how of an actual runner.

We walked down the block with a two foot distance between us, like we were together, but only friends. It felt good to have Kalif beside me, working the problem along with me, but not hanging on me, fuzzing my head. But though I knew it was stupid to plan even hours into the future, I couldn't help but think that the next time we were alone together, we were so going to finish that kiss we'd started against the car.

The Chinese place was open, but not busy. The tables inside the shop were crusted in the drips of other people's lunches. No one was in at the moment, though, probably because the stickiness of the floor and the flimsiness of the chairs all screamed that this was clearly a take-out place.

A girl with waist-length hair stood behind the counter, looking at her phone. She'd dyed it a blue-black, but her natural blonde showed through in patches. The effect was unnatural— exactly the kind of thing we couldn't replicate. She also had some acne scars along her jaw line, but those we probably could have gotten away without. People notice their own tiny scars, but at a glance, other people usually don't.

The girl looked up at us through a thick layer of coal-black eyeliner. "To stay or to go?" she asked.

"To go," I said. "But let us look at your menu."

She nodded and went back to playing with her phone. I sat down at one of the tables and looked up at the menu posted over the girl's head. I didn't need to pretend, though. She didn't look up from her phone again.

The restaurant held two registers, but they were parked right next to each other, so there was no way for me to distract her at one register while he accessed the second. Kalif pointed to the menu and whispered to me. "I'm going to look for an office."

He got up and headed down a narrow, wood-paneled hallway toward the bathrooms.

I made a show of studying my options, but instead studied the girl. She didn't look up at me even once to appreciate the performance I was giving her; pulling the wool over her eyes wasn't going to earn me an Oscar.

Kalif came back a minute later and hung in the hallway. "Ask for the manager," he mouthed at me.

I nodded, and he disappeared into the men's room. I walked up to the counter and waited an uncomfortable number of seconds for the girl to glance up from her phone.

"Did you decide?" she asked finally.

"No," I said. "But I have some questions about your Walnut Chicken. Is there milk in that?"

She shrugged. "I don't know," she said. "Maybe."

I sighed. "What about eggs?"

She wrinkled her nose. "I don't think so."

"I'm allergic to eggs," I said. "If I have even one tiny bit of an egg, I'll break out for a week. So I kind of need to be sure."

Her face was deadpan. "We have an egg drop soup," she said. "That has eggs."

"Obviously," I said. "But the chicken?"

The girl eyed her phone, like she wished I'd quit interrupting her already. "I told you I don't know."

I sighed again, heavier. "Can I talk to your manager?" I asked. "Does he know?"

Giving a long suffering sigh, the girl disappeared into the back. A minute later she came back with an Asian man in a white shirt and a pair of khakis. Given the state of his clothes, I couldn't imagine he was the one doing the cooking.

"All of our food is cooked near eggs," he said. "If your allergy is that bad, don't eat it."

Now that I had him here, it was time to start whining. "You really don't have *anything* I can eat? I mean, come on. Some people have allergies, you know. Don't you care about your customers?"

106

"Of course we do," he said. "I wouldn't want you to get sick. That's why I'm telling you."

"What about the egg rolls?" I asked. "Do they have egg in them?"

The long-haired girl actually snorted.

I heard a flush from the hallway, and then Kalif appeared at my side. "There's nothing I can eat here," I said to him. "Let's just go get some pizza."

Kalif shrugged. "Works for me."

And we both turned around and left.

When we were back out on the street, I nudged Kalif. "Did you get what you needed?"

He waved a flash drive at me. "I got their whole address book from the office computer," Kalif said. "Including the door code to Megaware. I can also get you into the local art museum, if you want."

This time I sighed for real. "When my father finds out I'm breaking into places to save him, he'll be ticked. If he found out I broke in somewhere for a date, he'd lock me up for life."

"Maybe later, then," Kalif said. "Work, then play." He laughed as I swatted him on the arm. "I'm sorry," he says. "You're such an easy mark today."

"Yeah, yeah," I said. I focused on the sidewalk in front of us, putting one foot in front of the other. If I was even remotely tempted to break into places just to flirt with Kalif, then I was in far more trouble than Mom had thought. "Let's get home," I said. "I need to change into some business attire."

NINE

spent the rest of the afternoon working on my Susan impersonation. I found a pants suit in Mom's closet that looked professional in a vanilla kind of way. The best thing would be to duplicate a suit Susan wore regularly, but I settled for an indistinct outfit that seemed to fit her buttoned-up style.

Standing in Mom's bedroom, I could feel her everywhere, like she was already a ghost, always flitting outside the edges of my vision. As soon as I had my clothes ready, I headed over to Kalif's. Even the possibility of being caught by Kalif's parents was better than the silence.

While Kalif worked on his computer, I studied myself in his full-length mirror, working on matching Susan's face. We had no way of knowing what she might have done to her hair after the company photo was taken, and so I pulled it back in a bun and threw a bell hat over it, the way a woman might if she had to go out in public but didn't have time to groom. That should eliminate the possibility of having to explain a sudden change of hair color, or six inches of overnight growth.

Aida only poked her head in once, thankfully after I was done rehearsing the physical transformation.

"Your dad will be out all night," she said to Kalif. "So don't worry about him."

Kalif nodded without looking at her. "Is he looking for Jory's parents?"

Aida shot him an annoyed look. "He's doing reconnaissance, yes."

Kalif's answer was clipped. "'Kay."

When Aida disappeared upstairs again, I sat next to Kalif at his desk. "What was that about?" I asked.

"It's nothing," he said. "It just means Dad's finally found an opening at Eravision." He'd been teasing me all day, but now the laughter was gone from his voice.

I rested my elbows on the edge of the desk. "We did that yesterday. How hard could it be?"

Kalif cleared his throat. "Yeah, well, Dad works differently from the rest of us."

I dropped one hand to the desk, knocking my knuckles against it. "Quit being cryptic."

Kalif's shoulders hunched. "He's seducing someone, okay? It's his preferred method."

My stomach turned. "Oh."

Kalif sighed. "Yeah."

We all did questionable things on jobs, but seducing someone for money wasn't just a betrayal of a stranger. It was a pretty sleazy thing to do to your real-life spouse and family. "I'm sorry," I said. "I shouldn't have pushed. I just didn't expect the answer to be so . . ."

"Disgusting?"

I grimaced. "That's a word for it."

Kalif shook his head. "He's always been like that. He says it's because people with their clothes off will tell you anything."

I squirmed. "Seems like it would be effective. But you don't believe that's why he does it?"

He gave me a look. "Would you?"

I cringed. "And he talks to you about that? Like it's normal?"

Kalif pushed his stool away from the computer. "Even if he didn't, I've seen the files. Sometimes I wish I didn't know the things I learn in there."

And to think I'd been jealous that he got to be so involved in that aspect of the job. "What about your mom?" I asked. "Is she okay with it?"

Kalif shrugged. "She deals with it. Better than being alone, I guess." His face was shifting to look more like his mom. It wasn't hard to guess whose side he took in all this.

I couldn't help but be a little relieved about that.

But my stomach twisted further, thinking about the mission files. If Kalif read about everything that happened on missions, he'd know all kinds of things I didn't. "What about my parents?" I asked.

He looked up at me. "What about them?"

I squirmed. "Are they . . . seducing people?"

Kalif shook his head. "If they're taking those jobs, they're not turning in notes about them."

My body relaxed. "I don't think they are. They're pretty careful about not hurting each other."

Kalif's face turned curious. "They seem like they're really in love. That's not an act?"

"No," I said. "Sometimes it gets pretty mushy."

He smiled. "Better than the alternative."

"Yes," I said. "Much better." I wrung my hands a little, and then shoved them into my pockets. "Sorry to bring all this up."

He put a hand on my arm. "It's okay. It's good to know that some people have functional relationships."

I suppressed the goosebumps sprouting up my arms. From the way he looked at me, I couldn't help but feel like he was thinking about *our* future.

The one that would be over as soon as we found my parents.

"Keep an eye on that tracker," I said. "We need to know as soon as Susan leaves."

And if Kalif noted my rapid change of subject, when he turned back to his computer, he didn't let it show.

At seven o'clock, Kalif's tracking program showed Susan's vehicle heading north. It stopped again two hours later; the GPS put it in a subdivision on the outskirts of Tracy. "Guess she didn't move closer," Kalif said.

110

"Sucks for her," I said, "but safer for me."

Kalif kissed me goodbye when I left. He sat on the stool, and I stood in front of him, my hands tangled in his hair. "I wish I could go with you," he said. "But I'm more help here."

I smiled down at him, backing away. "I'll be careful," I said. "I'll call you when I'm inside."

Kalif took both my hands in his. "What are you going to do if you get caught? If they're expecting shifters, you might not be able to just change and get away."

I took a deep breath. "I'll send you a blank text if anything drastic happens," I said. "And you can tell your parents. Just . . . don't let them leave me there."

Kalif squeezed my hands. "I won't. Believe me. Besides, I don't think they would treat you the same way as your parents. Dad's much more likely to think you're the sort of person who needs saving."

Ick. "Let's hope he's wrong about that." I squeezed his hands back, and our fingertips lingered as I moved away, breaking apart only when our arms could no longer reach. I'd lengthened my arm a little, to hold on longer. I couldn't be certain, but I thought he'd done the same.

As I left his house, the space beside me felt empty. But my mind cleared, no longer tracking his every motion. Today I'd work sharper alone.

At home, I changed into my Susan costume, and paced the halls until midnight, to be sure that Megaware was as empty as possible. Before I left, I checked myself in the mirror, making sure I could slip in and out of Susan's persona. The details of the face were the most important—people would notice right away if I got it wrong.

I drove back to Megaware and parked several blocks away this time, in a lot that was free after midnight. It wasn't until after I parked that I thought about the dangers of walking four blocks alone downtown in the middle of the night, but I got out of my car and tried to walk like it didn't bother me. I saw a few figures moving in the shadows, but I moved toward the Megaware building with purpose. At least I hadn't brought a purse—that was my excuse for going inside. I'd left it in my office, like an idiot, and I just *had* to have it back tonight. But it also meant I had nothing for a thief to snatch.

I moved to the back entrance of the Megaware building and up to the keypad. I pushed the button at the bottom of the pad, which lit up with the numbers zero to nine, in a scrambled order. I entered the code, and the door clicked.

Since this was a back door, it led into a hallway instead of a lobby. I eyed the sides of the wall, checking for cameras, and paid careful attention to the give of the floor as I stepped in, searching for anything that might indicate a pressure plate. I was so busy searching for shifter traps that it wasn't until the door closed behind me that I saw the card reader at the other end, in front of another door, a security camera pointed right at it. Classic man trap. I tried the door, but wasn't surprised to find it locked.

No shifter-specific tech in sight, but they'd cornered me with regular tech just as well. I didn't have a card. Even if that data had been in the profile, badge ID codes changed often in high security facilities. I checked the lock. It was sealed with bars triggered by electrical pulses from the card reader. We owned the equipment to foil it, but I hadn't brought it with me.

Instead, I picked up the emergency phone. *Dial 4 for Lobby*, the sign told me. So I did.

I waited for the guard to answer the phone, but instead a popping noise came through a speaker in the ceiling, which probably routed to his handheld instead of to the phone in the lobby. I hadn't noticed it, which was sloppy of me. One point for the guard, zero for me.

"Can I help you?" the guard asked, his voice crackling through the static. He was starting off polite. Good move on his part.

I turned my face up to the security camera so he could see Susan's features below the hat. "I'm sorry," I said. "I left my purse in my office, key card and all. Could you let me in so I can get it?"

There was a silence, probably as he checked the video feed.

"Oh, Ms. Aftland," he said. "I didn't recognize you in that hat."

I controlled my urge to twitch. If he knew to look out for shifters, the hat would be exactly the kind of discrepancy that would peak his suspicions. I needed to be more aware of those things—people who knew about shifters were rare, so I didn't have a lot of training in dealing with them.

But if I'd raised red flags, he didn't show it. "Couldn't wait until tomorrow, eh?" he asked.

I shrugged. "If it's not in my office I need to start calling the credit card companies. Don't want to give a thief a head start."

"All right. I'll be right down."

He wasn't just going to buzz me through. Two points for him. I just hoped he wasn't coming to get a closer look at my hair.

When he opened the door, I recognized the guard from the parking garage. His ID was pinned to his breast pocket—Aaron Fern.

"Thanks, Aaron," I said. At least that wasn't a name with common nicknames. I never knew what to call a Richard or a Michael or an Elizabeth.

Aaron nodded. He took a good look at me, but didn't seem to find anything out of place. "I suppose you'll need to be let into your office, as well?"

I gave him an apologetic smile. "Yes, sorry."

"Not a problem. That's my job."

He hesitated, waiting for me to go first.

My heart beat faster, and I controlled my breath and my skin tone, so my nervousness wouldn't show. I walked in front of Aaron down the long hallway, until I spotted the elevator. I went right to it, like I'd been walking there all along, and stood in the corner, letting Aaron man the control panel.

It turned out Susan's office was on the fourth floor. I edged backward in the elevator, so Aaron stood much closer to the door than me. When the elevator doors opened, it was only natural for him to take the lead.

And, thankfully, he did.

He led me to Susan's office, and unlocked the door with a proper key. I looked around once inside. The office was spotless, without so much as a paper out of place. And, of course, no purse.

Aaron waited in the doorway. Three points for him. If I didn't step my game up, this was all going to be for nothing.

"It looks like it's not here," I said. "That's not good."

"Sorry you made the trip back, then." Still he waited, but he didn't look alarmed. He probably wanted to make sure I didn't get stranded somewhere else in the building without my keys. I needed some reason to be alone.

"I'm going to call my husband for those credit card numbers," I said. Then it came to me. "Could you check with the janitorial staff to see if they found it, just in case?"

Aaron paused, and I held my breath. That was exactly the sort of thing he wouldn't do, if he thought I might be a shifter.

But he gave me a sharp nod. "Will do." And then he left.

I closed the door, giving the room a once over, looking for cameras. Was Aaron watching through a video feed outside, waiting for me to slip up?

I kept my persona up just in case, glad I'd given Aaron a reason to be on my phone. I sat down at the computer. Then I dialed Kalif.

"I'm in," I said.

"Is the computer on?"

"Not yet."

"Boot it up, then follow my instructions exactly."

Kalif gave me a series of keystrokes to hit, and I worked through the process of giving him remote access. From there he'd be able to get into the main system without having to deal with the firewall. By the time anyone found the security breach, he'd have transferred all the information we needed to our server, and then covered his tracks.

I was glad he was good at this, because I was clueless.

A minute after I finished, a knock came at the door. I stood up just as Aaron came in, hands empty.

"They didn't find a thing," he said. "I'm sorry."

"Would you believe it?" I said. "My husband went to get the numbers, and there was my purse, sitting right next to the filing cabinet. I swear I looked there twice."

Aaron smiled. "And after you made the drive. Isn't that how it always works?"

I tried not to wilt in relief. I left the office and shut the door. If Aaron noticed that I'd left the computer on, he didn't say a word.

I thanked Aaron again as he let me out. As always, I hoped he didn't get in trouble for what I'd done. He was good at his job.

I'd scored only one point against him, but as it turned out, that was the only one that mattered.

TEN

That night, I couldn't sleep, and Kalif didn't. He sat at his computer, looking through the information we'd stolen, searching for clues. I stared at my phone, checking to make sure it was on, waiting for the text message from Kalif saying he'd found out where my parents were. When my blinds turned yellow with daylight, he still hadn't texted me. I sent him a message instead: *Fall asleep?*

I wish, he answered. *Still looking.*

At nine AM he appeared on my doorstep with red-rimmed eyes. "Breakfast," he said. "But still nothing."

I knit my fingers together. "Will you be able to keep looking with your parents around?"

"I should be able to," he said. "They won't check what I'm doing on the computer. But it might take some more time."

He'd already been looking for so long, I felt bad pushing him for more. But they'd been gone for so many hours. If they'd been sold for research, they could be literally anywhere by now. "Is there anything I can do to help?"

Kalif shook his head. "I don't think so. I'm sorry."

I tried not to look sullen. Teaching me the skills I'd need to sort through encrypted data would take much longer than doing it himself. "It's okay," I said. "I'll bring my books."

For breakfast we had spinach quiche topped with feta, and delicious though it was, I couldn't help but think that if Mel and Aida put half the work into finding my parents as they did

116

into their breakfast food, my parents would have been home by now. Kalif scarfed his food down faster than I would have expected from someone who'd spent the night poring over data, and slipped back to his room before his parents had even served themselves. I ate more slowly. I wasn't in a rush to go hover over his shoulder, since that's how I'd likely be spending the rest of the day.

Mel walked through the kitchen and waved good morning. I met his eyes like everything was normal, and tried not to think about the things he'd been doing to find my parents. I hoped Aida wasn't mad at me, since my family was the cause of this particular philandering. Although, to listen to Kalif, it seemed like he didn't particularly need the excuse.

As I forked a bite of mushroom crust into my mouth, both Aida and Mel sat down across the table from me, looking somber.

I put down my fork. "Bad news?" I asked.

Mel nodded, his face grave. "Unfortunately. Things settled down over at Eravision, and I got in to see the security video. It looks like your parents were taken captive."

Instead of faking shock, I nodded like I'd expected that. "That seems like the only reasonable explanation for why they haven't come back."

Aida reached across the table and took my hand. "I'm sorry we haven't been able to find them. We're doing the best we can."

"Do you have any idea who took them?"

Aida and Mel exchanged a glance.

"We have a working theory," Mel said. "Do you remember, a few months before we met you, your dad ran a job for a company called Megaware?"

It was all I could do not to roll my eyes. I assumed that Aida and Mel had had this theory for a while, and just now felt they had to break it to me, but we were so far ahead of them that I could barely compose a civil response. "That's what I thought, too. They might have been following Dad, even after all this time."

"We're working on the lead," Aida said. "We just want you to be prepared. If your parents were kidnapped by people who know what they are . . ."

I tensed. "It's bad. I get that." And I certainly didn't need her finishing that sentence to add to my visions of torture and experimentation.

Mel gave me a sympathetic glance. "It might be a while before we find them. Why don't we rearrange our office room, and you can sleep here? We don't like the idea of you all alone and worried over there every night."

I considered that. Staying here would make it harder for me to sneak out at night, if Kalif and I needed to run more missions. Their office was right next to their bedroom; they might also be offering so that they could keep an eye on me. But as soon as Kalif found a lead at Megaware, we'd probably tell them what we'd been doing; we'd be stronger as a joint force than Kalif and I were alone. Staying here would put me closer to Kalif, and closer to the investigation.

"Okay," I said.

Aida smiled. "Pack some things today. I'll have the office all ready for you by tonight."

I nodded. "I'll do that. Thank you."

Hopefully they wouldn't pitch me out again when they realized I'd been making out with their son.

After breakfast I sat on Kalif's bed with his laptop, trying not to fume about Mel and Aida's refusal to let me help them. Kalif hunched over his keyboard, focusing on the data in front of him. I wanted to sit next to him, but kept myself glued to the bed. After all my lectures about how we should focus, I couldn't make a hindrance of myself now.

I meant to study, but instead I wandered onto Kalif's conspiracy forums, searching for images of dead shifters. Aida and Mel were right; I needed to be prepared for the worst.

The nuts on the conspiracy boards argued endlessly about how to spot a shifter, some claiming that we couldn't change our eye color, others claiming that we could only change at night. It was nonsense, of course. I told myself that their theories on death were probably just as nonsensical, but that didn't prepare me for the images of the bodies.

There were three of them in all; three people who'd died within days of the photos, according to the posts. Their faces were sunken, like their features had melted back into their skulls. Acute post-mortem myopathy, the morticians called it. The conspiracy nuts called them shifters.

I was so absorbed in the photos that I didn't see Kalif walk up next to me until he put his hand on my shoulder. "They're just crazies," he said. "It's not real."

I still couldn't rip my eyes from them. "The photos are doctored, then?"

He sat down beside me on the bed. "No, those are real. But it's some drug effect, something people do to disguise dead bodies. That's not us."

I leaned against him. "How do you know?"

He shrugged. "I guess I don't. But I also don't believe anything I read on those forums. Did you read that we can turn invisible? Or that we're all assassins? Or that one of us killed President Kennedy?"

I shut the laptop. He was right. I was clearly losing my mind. "Fine," I said. "They're crazy. Give me something productive to do before I join them."

Kalif wrapped his arms around me and squeezed. "Okay," he said. "Let me find something for you."

Kalif had me run some searches through the company email, but I came up empty handed. In the late afternoon, I sat watching the seconds tick by. Mom and Dad had been gone almost sixty hours. The chances of them staying awake that long were small, and they almost certainly wouldn't make it past three days. Even with training, that was just too long to go without crashing. That meant whoever had them knew about their personas, if they hadn't already. From here on, the layers of trouble just got deeper and deeper. If they were even still alive. We had to find them.

In the evening, Kalif closed his door. "Look," he said, "you aren't going to like this."

I drew a deep breath. "Just tell me," I said. "Whatever it is, I can take it."

Kalif looked down at the floor. "Megaware is clean. Or at least, there's no digital evidence they're involved."

The floor seemed to drop out underneath me. Anything but *that*. "They have to be," I said. As soon as the words were out of my mouth, I heard my own desperation. Black vans weren't proof. Likelihood wasn't a guarantee.

But if Megaware wasn't involved, then we had nothing. My voice was weak. "Can you check again?"

Kalif shrugged helplessly. "I've been through everything twice—emails, digital phone records, security footage. I checked their property holdings and their expense accounts. I found all the information I expected to about the correspondence with your parents. There's nothing suggesting that Megaware followed your parents, or that they have the facilities to hold people, or that they're hiding anything at all, besides their very legitimate software development. If someone inside did it, they did it without company correspondence, so I'm not going to find it here."

Kalif's voice seemed to grow quieter as he spoke, like someone was turning down the volume. All the sounds—the humming of the computer, the footsteps of his parents upstairs—faded as my mind emptied. "So we've got nothing."

Kalif took my hand, but I could barely feel it. "We'll keep looking."

But I couldn't think of anywhere to look that would help. "You need sleep," I said.

"We both do," Kalif said. "We'll think better in the morning."

The morning. Past the seventy-two hour mark. By then, my parents would certainly have fallen asleep. And if they hadn't been sold or dissected or tortured by then, after that they certainly would be.

My stomach turned. What if their captors decided to cut on them? Torture could leave marks, couldn't it? Then, even if they did escape, they wouldn't be able to shift to hide. We couldn't disguise open wounds or thick scar tissue.

It would be enough to bring new meaning to the phrase scarred for life.

Kalif touched my arm and I turned away instinctively. He quickly withdrew his hand, and I hated myself for acting like I blamed him. I wanted him to kiss me, but he still sounded so far away, I wasn't sure how I'd bridge the gap. So instead I just climbed up the stairs. I was dimly aware of him standing at the bottom of the staircase behind me. He must have felt so useless. I should have thanked him for looking. I should have assured him this wasn't his fault.

But I didn't have the strength to turn around.

ELEVEN

That night, while tossing and turning on the squeaking air mattress Aida had wedged into their office, I dreamed of searching through the Eravision building for my parents. The fluorescent ceiling lights glowed so brightly that I couldn't fully open my eyes, and I crawled from the elevator on my hands and knees, struggling to look up. I couldn't walk. I couldn't see.

I couldn't find them.

My fingers brushed cold flesh, and I pried my eyes open, catching barely a glimpse of the hall in front of me. Shriveled, blank faces lay before me, and I tried to scream, but couldn't make a sound.

I woke to cold sweat and a howling void in my chest. I rolled over, and bumped my elbow on Aida's desk, barely an inch from my mattress. My fingers creaked as I unclenched my hands, and my jaw and teeth ached equally. I sat up, fighting for breath.

My parents might be dead. We had no leads, so even if they weren't, we'd probably never find them. Even if the blank faces were a hoax, I still wouldn't recognize their bodies. Once their minds were gone, their subconscious selves would fade, like they never existed.

And I'd never know the truth about what happened.

I hugged my knees, shivering. I was all alone in the world.

Kalif, I thought. I needed Kalif.

I climbed out of bed, itching to pace, but the mattress filled the floor between Aida and Mel's desks, leaving me no space. I opened my door as softly as I could, and listened. Silence came from the direction of Aida and Mel's bedroom, so I tiptoed out into the hall, testing each of the floorboards before shifting my full weight on it. One of the stairs creaked a little, so I skipped it, stepping down to the next one. All this sneaking wasn't my usual way—my impulses told me to use a persona. But Mel would appreciate finding a stranger in his home even less than he'd like finding me sneaking down the stairs.

I half expected Kalif's room to be alarmed, but nothing happened as I pushed the door open. Streetlight shifted through his blinds, casting slats of blue light across him in his sleep. He had one arm tossed across him, and the other stretched toward the edge of the bed. A blanket covered his chest, but his bare shoulders were exposed. I stood there in the doorway, listening, but except for the hum of the refrigerator, the house was perfectly quiet. I stood there, frozen, watching Kalif sleep. His jaw wouldn't hurt in the morning.

I should just leave him alone. He'd been through enough of my drama, and he'd barely slept, helping me search.

But as I turned to go, the howling in my ears grew louder. I couldn't go back to that room alone, and I couldn't go home. If I told Kalif tomorrow that I'd stood here, needing him, and then let him sleep, he'd be disappointed in me.

So I stepped into his room and closed the door behind me. At the edge of the bed, I took his hand, pressing our palms together. He shifted to the side and opened his eyes, squinting up at me. Then he tightened his grip on my hand, and we each adjusted our temperature; me warm, him cold, then him warm, me cold.

Suddenly I felt like I needed a reason to be there, and I didn't have words to explain the emptiness that threatened to swallow me. "I had a bad dream," I whispered. Kalif nodded and moved over. I sat down on his bed and shifted his covers over me, filling the warm spot where he'd been. He was only wearing boxers underneath, but he didn't seem embarrassed. He propped himself up on his elbow and I lay down beside him with my head on his pillow.

He looked down at me, his face still wrinkled from the pillow. "Do you want to talk about it?"

I shivered. "Not really."

Kalif shifted the blankets out of the way, so that I could curl up to him. His foot hooked over my ankle, pulling me closer. My hands slid over his bare skin, and his mouth lingered gently on mine.

Kalif's body was warm in all the ways mine was cold. As our mouths moved together we rolled into each other, breathing as one. Kalif's hands worked up under my t-shirt, scratching gently over my hips. They hung there for a moment like a question. So I slipped my shirt off over my head.

Warmth hummed over me, rising to a fever pitch where Kalif's body touched mine. Our stomachs pressed together, and I could feel my body stretching and molding, fitting itself into the hollow of his. We reacted to each other instinctively, as if our bodies were made to fit with each other's. As if they already knew how. I closed my eyes, letting the song of him fill my ears, shutting out the pain.

Kalif kissed me softly under my ear, and traveled down to my jaw. He paused at my chin, whispering into my neck. "If my mother catches us, she's going to kill us." But he drew his body closer to mine, his teeth grazing my shoulder.

I couldn't breathe; I didn't want to. I stretched out on the mattress, letting his hands work up my back as his mouth worked down my neck. Our bodies arched, our hips moving together. I could feel my body shifting with him, becoming leaner, not to impress him, but to match him.

My heart raced. This wasn't what I meant to do when I came down here, was it? I kissed the sweat away from his chin and upper lip, but my toes stuck out the bottom of the blanket, tingling from the chill. And this thought pushed its way in: Kalif could be gone tomorrow. He could just shift away without warning, twist into something else and disappear forever. The cold seeped into my bones. I pushed my body up against Kalif's, trying to get warm again, but it was too late. The storm in my chest ripped free, howling in my ears. By the time Kalif's mouth hit my collar bone, I was choking on my own tears.

Kalif looked up at me and froze. I wanted to wrap back into him, to draw all his heat into me, but instead my body crumpled in on itself, drawing up into a ball.

"I'm sorry," Kalif said. He lay aside, regret stretching over his face. "I'm so sorry."

I sniffled against the sobs. "It's not you," I managed to say. A hundred times over, it wasn't him.

Kalif hovered near me, as if he wasn't sure if touching me would help or hurt. I pushed my face into the pillow, trying to stop the tears, but my chest kept heaving, and my breath wouldn't slow.

He put a hand lightly on my shoulder, turning me away from the mattress, trying to uncoil me. "Hey, it's okay," he said. "Can you talk about it?"

I sniffled between words. "I'm sorry,"

Kalif shook his head. "No, don't be. I shouldn't have—I didn't mean to take advantage."

I laughed, though my nose was running like a faucet from the tears, so I probably looked like a complete maniac. "I didn't mean to throw myself at you. That wasn't the plan."

He squeezed his eyes shut and cringed. "I wasn't exactly complaining. But I know you're a mess over your parents. I've been there. I know better."

Everyone's posture changes when they feel guilty. Shoulders slump, foreheads draw back, arms cross protectively over chests. But Kalif's whole face shifted, his mouth widening, his eyes rounding out. The changes were subtle, but millimeters of difference can have a profound influence on a face.

He looked so much more like his father.

I must have been staring, because Kalif rubbed his cheek self-consciously. "What?" he asked.

I tried not to smile. Laughing at him would only make him feel worse. "Your face is shifting. You look like your dad."

Kalif buried his head in his pillow. "I," he said, "am a bastard."

I smacked his shoulder. "Shut up," I said. "You are not. I'm the one who came down here and attacked you and then started crying."

Kalif sounded miserable. "Yeah, and I knew you were vulnerable, and I didn't care."

If he didn't care, he wouldn't be so upset about it now. I laid a hand on his bare shoulder. "Relax," I said. "I'm pretty sure I was the one trying to take advantage of you."

His face was normalizing now, whether by instinct or by force. "I still feel like a jerk."

Now I did smile. "And when you feel like a jerk you look like your father?"

Kalif looked disgusted, at himself *and* his dad. "Yeah, well. The shoe fits."

I sighed. "Look, don't blame yourself. I shouldn't have started any of this."

He looked like I'd slapped him.

"No," I said. "I didn't mean *any* of it. I just meant I should have let you sleep."

Kalif shut his eyes, his cheek squished into his pillow. "Am I a total asshole if I say that I'm glad you're here?"

I couldn't help but smile. His self-loathing was kind of adorable. I lay down next to him and kissed him on the forehead.

"Thank you," I said.

He opened his eyes, looking at me. "For what?"

I pressed my face against his so our foreheads rested together. "For being here."

He smiled and wrapped his arms around me, holding me tight against him. "For that," he said, "you are very welcome."

And we lay there like that, just holding each other, and for that one moment, I allowed myself to believe that I'd never have to let him go.

An hour later I felt warm from head to toe. Kalif had fallen asleep lying behind me with his head next to mine on the pillow, his chest pressed against my back. The clock on his desk showed four AM.

I rolled onto my back, and Kalif opened his eyes.

"Hey," I said. "I should probably go back upstairs."

Kalif reached for me, his arm settling across my stomach. "Do you have to?"

I groaned. "Only if we want to live to see morning."

Kalif sat up. "Are you going to be okay alone?"

"I'll be fine." Climbing out of bed, I felt like a scrap of metal fighting against a giant magnet. But I did it anyway, and shuffled through the sheets to find my lost shirt, and pulled it on.

Kalif reached out and took my hand. "We'll keep looking for your parents, okay? We still have all the records of their old operations, and their lists of enemies. We'll find something."

I sighed. We couldn't be sure that we would, but he was right. We needed to keep looking. If I were the one missing, my parents wouldn't give up. "Okay," I said. "Thank you." And though everything in me wanted to stay there with him, I dragged myself out of his warm room and into the drafty stairwell.

As I walked up the stairs to the main level, I heard a click up by the bedrooms. I walked over to the sink and turned it on, filling a glass of water. That step at the top of the stairs creaked, and Aida looked down at me.

Aida squinted at me. "I heard something."

I flailed a hand at the sink. "I'm just getting a drink. I couldn't sleep."

She nodded, but she also waited to close her door until I was safely shut back up in my room with my glass.

TWELVE

In the morning, I stayed in my new room, waiting to be called down for breakfast. I buried myself under my borrowed blankets, letting my cheeks burn, as if doing so would evaporate my embarrassment.

What had I been thinking? Crawling into bed with a guy I'd been kissing for a couple of days? When the only chance I had of staying near him was if my parents were *dead*?

I jumped when Aida knocked on my door.

"Breakfast," she said, as I pulled it open. She slid her hand in, and checked my signal before she went on. "Mel's already gone for today. He's following a woman who works at Megaware. Hopefully when he returns, he'll have news."

My stomach sank. I wondered if he was following this woman by his usual methods.

But it shouldn't matter. There was still a chance that Mel would find something Kalif hadn't, and any news at this point was good news. "Is there anything else we can do?"

"No," Aida said. "I'm going to make some phone calls. It's possible I'll turn something up before he does."

I looked at the floor. She wasn't even going to let me make *calls* for her. I was better off proceeding on my own. "Thanks for looking," I said.

"Of course," Aida said. She traveled down the stairs, and I heard a muffled knock as she called Kalif to breakfast as well.

He was probably exhausted.

I heard Kalif's door open as I came down the stairs. I was still wearing my t-shirt and sweats, but Kalif came upstairs fully dressed for the day, which meant he'd been up even before his mom knocked.

I met Kalif at the top of his stairs, just as he was reaching the kitchen. He took my hand and gave me our signal, the corners of his mouth turning up in a suppressed smile. Again he held on a moment longer than he needed to, only this time I was sure that he meant to. I squeezed his hand back. He turned his face away from the kitchen, so his mother wouldn't see his mouth slip into a full grin.

Aida looked at us sideways from the oven, where she pulled out a pan full of muffins. I dropped his hand, but it was too late. She'd seen.

If Kalif was worried about it, he didn't show it. He recovered his composure, and we both sat down at the table. Our plates were already overflowing with hash browns, and Aida topped them off with a blueberry muffin apiece.

"Thanks," I said.

"You're welcome." Aida watched us both eat. I wondered if she was regretting offering me a place to sleep here, or if she was starting to put together that I'd been down in Kalif's room last night.

After breakfast, Kalif turned to me. "Give me some more help with voices?" he asked.

I nodded. It was the perfect opportunity to spend some hours downstairs, figuring out what we were going to do next.

Aida narrowed her eyes. "Why don't you go on down," she said to me. "I need to talk to Kalif for a moment."

I gave him a sidelong look as I stood up from the table, but Kalif didn't look nervous. "Sure," I said.

When I got downstairs I closed Kalif's door behind me, leaving a crack between it and the doorframe. From upstairs it would seem I did that to give them privacy, when really I just wanted to stand in the doorway with my ear to the kitchen without looking obvious.

From here I couldn't hear every word, but I did catch Aida saying "respect" and "appropriate." I leaned against the wall, wishing I could shift into it and disappear.

Kalif said something in a reassuring tone, and then I heard Aida say, clear as day, "you stay downstairs, and she stays upstairs," which meant she'd raised her voice a little to say it. I swallowed. She knew I was listening.

Message delivered.

The stairs creaked, and I stepped away from the door and sat down at Kalif's computer. Kalif moved into the room, and I checked his hand again, just in case.

When we finished, I hugged my arms and whispered at him. "She knows?"

Kalif shook his head no. He closed the door, leaving it open a crack, just like I had.

My shoulders sank. "She told you not to close it?"

He smiled. "Yes. And you're not allowed in my room at night."

I put a hand over my eyes, mostly so I wouldn't have to watch him laugh at me. "So she does know."

"No," he said. "She was speaking hypothetically. If she knew, she'd still be yelling at me."

I groaned. "I'm sorry."

Kalif folded me into his arms. "Don't apologize," he said in my ear. "It's okay. Really."

I could feel tears burning in the corners of my eyes—more from embarrassment than relief. I buried my face in his shoulder. "I'm sure that'll be a comfort after I die of humiliation."

Kalif laughed. He probably would have been laughing with me if I could just join in. "Let's get some work done, before my mom decides she needs to forbid you from coming down here at all."

I winced. "Is she that uptight?"

Kalif shrugged. "I think she's mostly concerned that I show respect for you. That's always been really important to her."

I wondered what she'd say if she knew that *I* was the one crawling into *his* bed. "Is that because of your father?"

Kalif nodded. "She doesn't want me turning into him."

I eyed him. "Obviously she's not the only one who's worried about that."

He blushed. "Can we forget about that?"

Now it was my turn to laugh. "Oh, come on. It's cute."

He shook a finger at me. "Looking like my father is never cute."

"Fine," I said. "Forgotten. So is your mom mad we're . . ." I realized too late I should have structured that sentence differently to avoid labels.

"Together?" Kalif suggested.

My heart picked up. "Yeah," I said. "That."

He shook his head. "I'm beginning to think it's you who's the most upset about it."

"No, it's just—"

Kalif wrapped an arm around my waist. "I'm kidding."

Right. I clearly needed to locate my sense of humor. "But your mom? Do we need to worry about her spying on us?" We had plenty of surveillance equipment around, so she had the means.

Kalif thought for a minute. "Maybe."

I looked around the room, as if a camera would just be sitting out, obvious. "Really?"

He shrugged. "Wouldn't be the first time she did it, though it's been a few years since I've caught her."

My neck prickled, and I scanned the walls, looking for places to hide a camera. At places of business, having obvious cameras was a type of security in itself. In a bedroom, not so much.

Kalif watched me, sighing. "If she had a camera in here, she'd know about last night."

I scanned the ceiling. "Unless she doesn't have a constant feed." The only hole I could see was the light fixture, and I stepped up on the bed, examining the space where the bulbs screwed in. Thankfully I didn't see one. If she'd put a camera there, it would have pointed straight down at Kalif's bed—and any mother who wanted to spy on her sixteen year old son's bed via security camera had serious, serious issues.

Kalif sat down at his computer. "If you want to check the walls, there's a voltage detector in the second drawer."

Kalif started working on his computer while I checked the room. I didn't find any electricity in the walls, except for above the sockets and by the light fixtures, where I'd expect wires to be. I couldn't find any cracks or recesses where Aida might have planted cameras; I checked the outlets themselves, but none of them would afford a view of the room. I found a small screwdriver in Kalif's same desk drawer, though, and removed the plates in the wall, looking for microphones, but came up empty handed.

"Don't your parents spy on you?" Kalif asked.

"No," I said. "At least, I don't think so. We've talked about how I could change my face and run away if I wanted to, and they know that, so we have to base our relationship on mutual trust. I don't run off or hide important things from them, and they don't spy on me. I'm pretty sure, anyway." I put my hands on my hips and gave the room one more once-over. "I think it's clean."

Kalif nodded. "I'm pretty sure Mom hasn't spied on me in a while, but I'm never sure if she just got better at hiding the evidence."

"Doesn't it bother you, knowing your own parents don't trust you?"

Kalif shrugged. "You get used to it."

I didn't see how that could be true, but I let it drop.

"Can she watch your computer?" I asked.

"That's what I'm checking," Kalif said. "But no, I don't see anything."

"Okay," I said. Time to pick out our next lead. "If it wasn't Megaware that went after my parents, who else could it have been?"

"It would have to be someone who knew where your parents were going to be," Kalif said. "There's me, and my parents—"

"But if they wanted to get rid of my parents, they had lots of other opportunities—ones that wouldn't result in a botched job."

"Right," Kalif said. "So who else?"

I thought about it. "Could someone have hacked into your server, and read our files? They could have gotten enough information that way."

Kalif gave me a look over his shoulder. "I monitor the security."

"I'm not trying to insult you, I just thought—"

Kalif bent over his keyboard, grumbling at me. "You're right. It's a possibility. I'll check now."

"Other than that," I said, "the only other person who would possibly have is the client who hired Mom and Dad to do the Eravision job in the first place."

Kalif nodded. "Circom. They shouldn't have known they were working with shifters, though."

I stared at the ceiling. "Unless rumors have gotten around. If someone figured out that a group of shifters was operating in the area, it's possible that instead of hiring Mom and Dad to do a job, they were actually laying a trap. Think about it. That job was perfect for shifters, since they wanted to frame specific people. Maybe it was *too* perfect."

Kalif kept working on his server checks, but he nodded. "That's a plausible theory."

My parents always said that so many of us working together were bound to draw attention. Most of our targets could have figured out they'd been scammed by shifters if everyone told the whole truth, since we didn't kill people to keep them from talking. But people were more likely to assume someone was lying or had tampered with video footage than they were to leap to the conclusion that shape shifters had been stalking them. We were far outside most people's comprehension of reality. Our jobs were easier than they would have been in centuries past, when magic was a possibility. Perhaps that's why Hassan-i-Sabbah's assassins inspired so many legends and we didn't.

"Give me the files on Circom," I said. "I'll look over them while you check for hacks."

Kalif opened the files on his laptop, and I sat cross-legged on his unmade bed, searching.

Still, it was hard to concentrate while sitting on Kalif's bed. The blanket bunched under my knees, and I closed my eyes, remembering the way his arms felt around me. Mom said things were intense when you fell for your first shifter, but intense wasn't the same as lasting. She'd probably emphasized that part for my benefit, and now I could see why.

"Do you ever worry," I asked, "that you only like me because you don't know any other shifter girls?"

Kalif didn't even take his eyes off his screen. "No."

I glared at him. "Just no? You're not even going to speculate with me?"

"Sorry," Kalif said. "Why, do you like me only because you don't have other options?"

"I asked you first."

"And I answered you."

I sighed. "You did, but your answer wasn't very interesting."

Kalif laughed. "What do you want me to say? To some extent, all relationships are about proximity. You don't fall for someone you've never met, and the more you're around someone, the more likely you are to like them."

I slumped back on the bed. "So the only reason people get together is because they're near each other?"

"No," Kalif said. "Proximity is part of it, but it's not everything. You're not the first shifter girl I've met."

I sat up straight again. "Really?" There were so few of us, I'd just assumed that my family was the first set of shifters Aida and Mel had met outside their families.

Kalif glanced at me over his shoulder. "Really. When I was thirteen my parents were working with another spy, a guy from

Belgium, actually. He was in a mixed marriage, and he had a shifter daughter—Helene was her name. I didn't like her at all."

"Why not?"

"She was always going on about how bad her life was, how hard it was to be a shifter, how she never knew who she was. I always figured she'd have had that same problem if she'd been normal. I don't know for sure, but it wasn't attractive."

"My life was pretty good, before my parents disappeared." I looked at Kalif. "I guess it's still pretty good, considering."

He turned around again to smile at me. "See? You think differently than she did. So there you go. I like you for who you are, not for convenience."

I raised one eyebrow. "And you never worry about whether I feel the same way?"

He rolled his eyes. "Would you want me if I was a jerk to you?"

"No," I said.

He nodded sharply. "There you go."

I flopped backward, bring the laptop onto my knees. "I just don't see why you have to be so sure of everything all the time."

"Not everything," Kalif said. "Just you."

My breath caught. "How can you say that? It's only been a few days."

Kalif's face turned serious. "Jory," he said. "It's not like I just met you."

I lay back on his bed, staring up at the ceiling. I didn't know what I did to earn that kind of faith from him, but I wanted more than anything to keep it.

THIRTEEN

Circom was supposed to be our client, not our mark, but Mel had done a complete security workup on them anyway, just in case. From the looks of his report, Circom's security was top notch. That made sense; if they had enough money to hire spies and saboteurs, they had money to protect their assets. Their budget for installation was big and their budget for maintenance matched its magnitude. We would probably be looking at a design that didn't cut corners, which was a shame, since cut corners were my friends.

That was doubly true when I was dealing with another company who might already know about shifters. If I left evidence behind, I might put Mom and Dad in even more danger. Better to play it safe. Always.

"I have some good news, and some bad news," I said to Kalif.

"Is the bad news that their security is airtight?"

I sighed. "You knew?"

"That's what I remember."

"Well, the good news is their footage is transmitted wirelessly," I said. "But if their network security is as intense as the rest of this, we'll want to get me inside first, like we did at Megaware."

"You'd need a profile for that. Got any leads?"

I pulled up a map search program and plugged in Circom's address. When the cross streets popped up, I smiled. Here was the first piece of truly good news about Circom; they were located comfortably inside the district of my favorite fire marshal. "Bingo."

Kalif spun around on his stool. "What?"

I smiled. "I think it's time for Circom to get a visit from Sergeant Menendez."

The first thing Mom and Dad did whenever we moved to a new area was to get to know—and profile—the local fire marshals. When one was promoted last year, Mom and Dad let me profile his replacement. Some of the profiles we did made me feel sad for the pathetic lives of our subjects; others made me feel sick because of how awful people could be. But the profiling of Mike Menendez just made me happy. Mike was a nice guy with two little kids and a wife who owned her own hair studio. In his spare time he ran a side business doing controlled burns of abandoned buildings to teach people fire survival skills. He was built like Barney Rubble and laughed like Santa Claus. And most of all, he ran all of his fire inspections exactly by the book.

I liked him so much that I had felt bad when Kalif had hacked into his personal phone to secure his inspection calendar, which he kept in an online calendar app. Luckily, we didn't need that information to frame him for anything—we just needed to be sure that Mom and Dad didn't show up for a surprise inspection in the same place that he did. For extra safety, we always scheduled those sorts of pop visits during time he'd also allocated for inspections, so if any of the companies called to follow up with his office staff, they wouldn't be confused unless they spoke with Menendez in person.

This time we couldn't wait, so I'd just make sure to find nothing wrong. That way there'd be nothing for them to follow up about. "I'll need to figure out what I'm inspecting," I said. "And beef up on my fire code. Do you know what I need to do once I'm inside?"

Kalif closed his server stuff and opened a web browser. "Give me ten minutes," he said.

When Aida came down to check on us, Kalif clicked over to

a server maintenance program. I kept my screen pointed away from the door. I squirmed under her scrutiny, acutely aware that I was sitting in the middle of Kalif's unmade bed.

But she didn't protest. She brought us a plate of sandwiches and left again, giving Kalif a pointed look. The message was clear—she could come down any time, so we'd better behave ourselves.

Her trouble was that she was looking for the wrong behaviors.

Two hours later I was headed over to Circom in Mom and Dad's car. This was our third mission with the same car, which was bad for our cover, but couldn't be avoided. Kalif stayed behind to make excuses for me, and to get the info as soon as I gave him access from inside. Mike's uniform was laid out on the back seat, complete with a warm pair of thick, clunky boots. I'd never asked where Mom got it, but we used it often.

I parked the car in a metered spot about a block and a half away from the Circom building. I needed to be far enough away that no one noticed it, but close enough that I didn't have far to go in a fire sergeant's uniform.

I walked up to Circom and through the Hurculite front doors, which were made of solid glass with no frame. I was glad I wasn't trying to break in—electrified locks on those kinds of doors weren't easy to bypass.

Inside the lobby, a desk spanned the center of the room, reaching from wall to wall in a horseshoe shape. Turnstile openings in the desk led to the elevators near the back of the building—past a security guard in a pinstripe suit.

The guard smiled at me as I came in. "How can I help you?"

I forced myself to smile. The guard hadn't called Mike by name, so I had to assume that they had no history, but not say anything that would seem out of place if they did. "I'm here for an inspection." I flashed Mike's badge—another piece of Mom's handiwork. "I'll need someone to show me around."

The guard took it, and then pulled out his radio. "Hey Sam," he said, "Sergeant is here for a fire inspection."

My thick, calloused palms began to sweat. Sam Weisner was the contact Aida had used for the Eravision job. That probably made him middle management—the higher ups didn't usually do the dirty work themselves, so they'd have someone to pin it on if their espionage made the front page news. It also made him the guy most likely to know there were shifters involved, if in fact these were the people who kidnapped my parents. It took all my training to keep smiling.

"I'm not expecting anyone today," Sam said over the radio.

I shrugged with one shoulder. "That's kind of the point of a surprise inspection."

The guard nodded at me. "It's unscheduled. You want to show him around?"

There was a long pause, and then Sam's annoyed voice blared through the speaker. "Be right down."

Sam was a wiry man about eight inches shorter than Mike. He had his head shaved clean, and his eyebrows were such a pale blond that they disappeared into his ghostly skin. I might have interrupted his plans for the day, but when he got to the lobby he was all smiles. "Surprised to see you today, Sergeant."

I looked Sam in the eyes. This might be the guy who took my parents, but Mike would have no reason to hate him, so I smiled casually. "Oh, you know. I have to keep you on your toes. Give me a look at your emergency lighting and I'll be on my way."

This time Sam's smile looked a little more uneasy. I wanted to chalk that up to his guilt, but it was probably because of the inspection. No matter how many years you spend out of school, nobody likes a pop quiz.

Sam showed me to the elevator. I pretended to survey their wiring and conduits on the way, when really I was looking for signs of shifter detection equipment. Mike was a big guy, so if they had them, I was already in trouble. But if there were any floor plate camera combinations on the way upstairs, they were well hidden. There wasn't any way to know for sure if the floor was wired without ripping the place apart.

We stepped out of the elevator onto the second floor, which was a maze of cubicles. I could hear keys typing away, pages turning, and somewhere on the other side of the room, a phone ringing. I looked at my watch. It was three in the afternoon, so nearly everyone here would still be at work. The cubicle environment was too open. "I'll need you to cut the power," I said. "I'm going to walk the floor and check your signage."

Sam narrowed his eyes. "You need to cut the power while they're working? That's pretty disruptive for an unscheduled visit."

It was, but if I wanted to get to a workstation with a rebooting computer in a time crunch, cutting the power was my best bet. I needed Sam to do what I wanted. If that meant I needed to put him on the defensive, so be it. I came in wearing this uniform for a reason. But if I went too far, he might call the fire department to complain, so pushing him around was a bit of a tightrope walk. "You have a point. Where are the breakers?"

He pointed at the back wall.

I craned my neck to see the panel over the top of the cubicle walls. "For every floor?"

"This one," Sam said. "And the one above us."

I nodded. "What's upstairs?"

Sam gave me a dry look. "Offices."

Offices. Perfect. "Cut the power upstairs, then. I'll disturb fewer people that way."

Sam gave a belabored sigh, but took out his radio and warned the offices upstairs via the intercom.

"Great," I said. "Give me a head start, and then flip them off. Wait a few minutes, and then turn them back on. I'll come back down and let you know if I need you to flip them again."

I left Sam standing there with a sour look on his face. I hoped he was the one who'd kidnapped my parents, partly because otherwise I shouldn't be taking pleasure in pushing him around.

I took the stairs up to the third floor. Sam cut the power when

I was only half-way up, so I got a good look at their emergency stairwell lighting and glowing exit signage. I was no expert, but it looked up to code to me.

When I stepped out onto the floor, I found a row of closed office doors. This was what I needed. With the power cut, the security cameras should be down. I checked the door handles. The first two doors were locked, but the third swung open. I found a woman sitting behind her desk, bent over a pile of papers. Her lights were off, but there was plenty of light streaming in her window to work by.

"Pardon me," I said to her. "Just checking the lighting." Then I pulled the door closed again.

I sighed. Sam would be turning the lights back on any minute, so I needed to find a private workstation, quickly. I moved back down the hallway, checking doors again.

Then I found it. An office with a name placard on it: Sam Weisner. I tried the door; it was unlocked.

I stepped into Sam's office just as the lights turned back on. The computer didn't come back on by itself, so I had to start it up and then quickly type in the sequence Kalif had given me, which was only slightly different from the one I'd used before. I wished I had time to text Kalif to make sure he'd gotten in, but I barely had time to step back into the hallway and close the door before Sam appeared at the end of the hallway.

"Are we finished here?" he asked.

I glanced around, like I was still surveying. "Everything looks up to code."

Sam gave me a satisfied smirk. "Then I'll walk you out."

I wavered. I already had the main thing I'd come for. But if I wanted to make the most out of my visit, now was the time for the long shots. It was unlikely that Circom would be holding my parents on site, but if they were, the quickest way to determine that would be to try to look over every inch of the place.

"I need to check the basement," I said.

"We don't have a basement," Sam said.

I nearly peed my pants. Mike would have known that. He'd have looked at all the building plans before he came, but in my haste, I'd forgotten.

On the other hand, that was also what he would say if they did have a basement, and had captives hidden inside it.

I crossed my beefy fireman arms across Mike's broad chest. "No boiler room?" I asked. "No climate control down there?"

Sam gave another longsuffering sigh. "We do have some utility access, yes."

I smiled. "If it's got access, it has to have lighting," I said. "Let's check it."

Sam followed after me, looking like a scolded puppy. I hadn't been managing my persona well enough; Mike would have done all this with a jibe and a joke, instead of making Sam feel like he was being bullied.

The boiler room was a dead end, literally. When I had Sam cut the power, the room was utterly black except the tiny green strips of emergency lighting on the stairs and below the door. When the lights turned back on, I searched for doors, street access, anything that might allow prisoners to be held below the Circom building. I found nothing.

Then I had another thought. "I'll just need to check the parking garage, and I can be on my way."

Sam raised an eyebrow at me. "Of course."

The parking garage was adjacent to the building, and Sam had to unlock a control closet to get to the breakers and shut down the power for me. While he worked the breakers I walked up and down by way of the stairs.

As I rounded the corner up to the third floor, I froze. A row of four black vans were lined up on the far side, each indistinguishable from the one that had driven away with Mom and Dad. I curbed the impulse to tug at the van doors, as if Mom and Dad would still be inside.

This is it, I told myself. *Think.* I made note of the license plate numbers, so I could write them down when I got back to the car. I wished I could tattoo them on my skin, but unnatural marks were outside of my shifting capabilities, and holding on to a complex pattern of freckles would be harder than remembering the numbers.

I forced myself to breathe. I could always come back, in a different persona—with forensic equipment, even, if that's what it took. That was the benefit of being a shifter; I could nearly always try again.

Instead I walked up behind the vans, taking a good look at the area around the plates. On the one parked farthest from me, I found what I was looking for—grey, rectangular marks on the paint at the edge of the license plate. I bent over, running my hand over it. It was tacky to the touch.

I pulled my hand back, like it had been burned. These were remnants of adhesive, left by pieces of tape.

"Will that be all?" Sam asked.

I jumped. I hadn't seen him come up behind me. Startling like that was out of character for Mike, and now I'd let Sam see me examining the van. I wanted to use Mike's muscled arms to shake Sam by the shoulders and demand to know where my parents were. I wasn't much stronger in Mike's body than I was in my own, but I was a good bit taller than Sam. I might have gotten the information from him on intimidation alone.

That would give me away, though, and I was on Sam's turf. Who knew where his black-clad assailants might be hiding. I couldn't imagine Sam did his own dirty work, but if he suspected me of being a shifter, he wouldn't be standing this close without backup somewhere nearby.

Time to go. I'd done enough damage for one day.

I forced myself to give Sam a friendly smile, and clapped him on the shoulder with a heavy hand. "Looks great. Thanks for the tour."

Sam gave me a sharp nod. I hoped for my sake that my fake smile looked more real than his. "Any time," he said. Though he clearly meant otherwise.

I texted Kalif with shaking hands when I got safely back to the car, but didn't receive a response. He was probably absorbed in digging up the information he needed. I didn't know how much time I'd bought him; he was probably in a rush. I hoped he was working quickly, because this was the one—the company that had my parents. It had to be.

When I got back to Kalif's house, I didn't run into either Aida or Mel. The door to Kalif's room was closed, so I knocked once.

"Come in," Kalif said. He was hunched over his computer, his screen a wash of text, but he paused to check my hand.

I leaned over his shoulder. "Find anything?"

Kalif didn't look up from his computer. "Yes," he said, opening a different window. "These are some emails from one of the site managers to an external contractor, talking about borrowing a van for some shipping the night your parents disappeared."

I drew a sharp breath. "That's it," I said. "That's the van, right? I saw four just like them in the Circom parking garage, and one of them had tape residue next to the plate."

Kalif nodded. "It looks like the one."

I rubbed my temples. "So all we have to do is follow the contractor and we'll find my parents, right?"

"That's what I'm doing. The name for the contractor didn't turn up much, but I tracked the IP address from the email. It's routed to hide its origin, and the masking is pretty intense."

"But you can track it, right?"

He wobbled his head from side to side.

"Cut the modesty," I said. "It doesn't become you."

"I know," Kalif said. "Believe me. But whoever set this up is not just good. He's amazing. I haven't seen security like this in a long time. Maybe ever."

I collapsed on the bed. "You don't need to sound so excited about it."

"Seriously, though. I could spend *months* pulling this apart."

I pulled off my shoe and threw it at him. It struck him in the shoulder, and he looked at me over his shoulder. "Sorry," he said.

"I know we don't have months. I'm working on it."

I dragged myself off the bed and looked over his shoulder. "I'm not going to spend days waiting for you again. Give me something to do."

"This is seriously tough," he said. "I mean, take a look at this for instance. The IP address looks like it's coming from Ecuador. I follow it there, and it looks like it's coming from Taiwan. Those are the same locations I use to mask our emails. So is it a coincidence, or is this guy showing me mirrors of my own system? If he can do that, I need to figure out how."

The blood drained out of my face. "What do you mean, your own system?"

"My own security work," he said. "The way I've masked our IP."

I climbed off the bed and put a hand on his shoulder. "And you checked our system, right?" I said. "To make sure that's not where the emails came from?"

He looked up at me, and all the thrill drained out of his eyes. I squeezed his shoulder harder. "Right?"

He turned around slowly in his chair, looking at the data. "No way," he said.

He opened up his own server files, poking through them. After typing in a password, he found it. A copy of the email he'd been tracing.

"The best security you've ever seen, huh?" I said. On another day, I would have ribbed him for that for hours. But today, we just stared at the email, sent to Circom from Kalif's very own server.

"One of us borrowed the van," I said, trying to piece it together. "The van that was used to kidnap my parents."

Kalif's hand shook as he pointed at the top of the screen, to a sender email address I didn't recognize. "It was my mother," Kalif said. "The person who borrowed that van the night your parents disappeared was my mother."

FOURTEEN

We both stared at the screen in silence. This *couldn't* be right. They'd been a step behind us, but I'd thought it was because they were playing it too safe, protecting themselves. "If your parents wanted to kidnap mine," I said, "they could have taken them out of their beds. They could have drugged them—we eat at your house all the time. Why botch the job?"

"They wouldn't," Kalif said. "There's got to be another explanation."

I waited. His eyes crinkled as he focused on the screen.

"Not coming up with anything?" I asked.

He shook his head. "I will if you give me a minute."

"There has to be one," I said. "This was too theatrical. That's not the way your parents work. It's almost as if . . ." A realization sank through me like a stone to the bottom of the ocean.

Kalif looked at me. "What?"

My head throbbed. There was no reason to grab my parents in the middle of a job unless they were trying to throw someone else off their trail. It couldn't be my parents they were trying to fool—they'd been captured, so they weren't looking at the security tapes.

But there was someone else Mel and Aida had to worry about. There was me.

"They knew I'd go looking for my parents," I said. "That's why they borrowed the van. They were setting up a story, one that I

146

could follow to Eravision, and to Megaware, and to Circom . . ."

Kalif closed his eyes. "But you wouldn't look here."

I balled my fists, ready to punch them square into Aida's jaw. It was classic diversion. My parents trusted Aida and Mel. I wanted to trust them, too, so I didn't stop to think that the pieces of evidence diverting suspicion away from them might have been planted *by* them, for just that purpose. "But when we looked at Circom, we found the email," I said. "They left a trail. They wouldn't have done that if they thought we were going to look."

Kalif shook his head. "My parents both encrypt their email, so that I can't read it."

I stared at him. "They know how to do that?"

"No. They hired someone to build the program for them. It was good work."

"But you *did* read it."

Kalif waved his hand at me dismissively. "I broke through their encryption long ago. Took me a good month, though. It was a real challenge."

I sank onto a stool. "But if you've been in your parents' email all this time, why didn't you know about this before?"

"I don't ever read it," Kalif said. "I just wanted to see if I could break into the program. I've never had a reason to use it until now."

I stared down at my hands. "I can't believe I didn't see this."

Kalif held up his hand. "It's still hypothetical. There could still be other explanations. Think about it. There's no reason for my parents to want yours to disappear. It was their idea that we all work together in the first place. And why now, after all this time?"

I rolled my shoulders back. He was right. Answering one question didn't make the whole story true. The folds could go even deeper than that. Maybe all the evidence pointing to Aida and Mel was also a setup, placed there by someone who wanted to frame them.

After all, there'd been more than two assailants at Eravision the night my parents disappeared.

I closed my eyes. "If your parents did it," I said, "who were they working with? And where are my parents now? We don't hold people for long periods of time—it isn't secure. Are they . . . ." The word *dead* hung in the air, unsaid.

Kalif put a hand on my arm. "Hey. We don't kill people, right? So if my parents did it, that'd be good news. Your parents would still be alive."

I shrugged. Anyone who double crossed us like that might be playing by a different set of rules. "You should look through the rest of their email," I said. "See if there's any more evidence."

Kalif nodded, but his fingers tightened on my arm. "I need to tell you something, though. Something I probably should have told you before."

Blood drained from my face. "What?"

He looked down at the floor. "Remember that other shifter girl I told you about? Helene?"

I spoke slowly. "Your parents were working with her father. So?"

Kalif rubbed his eyes. "They just disappeared one day. They all ran a job together, and the next day, the whole family was gone."

I blinked. "You said the mom wasn't a shifter."

Kalif looked up at me, his face suddenly taking on all those hours of exhaustion. "She wasn't. But regular people can disappear, too."

I bit my lip. "Why *didn't* you tell me about that?"

He shook his head, staring. "I didn't think anything of it," Kalif said. "Shifters disappear. The ones with normal spouses relocate their relatives. It happens. But if my parents did something to yours . . ."

I nodded. "They might have done the same thing to your friend and her family."

Kalif's voice was quiet. "Right. I just thought you should know."

I wanted to ask how this could have happened without him knowing, but he was obviously upset enough about the fact that it had. I took his hand and squeezed it. "Let's start looking."

I sat down beside Kalif at his desk, and he pulled up his parents' emails. We all used multiple addresses, one for each new persona. That was a lot to manage, so Kalif had them all route to a single inbox for each of us, covering the forwards, of course, so no one could follow the trail. I leaned over his shoulder, watching as he ran the same searches he'd used for the Circom data. He came up with a series of emails from Sam involving the vans. These were sent after my parents disappeared, on the same day that Mel told me they were cutting loose from the client.

I don't understand what you thought you were doing, one of them said. *Using our van to kidnap Cambrian and Delacruz? What the hell kind of frame job is that?*

So Sam probably wasn't in on it. That was a shame; it meant my dislike of him was mostly unfounded. "Did they answer?"

"I don't see a reply," Kalif said.

"Would they have deleted the emails?" I asked. "That's what I would do if I'd been doing something suspicious."

"Maybe," Kalif said. "But even if they used a scrubber on the files, I have backups." He started typing.

I paced back and forth behind him. Then he swore.

"What?" I asked.

Kalif gripped the edge of the desk. "There are some deleted emails. But more than that, some of the files from the mission log have been deleted."

"Okay," I said. "And?"

He threw his hands in the air. "What do you mean, 'and'? They deleted files on *my* server."

I sighed. That seemed a little beside the point. "Clearly that's bad."

"It *is* bad," Kalif said. "No one messes with the files without me noticing."

"But you didn't notice until now."

149

Kalif glared at the screen, but I was pretty sure he meant the look for me. "Rub it in."

I put a hand on his shoulder. "I'm not trying to criticize you," I said. "It's a big server, right? Of course you didn't notice."

"Yeah, thanks." Kalif hunched forward. That was clearly not the answer he was looking for.

"Can you recover the files?"

"Of course. That's not the point."

"Pull them up on your laptop when you do," I said. "I'll go through them while you keep looking."

Kalif worked for a minute, his fingers striking the keys harder than was strictly necessary. After a minute he switched to the laptop, then handed it to me. I settled in on his bed, with the screen facing away from the door. I hadn't heard either Mel or Aida in the house, but given what we were doing, we couldn't be too careful.

What if they returned before we'd verified our suspicions? I wanted to spit the truth in their faces, to confront them and make them explain.

But I'd have no way to recognize the truth among their new lies. If I didn't have sufficient evidence, they'd deny everything. It was smarter to wait until we were sure. Then we could plan what the next move should be.

I started with the files. "These don't look important," I said to Kalif. "It's just some mission my parents ran." I remembered it, vaguely. They'd been working on personas to break into a factory in Stockton, to steal a prototype microchip. At the last minute, Mom got wind that the person they'd been studying was fired, which marked both the last moment they had to impersonate her, and the best moment to frame her for the theft. They'd left late at night, on only a few hours notice, but after that, Mom had told me everything was smooth sailing.

I read over the whole mission twice, in case there was some clue there as to why Aida and Mel would have taken my parents, but I couldn't find anything.

"What about the emails?" he asked.

I looked through them. Most were spam, and a couple further complaint emails from Sam, including a threat to get his lawyers involved. He wouldn't do that, of course, but he must have felt pretty powerless if he made the threat. It was hard to feel sorry for him, though, since he'd only hired us for revenge.

There were a few emails from last week that caught my attention—a whole chain between Aida and someplace called Asylum. *I'm sending the profiles over today*, Aida wrote. *They should arrive tomorrow by mail, so watch for them.*

We sometimes sent things by mail, always from post offices so that our original location couldn't be tracked. "Can you do a search for me?" I asked. "See if you can find any more emails that reference Asylum."

Kalif nodded. "Does that name mean anything to you?"

I shook my head. "No, you?"

"Never heard of them."

"Your mom sent them something in the mail last week, a few days before my parents disappeared. Then she deleted the email."

Kalif took a moment to respond. "There aren't any more emails using that name. What's the domain name?"

I brought the laptop over to the desk so that Kalif could check the data on the email in question, and cross-reference it with Aida's inbox.

"There's nothing here," Kalif said. "Let me see if there're any more deleted emails from further back."

Kalif pulled up a few more exchanges, all similarly vague. *How is the project?* Asylum asked. *We've found evidence*, Aida replied. *Give us more time.*

"That's odd," I said.

"Why?"

"She doesn't routinely delete emails from clients, right? Or that pile of deleted emails would have been a lot bigger."

"True," Kalif said.

151

"And she seems to be giving them information over email, but there are pieces missing. Like the address that she was going to send the profiles to."

Kalif nodded. "It's possible she was also talking to them over the phone."

"But if she got the address over the phone, she would have told them these things, too."

"Maybe it's in the mission logs," Kalif said. "Let me check there."

But if it was going to be there, I imagined Kalif would already know about it. If Aida hadn't logged the mission, that meant she was hiding something from my parents. Or Kalif.

Kalif swore. "I'm not finding anything," Kalif said. "What the hell is going on?"

I leaned toward him. "Can you trace the emails to the source?"

"Of course I can," he said. "Let me work."

While he did, I looked over that deleted mission again, searching for any connection to Asylum. I couldn't find anything. Maybe these files had gotten deleted accidentally. Those things happened, sometimes, whatever Kalif thought about his infallible records.

"Ugh," Kalif said. "They're masking the origin. This is going to take a while."

"Okay," I said. "Put that on hold. Let's try to piece this together with what we have."

Kalif spun around on his stool. I sat on the edge of his bed, facing him. I'd never seen him look so grumpy. "I'm sorry about your files," I said. "Really."

He sighed and shook his head. "It's not that. How could I not have known about this?"

I set the laptop aside. "We haven't proven anything."

Kalif planted his elbows on his knees, his fingers knotted together. "But my parents had something to do with those vans. Something they deliberately hid from me. How did they think I wouldn't find it? Do they think I'm stupid?"

"They think we're kids," I said. "Which amounts to the same thing."

He rolled his eyes. "Yeah, well. They also think when you delete a digital record, it's gone. In that way, they're just like most of the rest of the world."

I sat on the edge of the bed. He needed a lead. We both did. "Let me ask you this," I said. "If your mom sent something through the mail, she'd have kept a copy of it, right?"

He thought about that. "Probably," Kalif said. "But I didn't find anything on the server."

"She wouldn't put it on the server if she didn't want you to see it."

"Right," Kalif said.

"So where would she keep it?" I asked. "Paper files she didn't want you to see. Where would they be?"

Kalif dropped his hands to the side. "In her office."

I shook my head. "She's been letting me sleep in that office. We can look there, but if she had files she didn't want me poking through, she'd have moved them."

"Their bedroom, then. I never go in there."

I nodded. "So that's where we need to look."

We were both quiet for a moment. We were about to cross a line—one we wouldn't be able to step back across easily. It was one thing to investigate behind Aida and Mel's backs, and quite another to investigate *them*.

"They're both out, now," Kalif said. "They said they were going to check on Circom."

"If Circom is a diversion," I said, "who knows where they *really* went." Next time, we could try following them, but for today it was too late.

Kalif stood, his palms slapping his legs on the way up. "I'll watch the front of the house. You go up and see what you can find."

I stood, too, hesitating by the end of his bed. "Are you sure?"

Kalif rubbed his forehead. "Yeah," he said. "Do it."

153

I wanted to hug him, to make him tell me that things were going to be okay, but he was already headed up the stairs. And that was smart; his parents wouldn't be gone forever. So I followed him up.

Kalif sat in the living room, watching out the window for Mel and Aida's cars. He'd also be there to stall them while I extracted myself from their room, if necessary.

I moved up the stairs, alone. I started in their office-turned-my-bedroom, looking through the closet and desk drawers. They'd obviously moved a lot of things out, as most of the spaces were empty. That made practical sense, if they were turning the room over to me, but was also unfortunate. We had no way to know what else they'd been hiding.

I hesitated outside their bedroom door, checking the doorframe. No wires were visible from the outside, though if I were going to alarm a bedroom door with a visible mechanism, I'd have put the device on the inside. Better yet, I'd remove the door frame and carve a place for it inside the wood. I checked the frame, but the paint wasn't disturbed. I fetched a flashlight from Kalif's bedroom and shone it through the crack, looking for sensors, but didn't find any.

I took a deep breath, turned the knob, and pushed the door open.

I froze in the hallway, half expecting an alarm, though if there was one, it would almost certainly be silent, routing alerts to their computers or cell phones. I checked the inside of the door frame, but it was equally clean. If Aida or Mel had installed sensors here, I couldn't find them. I scanned the room for cameras or motion detectors, but there weren't a lot of places in this room to hide things. It looked like a hotel—clean, fluffy bedspread made over a king-sized mattress, nightstands with lamps, but no adornments, and a natural wood bookshelf with photos of skylines and beaches, but, of course, no family photos.

I started with the closet, checking the boxes at the top and the shoe racks at the bottom. That was the only sign that shifters lived here; the closet and dressers were both filled to bursting with clothing in all sizes, appropriate for both genders. In a normal house, there was no way this wardrobe would be in use by just two people. Twenty might be pushing it.

In the bottom dresser drawer I found many of the things Aida and Mel had moved out of the office: pads of paper, stacks of bills in several different names, pens and pencils, staplers and tape. But no records, no files. Those were all supposed to be kept digitally, after all. That's what they'd told my parents when we first starting working together. Digital encryption was safer than paper.

I spun around, despair clogging my windpipe. If there was nothing here, then what? I could confront them, but without evidence, they'd only lie. There had to be something else here.

I stepped up to the bed—the last unchecked piece of furniture in the room. I pulled up the edge of the comforter, and that's when I saw it. A locked briefcase, tucked up under the foot of the bed. Exactly the sort of place I'd keep paper files, if I wanted them to remain secure.

I tried to pop the locks as they were, but of course they'd been latched securely. I left the case where it was, so Mel and Aida wouldn't catch me with it, and ran downstairs.

Kalif sat on the couch, watching the driveway through the sheers.

"I found a locked case," I said, "but I need lockpicks."

His eyes widened. "There're some in my bottom desk drawer. Do you need help?"

I wanted him to come with me, to use his steadier hands to do the picking. But what he was doing was important. If Mel and Aida came home, I wanted a warning. "No," I said. "I've got it." I ran down and grabbed the picks, then headed back upstairs to the lock.

I held my breath as I manipulated the pins, keeping my ear to the side of the case so that I could hear the tiny, insulated clicks. The first lock popped open, and then the second.

I drew a slow breath. "Still clear?" I called downstairs.

"Still clear," Kalif called back.

I pulled the case into the middle of the floor, and opened it up.

Inside were stacks of paper—printouts, photocopies, emails. I lifted the first stack, sifting through it. From the bottom of the pile, some photographs slipped out—pictures of a body lying in a pool of blood.

I dropped the papers, but the picture of the blood slid onto the floor, where I stared at it. The man in the photos was stocky, with brown hair down to his shoulders, now matted. His head twisted to the side. Nothing but a red-black pit remained where his eye had once been, and blood had smeared all down his face and pooled in the creases formed by his collar bones. My heart beat double time. Could this be my father? If it were, how would I ever know?

I swallowed. We were going to have to go through these in more detail, which meant probably not in the house, where we could be so easily caught. I shoved the photo of the body back into the stack, and forced myself to gather the rest of the papers into my arms, ready to relock the empty briefcase and slide it back under the bed.

As I lifted the last of the papers from the case, I froze in place. A small, flat box lay in the bottom of the briefcase, a tiny red light flashing on the side. The wires from the box had been slipped underneath the lining, running up to the second lock.

An alarm, transmitting.

I dumped the papers on the floor. "Kalif!" I yelled. "Alarm!" I broke the signal box open in my hands and popped out the battery, but it was too late. It would have begun transmitting the moment I opened the box.

Kalif pounded up the stairs. His eyes widened when he looked at the box in my hands.

"Where does the signal go?" he asked.

"I don't know," I said. "Their computers? A cell phone?"

"Laptops," he said, looking around the room.

Then Kalif's cell phone rang in his pocket.

We both froze, looking at each other in horror.

I recovered first. "Answer it," I said. "If it's them, you can play it off. Say you'll check upstairs. We can find the box and break it open."

Kalif's fingers twitched. "Okay," he said. He looked at the caller ID, and then punched a button to answer.

"Hello?" he said.

Mel's voice was loud enough on the other end that I could hear him. "What are you doing upstairs?" he asked.

"What?" Kalif asked. "I'm in my room. Why, is there a problem?"

Even though he was shaking, Kalif's voice sounded casual. I had to give him points for the cover.

Mel, however, didn't. "Don't lie to me," he said. "I can see you right now."

We both spun about the room, looking. As I stepped closer to the bookshelf, I found it: a recessed square had been cut from the underside of the top shelf, with a tiny notch in the decorative lip for the lens to poke through. A camera was glued in there, the kind that parents might use to spy on babysitters. The craftsmanship was good; from as little as a foot away, the lens was indistinguishable from the knots in the wood—that's why I'd missed it the first time.

The alarm must have triggered an alert to Mel's phone, and then he'd checked on us through the transmitting visual. I turned away from the camera before I cringed. If I'd checked more thoroughly, I could have covered the lens before looking.

Now we were caught.

Kalif looked at me with wide eyes.

"Hang up," I told him.

He shook his head and glared at the camera. "Where are Jory's parents?" he asked. He dropped the phone from his ear, switching it to speaker.

157

Mel barked over the phone. "Just stay where you are. We'll be there in a minute."

I shook my head at Kalif. "Hang *up*."

This time, he did.

I grabbed him by the arm and pulled him toward the door. Mel and Aida would be on their way already. "We have to get out of here. Get everything you need, but be quick."

Kalif's phone rang again, and he looked at it.

"I think we should talk to them," Kalif said.

I spun around to face him. "Are you crazy?"

He shook his head. "Not here, but someplace open."

I hauled him out of the room and away from the camera. When we got to the stairs, I paused. Kalif's phone still rang in his hand.

"You'd probably be safe talking to them," I said, "but they might do the same thing to me as they did to my parents." My heart beat faster as I thought about that body in the photo.

Kalif put a hand on my shoulder. "They won't hurt you. I won't let them."

I took a step downstairs. In a physical fight between him and his parents, I knew who I'd put my money on. But if we did meet somewhere open, I might have a chance to get away.

The information about where my parents were might be in the papers I held in my arms. But if it wasn't, talking to Aida and Mel might be the best course of action, even if they did lie to me. Mom and Dad often deduced things from people's lies that they'd never have found out from the truth.

We needed someplace that was not just open, but nearby. "Tell them to meet us at the park down the street. But they have to come right away. Don't give them any time to prepare."

Kalif's phone stopped ringing, but he began to dial as we charged down the stairs.

I wished I'd brought the case to carry the papers, but if it was bugged it might also have a tracker in it, and I didn't have time to stop for a bag or a purse. I clung to them as I ran out the front door and moved around the block of houses to the back alley. Kalif followed behind me, phone to his ear. A thought came into my mind, one I immediately wanted to squash. If Aida and Mel were against me, who was to say that Kalif wasn't in on it?

Stop, I thought. He'd let me search his parents' room, where the evidence was. He'd let me take the papers. He'd found the emails himself.

My feet hit the concrete with heavy thuds. That was the way a con worked, though. You gave the victim just enough evidence that you were on their side, just enough clues to keep them trusting you.

And then you led them in the wrong direction.

I slowed a little, to catch his conversation.

"The one on the corner," he was saying. "Now. Come fast, or we'll be gone."

Then he hung up.

I hurried to the park on shaky knees, Kalif following behind. He'd brought all this to me, even when he realized his parents were involved. He'd told me the truth when he could have hidden it. But a creeping voice deep in my mind asked me why he should be any different. If Mel and Aida were against me, how could I ever know for sure that Kalif wasn't the same?

159

FIFTEEN

The park down the road was more of an appendage playground attached to a large soccer field. On the far side of the fields were buildings that used to be an elementary school, but the school had been closed so long that the original playground had been demolished. A new playground had been added closer to the street—a small neighborhood park on the edge of the forgotten buildings.

Kalif and I picked a corner of the field near the old school buildings. The padded pit where the old playground used to be was a few feet away—I could see the stumps of poles still sticking out of the ground where the slide had been. Standing in the open in our home bodies made me feel exposed, but I wanted the truth, and that meant that I needed to resist the urge to hide. We were far enough from the buildings that Aida and Mel wouldn't be able to sneak up on us, but not so far that we'd be caught entirely in the open, with nowhere to run and shift. I kicked myself for not bringing a change of clothes, but it wasn't safe to go back for one, now.

Kalif took my hand. "I'm so sorry."

"For what?"

He gestured toward home. Or what used to be our homes. I couldn't go back now. "Not protecting you from this," he said.

He glared in the direction of the parking lot, where I expected his parents would come.

"You didn't know," I said. And then I couldn't help but add: "Right?"

He squinted. "I should have. All the pieces were there."

I squeezed his hand. Of course he didn't know. But I wished I could quiet the niggling doubts. My parents thought I needed more training, but at least in the area of suspicion, I clearly had too much.

This wasn't the time for those, though. We needed to prepare. I drew my hand away and gave him part of the stack of papers. "Look through these," I said.

I read through the second half of the stack of papers while keeping one eye on the parking lot. A mother and her daughter walked up to the playground, the little girl running ahead, pigtails bouncing, with a shovel in one hand and a bucket swinging in the other. That could have been them—anyone could. But I hoped these were innocent bystanders, because the more witnesses we had, the safer we'd be.

I flipped through the papers in my hands. They were profiles, in the same style as the ones Kalif managed on the server. But all these people had been murdered; most of them shot in the head. Aida and Mel had collected information as if they were building profiles on these people to impersonate them, but they'd also collected the details on the crime scenes, the newspaper reports of the killings, and the obituaries. As I shuffled through, I watched my parents die a thousand times before my eyes. But these deaths were too old. Not one of them had occurred in the last week.

"What is this?" I asked.

Kalif shook his head. "Not your parents." He looked up at me. "That's good news, right?"

No news wasn't good news. Just because none of these bodies belonged to my parents didn't mean my parents weren't dead.

I was about to ask Kalif for theories about the deaths when Mel's SUV pulled into the parking lot on the far side of the field. Kalif tensed as Aida and Mel both got out of the car wearing their home bodies. If they hadn't already been together, they'd taken the time to meet up before finding us, which meant they'd had time to align their stories. We'd forced them to meet us quickly, but not quickly enough.

The two of them began across the field at a measured pace.

I flexed my fingers. Every muscle in my body wanted to run. I must have looked it, too, because Kalif put his arm around my shoulders, steadying me.

"We could go now," I said. "This might be our last chance."

"They're my parents," he said. "They aren't going to shoot us on sight."

I hoped I was overreacting, and that there was a reasonable explanation for all of this. That would be the best possible scenario, all things considered.

Aida and Mel walked toward us. Aida had her arms folded over her chest, and Mel was already glaring.

Since they were already on the defensive, there was no sense trying to keep things civil. When they got within a few paces, I held up my hand for them to stop. "Stay there," I said.

To their credit, they did.

Aida held out her hand, as if to shake mine. "No," I said. The odds of this being other shifters was slim, especially since Aida had offered me her hand. But once she had hold of my wrist, she could easily overpower me, if that's what she wanted to do. I had training, but I couldn't help but remember how brutal the kidnappers were when they wrangled my parents into the van.

If my parents couldn't fight those people, neither could I.

I squared my shoulders to them, drawing a couple extra inches to my height, and stilling the tremors in my arms. I kept my voice calm and even. "Where are my parents?"

Mel shook his head at me, his jaw set like he was barely holding back his anger. "We were in the middle of looking for them. We might have found something, if you hadn't interrupted."

Right. They hadn't found anything in days, but these last few minutes were the key to everything. He was just trying to make me feel guilty.

Tough luck. "You borrowed the black van that kidnapped

my parents," I said. "I think you know exactly where they are."

I studied their faces, looking for cracks in their façade. But Mel and Aida were professionals. They shot each other a confused glance that was so convincing, it might have been scripted.

"That's ridiculous," Mel said. "You must be confused."

For a heartbeat, I panicked. What if the information we had was wrong? Who might have planted that evidence?

Kalif. He'd led me right to it.

I kept every cell in my body locked and still. Kalif wasn't the bad guy. He was working *with* me. He'd never have suggested meeting with his parents face to face if he was trying to set them up. It would be stupid to allow them a chance to explain.

Kalif spoke next. "We're not confused. You arranged it by email. You left a trail."

A flash of malice crossed Mel's face, just for an instant, and then he had himself back under control. He should have been able to cover better than that, but my dad always said no one gets under your skin like your own kid.

So we were right. They *did* kidnap my parents. "Where are they?" I asked.

Aida and Mel exchanged glances again, more measured this time. My parents could read each other so well, they could slip each other cues that no one else in the world would recognize, not even me. If Aida and Mel were having that kind of silent conversation, I couldn't read it, either.

I waited, standing perfectly still, as if suspended in time. All I wanted at that moment was for her to tell me something that made sense—something that meant my parents were fine. Something that meant our lives could just go back to the way they were before.

"Your parents," Aida said finally, "are in holding cells."

I took a step back, imagining my parents cowering behind bars. Kalif stepped up just behind me, letting me lean against him.

"What?" I asked.

Aida's eyes flicked toward Mel, just for a moment. He stared straight at us, not even sparing her a glance.

"Holding cells," she said again, slowly. "We had to detain them."

If Kalif hadn't been supporting me, the asphalt might have opened up and swallowed me whole. "They're alive?" I asked.

Aida nodded.

I forced myself to breathe. Everything else was fixable, as long as they stayed that way.

I'd never seen Kalif angry before, but he was seething now. "How could you not tell us this?" he asked. "You made Jory worry her parents were dead, when you knew all along where they were. Do you have any idea how scared she was?"

Is, I thought. "What happened?"

Mel pointed at the papers in my hands. "You've got the evidence right there," he said. "I thought you'd put everything together." He was baiting me, waiting for me to give up what I knew, so he could tailor his answers to it.

Not likely.

I should have figured things out before confronting them, but the alarm had forced my hand. What I needed now was a good bluff—one Mel couldn't immediately call.

I looked down at the photo on top of my pile of papers—a man lying in a pool of his own blood.

"Take a good look," Mel said. "Because your parents murdered him."

The blood drained from my face. Kalif's fingers laced through mine. I kept every muscle still, so my body wouldn't betray any reaction. "That's ridiculous," I said. I kept my voice so flat that it came out monotone, and Mel's lips curled into a slight smile. He knew he had the upper hand. "My parents don't kill people. Not ever, not even in self-defense." My mind raced for the right answers—to piece together what had really happened here, so I could spit the truth in Mel's face. But I didn't know. I hadn't had enough time to prepare.

Kalif followed up for me. "Who did you give them to?" he asked. "There aren't any shifter police. But we saw the video. There were at least four kidnappers. You were working with someone."

Aida spoke slowly, cutting her eyes sideways to Mel, as if asking for permission. "There are some who look out for our interests."

The hairs on my neck prickled. "Asylum," I said.

Mel's smile widened. A heavy weight settled in my chest. The only reason for him to be that happy about the connection was if the truth was more terrible than his bluff.

Kalif waved an arm at Aida. "This is ridiculous. If there are shifter cops, why have I never heard of them? We've done thousands of things they should have busted us for."

That was true, but police worked for governing bodies, and governments worked by popular consent. I sure hadn't consented to be governed by them, and I was certain my parents hadn't, either. "They aren't cops," I said. "They can't be."

"Then who are they?" Kalif asked. His face contorted in anger and disbelief. "Vigilantes? Is this what happened to Helene and her family?"

Mel gave Kalif one patronizing shake of his head. "Helene is fine. She and her mother moved back to Europe, to be near her mother's family."

"And her father?" Kalif asked. "What did you do, drag him off in his sleep? Or did you kidnap him on a mission, like you did to Jory's parents?"

Mel straightened, his chest and shoulders bulking slightly, like a gorilla making himself known as the alpha male. "You may get to help around here," Mel said, "but you don't get to talk to me like that."

Kalif set his jaw, which told me he took Mel's sidestep of the question for an admission of guilt. "Right," he said. "I'll just get back to facilitating your work, then. As long as I don't ask what it's for."

Aida looked from Kalif to Mel, as if she didn't know whose side to take. Finally, she turned to me, her face pleading. "I know it's hard for you to believe, but your parents did murder those people." She pointed to the picture of the man, lying in blood. "That's Ruben Ferreira. They killed him before he could testify in a court trial against a mob boss in Chicago. He was under police protection, but they took on the identities of the officers he was working with, gained his trust, and then shot him in the head."

"Please," I said. "When were my parents in Chicago?"

"Before you were born," Mel said. But he kept his eyes on Kalif, and Kalif stared back, like he was daring his dad to come near me.

I wanted to tell him to knock it off. Provoking Mel wasn't going to help anything. But I didn't dare show the smallest crack of tension between Kalif and me. If I did, his parents would use it as leverage.

That's what we did. We manipulated people. But we didn't kill. How many times had my father told me—ordered me—never to take a life? It was the first rule. The only rule. There was no way he'd broken it once, let alone enough times to leave this pile of evidence. I lowered my voice, looking directly at Aida. "Someone must have set them up."

Aida's eyes were sad, like she wished, for my sake, that I was right. "They hid it from us," she said, "and I'm glad they hid it from you. It shows they had shame."

Shame. *A regular person can kill someone in self-defense*, he'd said. *But we have an edge over them. We're powerful. We don't dare cross that line—not ever.* Those weren't the words of a murderer, past or present.

Aida sighed. "The evidence is right in your hands. Go ahead and keep it. Look over it."

"Evidence of what?" I asked. "Murders from years ago? You can't possibly know it was them after all this time."

"If they'd left it in the past," Aida said, "then we never would have caught them. But they killed another man just a few

166

months ago. They made it look like a drug deal, and the cops believed it. But Mel did an investigation, and traced it back to your parents." She pointed to the papers in my arms. "Read. You'll see."

"I followed them that night," Mel said. "I saw the whole thing. Your parents were good. It took us a month to trace back to the client, and the rest of these murders."

I crossed my arms across my chest. We were all trained liars, so I couldn't tell if even they believed the things they were saying. This could just be another layer of lies, designed to keep me from discovering the truth. Nothing they could say would prove otherwise.

"I want to see my parents," I said.

"Of course you do," Mel said. "You think because you can do a little reconnaissance you can break your parents out of a shifter facility?" He scoffed at me. "You don't stand a chance."

Aida's voice shook as she spoke. "No one escapes," she said. "They can find you anywhere."

I narrowed my eyes at them. "If you believe that," I said, "then there's no harm in letting me know where they are, is there?"

Aida shook her head vehemently. "I don't want you in danger."

I held my arms out to the sides. "How am I not *already* in danger, if no one escapes?"

Aida cringed. "You're not a murderer. They know you exist. That's more than you want them to know."

"Then what?" I said. "My parents are going to be prisoners forever? I'll never see them again? And I'm supposed to be okay with that?"

Mel gave me a look of disdain. "We have an obligation not to let each other go running around killing people. Can you imagine what will happen if a shifter assassin gets caught by the government? There could be genetic tests, weight detectors, kill orders."

I stood frozen to the spot. No. Of course they wouldn't let them go, if they believed my parents posed that kind of threat.

"You're going to execute them," I said. My voice sounded flat again, but better flat than hysterical.

Aida cringed, and gave Mel a look of reproof. I couldn't help but wonder what softer way she'd planned to break the news. Maybe over some pancakes. *Sorry, honey. We're going to kill your parents.* "You can't do this," I said. Though that was stupid, as they obviously already had.

Aida's voice was pleading. "You have to understand what a risk that is. When people feel their lives are threatened, they'll do anything to feel safe again. There'll be witch hunts. People will die."

"You mean you'll die," I said. "That's what you're really afraid of."

Aida looked past me. She knew, rightly, that I would never understand. The one she was worried about persuading now was Kalif.

He stared at her over my shoulder, and I couldn't help but wonder if he'd positioned me between him and them as an unequivocal statement of whose side he was on.

I resisted the urge to shake myself physically. Kalif and I needed to extract ourselves from this situation, before it escalated. If Aida and Mel were among my parents' masked assailants, they could take us down easily, and I didn't think that the mom and child in the park would come to our rescue.

What else did I need from them? What would I wish I had asked, while I had them talking? "If my parents are going to die," I said, "why hasn't it happened yet?"

"We need to get as much information from them as possible," Aida said. "To make sure we can trace anyone else who's been working with them."

I squinted at her. "I suppose I should count myself lucky that you didn't turn me over, too."

"You're a child," Aida said. "No one wants to hold you responsible. That's why we kept it from you. We want to protect you. You don't need to be tortured."

I didn't miss the veiled threat.

Aida must have sensed I wasn't buying it. I'd been hit with too much—it probably showed on my face. She lowered her voice, as if afraid to speak the words too loud. "Really, Jory," she said. "You have no idea what you're messing with. If you go after your parents, they'll kill you. They'll kill Kalif. If they think we helped you, they'll torture us, too."

Kalif's voice was dry. "Nice friends. I see why you work with them."

Aida looked down at the ground. Even Mel wasn't smiling anymore. And for a split second, I thought I saw Aida's fingertips tremble.

Was it an act? Was she truly afraid for me?

Or was she afraid *of* me?

"When did you plan to tell me?" I asked. "After they were dead?"

Aida couldn't look me in the eye. "We thought it would be better if you didn't know."

I let my voice turn to steel. "You thought it would be *better?*"

Mel took a step between Aida and me, as if shielding her. "It's not your fault what your parents did. It's hard for shifters to be alone in the world—worse than it is for regular people. You *need* us."

I could feel bile rising in my throat. They wanted me to fold into their family, like nothing happened. I wanted to scream, to beat Mel's puffed up chest with my fists and demand to see my parents. But that wouldn't do anything to get me what I wanted.

"Come back to the house," Mel said. "You'll need some time to think and go over the files."

My body tensed. I could make a run for it. From the way Kalif glared at his parents, I was pretty sure he'd come with me. I had the papers, but I needed more—both supplies and information.

"I'll think about it," I said.

Mel had the nerve to smile. "I know it's hard," he said. "But we can take care of you. You don't have to be alone."

If I hadn't been afraid to get close to him, I would have punched him right in the gut.

"Give us a minute," Kalif said.

"No," Aida said. "You'll come home with us now."

"And if we don't?" I asked. "Are you going to execute us?"

Aida and Mel looked at each other. If they insisted on taking us home with them, they were as much as admitting their ill intentions toward us. Kalif and I were shifters. We could disappear at any time.

Aida crossed her arms, assuming the pose of the protective mother. And as she did, I couldn't help but wonder if that had always been an act. Maybe she wanted Kalif and me together, to motivate me to stay with them.

"Fine," Aida said. "But I expect to see you both for dinner."

And they turned together and walked back to their SUV, probably to congratulate themselves on how well I had taken the news.

SIXTEEN

Kalif and I stood there, hands locked, until Aida and Mel got into their car and drove away. When they were out of sight, I stumbled toward the edge of the grass, a cold, queasy sensation seeping over me. My body folded over, knees sinking onto the edge of the asphalt, and I vomited into a bed of weeds.

When my stomach stopped heaving, I stayed on my hands and knees. My nostrils burned with bile, and my whole body broke out in a cold sweat. My wrists and elbows shook. I knew I should be planning what I was going to do next, but for that moment, I couldn't do anything but tremble.

Kalif's hands rubbed my shoulders and wiped the sweat from my forehead.

When I was sure I could trust my knees, I stood and walked to the drinking fountain to rinse out my mouth. When I surfaced from the fountain, Kalif stood in front of me, arms hanging helplessly at his sides.

"I'm trying to think of something brilliant to say," he said. "This is all I can come up with."

I laughed, even as tears leaked into my eyes.

"I can't believe that my parents would do this," Kalif said. "I'm so sorry."

I put a hand on his shoulder. "They lied to you, too."

"Yeah," he said, "but it doesn't compare. I don't blame you if you want to split now."

I nodded. I would, without question. But not yet. "We need the data from your server. Can you still track that deleted email?"

"Yes," Kalif said. "It'll take a while, but I can do it."

"That's our best lead," I said. I hesitated. Aida had said that if we went after my parents, we were as good as dead. "Are you still going to help me with this?"

"Of course," Kalif said. "I'll do the best I can. My parents will watch me more closely, though, now that they know what we're capable of."

I fidgeted with the edge of his sleeve. We had to get away from Aida and Mel. But after these last few days, running away together had all sorts of romantic connotations that I hadn't even considered yet. "I can't stay here long," I said. "Are you going to come with me?"

He kicked the edge of the water fountain with his toe. "Yeah. Of course."

And as much as I wanted to grill him about what exactly that meant for our future, this was so not the time. "We'll need to take some equipment. And the data from your server."

Kalif nodded. "Do you want me to crash the server, too?"

His face looked pained. That would sabotage all his work. "Not yet," I said. "Could you do that from a distance, if we needed to?"

He nodded. "Sure. I can get through my own security."

"Okay," I said. "Let's not do anything to alert them that there's a problem. We'll leave tonight."

Kalif nodded. "Done. But you're a better person than I am. I'd want to take everyone down with me."

I swallowed. "Don't give me too much credit," I said. "If it wouldn't interfere with getting my parents, I wouldn't mind making them pay."

Kalif nodded, but the pain still showed on his face. I kicked myself. These were still his parents. How would I feel if the situation were reversed?

Would I be willing to walk away from my parents for him?

When we returned to the house, Aida and Mel sat at the kitchen table, sipping one of his gourmet coffees. I walked right past them and down to Kalif's room; they must have figured it was time to give me space, because neither of them tried to stop me.

When we reached Kalif's room, he closed the door behind us. No use following his mom's rules now, I supposed. They were probably always for show, anyway.

Kalif pulled over his laptop, and an external hard drive. "We can use these to transfer the data. I'll show you which files to copy, and then I'll go talk to my parents. If we both hole up down here, they'll suspect that we're planning something."

I was sure they suspected anyway. "Can you cover?" I asked.

He nodded. "I may suck at impersonations, but I have plenty of practice lying to my parents."

"What are you going to tell them?"

"I'll just say you needed some time to think, and go over the files. My room is more secluded, plus there's the emails and things for you to look at again."

"Okay," I said. "Thank you."

Kalif pointed the files out to me, and then he turned and left. I closed the door, alone with his computer.

I started by copying the email records between Kalif's parents and whoever these Asylum shifters were. Then I dumped the mission files from Kalif's computer onto the external drive. Some of the folders Kalif indicated contained files I didn't recognize—several of them programs. I dumped them all, trusting his expertise.

As I sat there, doubt gnawed at me. Kalif had agreed to come with me, maybe too easily. If he were secretly working for his parents, this is exactly what he would do—come along to spy.

I unearthed a flash drive from Kalif's desk drawer and pulled up the folders with the mission data and the email again. I made a second copy of those on the drive, and shoved it into my pocket. I had no real reason to suspect Kalif, but it was better to be safe than sorry. Information was my trade, and if I was going to work alone, I had to be prepared.

When the files finished, I unplugged the external drive and stashed it and the laptop in one of Kalif's carrying cases. There was nothing left to do—at least, nothing I could think of at the moment. I sat on Kalif's stool, looking at his computer screen. I loosened my jaw, hearing it pop. My teeth ached from clenching.

The basement door swung open again and Kalif stepped in. I took his hand and exchanged signals with him before either of us said a word. "You okay?" he asked. He jerked his head in the direction of the kitchen, and put a hand to his ear. His parents were listening.

"No," I said. "But I'll live."

He nodded. "I'm sorry about your parents." I wanted to congratulate him on sticking to things he could say sincerely, but I couldn't without breaking the act.

"Thanks," I said.

"I'll show you that program again. To get your mind off things."

Kalif walked past me into the room, and then closed the door.

"I made the copies," I said.

"Let me see what you've got," Kalif said, unpacking the computer again. "Make sure it's everything I'll need." As he leaned over the computer, though, his shoulders shook. There was a hardness in his eyes I hadn't seen before.

"What did they say?" I asked.

His fingers stabbed the keyboard. "They asked me to watch you. They want me to inform them about what you find when you keep looking."

I closed my eyes. The fact that I let that surprise me meant I still wasn't on top of my game.

"What did you say?" I asked.

"I told them I'd do it, because that's what they wanted to hear. But I'm not going to let them use me against you. We need to

174

make a clean break. Otherwise, they'll find a way to get to you through me."

I spoke slowly, trying not to sound desperate. "So that's why you're coming? Because you don't want them to use you?"

He put a hand on my wrist, squeezing it gently. "That," he said, "and I can't stand the idea of letting you go alone."

I could have melted through the floor. He was still facing the computer, but I grabbed him around the waist in a sideways hug, nearly knocking him off his feet.

Despite himself, Kalif laughed.

I bit my tongue, squeezing him tighter, trying to convince myself I'd never have to let go. I couldn't begin to imagine what life would look like after this, but I was certain Kalif's parents wouldn't welcome me back in any case, and I couldn't imagine my parents would be happy to have him come along with us.

Bringing him with me only prolonged the inevitable. But I was going to cling to every moment I could get.

I spent the rest of the evening in my office room, wishing I had a square foot of carpet on which to pace. We'd decided it would be easiest to leave after Aida and Mel went to bed, as usual. We couldn't take Mom and Dad's car this time—it'd be too easy to trace—so I used Kalif's laptop to look up local bus routes. Most of the buses shut down late at night, but there was one night bus that would stop a few blocks away. We'd take that downtown, to a stop near a hotel.

I tried not to think about the reality of staying in a hotel with Kalif, but of course that was all I could think about. My mind kept wandering to the way his hands felt on my back, that night we'd spent in his bed. Then thoughts of my parents cut through. In my mind, I saw them locked in dank cells, separated, starved, tortured. Waiting, praying I'd come for them. And all the while I was thinking about spending the night with a boy I'd been dating for less than a week.

I lay on my back on my mattress and crossed my arms over

my eyes. I wished Kalif was next to me, even then. Thinking about him was infinitely preferable to thinking about what my parents were going through.

I met Kalif downstairs half an hour after I heard Aida and Mel's door close. He was waiting on his own stairs, wearing a black hoodie that he could easily pull over his face. He tossed me another hoodie—this one brown. They were plain, so Aida and Mel wouldn't necessarily recognize them from the communal wardrobe, but they'd also give us quick cover if we needed to shift on the fly. He took my hand, passing me his signal.

"Are you ready?" I whispered.

Kalif nodded. "I grabbed a few more files, just in case."

I listened for movement upstairs, but all was quiet. "Your parents will be expecting us to slip out, won't they?"

He shrugged. "Maybe. But I told them that you were too scared to run off on your own, and when I told you I wouldn't go with you, you decided it was best to stay here."

It was a good cover. "How'd they take that?"

He gave me a grim smile. "Oh, you know. They couldn't be prouder of me for selling you out."

I cringed. "I'm sorry," I said. This whole thing was getting to be as painful for him as it was for me, which wasn't what I wanted at all.

Kalif shook his head, resigned. "It's okay. Just makes this easier."

I looked at the bags in his hands. "Do we have everything we'll need?"

Kalif nodded. "I think so. I knew where Dad kept the emergency cash, so we'll have enough to get someplace to stay, and anything else we've forgotten."

I looked nervously up the stairs. I was sure there were more things here we were going to want, but most things we'd be able to acquire elsewhere if we needed to, one way or another. "Let's go."

We slipped out the front door and walked quickly away. When we hit the main street, I looked back over my shoulder.

The windows to Kalif's townhome were still dark.

"Bus stop is this way," I said. "You have change?"

"Got it," Kalif said.

We strode down the street and took shelter inside the bus stop, tucking our bags far under the bench and pulling our hoodies over our faces to get ourselves into character. Kalif shortened his hair to a buzz cut and rounded his face out. In the streetlights, I couldn't tell exactly how much he changed his skin tone, but with his dark hair and changed features, he looked Hispanic. I changed my hair and skin tone to match. A pair of Mexican teenagers would fit in as well as anybody on the San Jose streets.

We'd been waiting about four minutes when Mel's car rounded the corner. "Don't look," Kalif said, pulling at his hoodie. "Act like it's just another car."

"I won't look," I said, "if you won't fidget."

Kalif glued both his hands to the bench.

The car drove slowly toward the bus stop. I didn't look, but I knew Mel must be scrutinizing us. The car moved slower and slower, until it came to a stop in front of the bench.

Kalif turned toward the car, and Mel rolled down the passenger side window.

Kalif wrapped his arm tight around my waist, holding me protectively.

"Hey," Mel said, leaning across the seat. "You see two kids out here?"

"Little kids?" I asked, making sure my voice was higher than normal. "It's kind of late."

Mel sneered at me. "Not little kids," Mel said. "About your age."

Yeah. We really needed a new shtick. "Oh," I said. "Why didn't you say so?"

He frowned. "I *did*."

I sighed. Mel was watching us now, judging our reactions, hoping if it was us we would slip up and act like ourselves. This was my department. I needed to think of something to say that would get him to leave, even though there was no way I could prove to him that we weren't exactly the people he was looking for.

Kalif beat me to it. He stood up, squaring his shoulders at Mel. He did a much better impression of a territorial silverback than Mel had. "Get lost," Kalif said. Then he swore at Mel and spit in the direction of the car. It all would have been too much if his posture hadn't been so very unlike the real Kalif. It was the dead wrong thing to do if we were facing down cops or security guards, but I didn't imagine Mel wanted to pick a fight on the street tonight.

Mel considered Kalif dryly for a moment, and then rolled up the window and moved on.

"Wow," I said. "I didn't think you had it in you."

Kalif watched Mel's car roll slowly up the street. "Neither does he. That was the idea."

"He's always talking you up," I said. "You really think he'll underestimate you now?"

"It's just a cover," Kalif said, "for how disappointed he is that I'm not as good a shifter as you are."

I gave him a look. "No way."

"Yes. That's why it needed to be me who convinced him to go away. Plays into his idea that I can't function in the field."

"Technically," I said, "I could have been the guy, and you could have been the girl."

"Yeah, but Dad knows I can't turn into a convincing woman, so he won't be expecting that."

I smacked him on the shoulder. "You function in the field just fine."

"Sure. As long as you're there to nudge me when I mess up."

I rolled my eyes. "Yeah, well. It would be smarter for us to quit turning into a teenage couple."

Kalif laughed. "You're right," Kalif said. "Two fat guys would be less predictable."

I elbowed his ribs. "We should have brought bigger clothes."

As the bus arrived, I wished I hadn't made my hair quite so

coarse. My new bangs hung in my face, causing my forehead to itch. We climbed aboard, and the bus driver barely glanced at us as we fed our money into his machine. I sat against a bench, facing Kalif. He stared listlessly out the window, as if he wasn't nervous at all, and I leaned back, too. I had to relax. This new persona shouldn't have a care in the world. Cares drew attention.

Kalif got up to leave the bus a few blocks from downtown, and I followed. Once the bus pulled away, I tugged my hoodie down over my forehead and fixed my hair, making it less thick and stretching it long enough to tuck behind my ears.

"You know where we're going?" I asked.

"There's a motel on the next block," Kalif said. "It's not nice, but it's something."

Blood pounded in my ears. The reality of what we were doing started to set in. I was running away. To a seedy motel. With Kalif.

But if Kalif was nervous about it, his persona didn't show it. He just plodded forward like he could take it all in stride. He walked with his shoulders slumped forward, which didn't look like his normal walk at all. I was proud.

Kalif made himself look a bit older when he went into the motel office alone. I hung out in the parking lot. Persona or no, I didn't want to deal with snide looks from the motel clerk.

Kalif re-emerged a few minutes later with two room cards and a number. "I reserved the room for one night. We should probably move every day."

I shoved my hands in my pockets to keep them from fidgeting. "Good thinking," I said. I needed to get my head in the game, and think of these things myself.

I followed Kalif to our room—a double bed on the ground floor. I stepped in, looking anywhere but the bed, trying not to wonder if he'd gotten one bed on purpose, or if that's all they had available.

Kalif locked the door, and I pulled the heavy drapes shut. In the darkness, my body melted back into my normal self. The room was dark except for the line of yellow from the street lights showing at the top of the curtains. And even though he didn't touch me, my whole body was aware of Kalif, standing just a few feet away, lowering his bags to the floor.

We could fumble awkwardly around it, or get straight to the point. I wasn't going to be able to focus on the search for my parents without some sleep—and without getting his nearness out of my head.

Kalif ran his hand along the wall, searching for the light. I caught his wrist before he found it.

The curtains behind me stirred, and a thin line of golden light cut across his face. He'd also shifted back into himself, and his dark eyes watched me as he stepped closer.

My hands were shaking. I stepped toward him, and Kalif folded me into his arms. I leaned against him, pressing my face against his shirt, feeling his body against mine.

"No one is going to find us here," he said into my ear.

His warm breath sent shivers down my spine. "I know," I said. "I just feel like I'm made out of eggshell. If someone squeezes me too hard, I'll break."

He rested his chin on the top of my head. "You're going to feel like that until we find your parents."

"Maybe. But I'm not sure even that can fix it." Once we found them, I'd have them back, but he'd be gone.

Kalif reached down for his bag. "I'll track that email. Pull out those files on your parents. You'll feel better once we get to work."

I caught his arm, pulling it back around me. I didn't want to think anymore. I just wanted to forget. Our mouths crashed together. Kalif kissed me back, but when his arm rose, it wedged between us instead of wrapping around me. He pushed on my shoulder, leveraging us apart.

"Hey," he said. "I didn't come along to take advantage of you again."

I stood on my tiptoes, lengthening my legs so I could bring

our eyes even. "Maybe it's a perk."

His face grew serious.

I kicked myself. That was clearly the wrong thing to say. "I was joking."

He dropped his arms. "No, you meant it."

I took a step toward him, but he backed away. "Look," I said. "It's not taking advantage if I want to, is it?"

Kalif looked up at the ceiling. The light from the top of the curtains lit his face from above. "You're stressed," he said. "This isn't about us."

I wanted to tell him he was wrong, but I couldn't. I squinted at him in the darkness. "Is that a problem?"

He sighed. "It is for me."

I could feel him slipping away from me with every word. I dug my fingernails into my palms. I was ruining everything.

Tears threatened my eyes, and I squeezed them closed. I wasn't going to start bawling this time. Not again. "This isn't how I wanted things to be," I said quietly.

Kalif edged toward the light switch. "Me, either," Kalif said. "And I keep thinking that if I screw this up, things between us will never be the way I want them to be."

I wanted to sink through the floor. He was right. So why did it still feel like a rejection? "Do you mean that?" I asked. "Or are you just blowing me off?"

Kalif leaned back against the door and moaned. "I wish I didn't mean it. You are really stretching the limits of my dedication to being a responsible boyfriend."

My heart double-beat. That was the first time either of us had used that word. "Are you?" I asked.

He looked at me miserably. "What? Responsible? Dedicated?"

"Boyfriend?"

He gave a rueful laugh. "Oh, that. No, I thought I'd run away with you and then break up immediately."

I sighed. "When you put it that way," I said, "I wonder when I got so needy."

He knocked his head back against the door. "Maybe when your parents were kidnapped and then you had to run away, leaving everything behind."

Everything. I hadn't given a second thought for any of my personal things. That was my training in action; we always had to be ready to drop and run. Things weren't important. But my parents? Kalif? They were. "Thanks for making me sound like I'm not crazy."

He shrugged. "You're not. But I don't want fear to be the only reason we're together."

"It isn't," I said.

He stepped toward me and put a hand on my arm. I wasn't sure whether he wanted to touch me, or hold me at arm's length.

Probably both.

"I believe you," he said. "So let's not rush it, okay?"

I flopped onto the bed. "Responsibility must be your second superpower. You're in a dark hotel room with a girl who can be anything you want, and you turn that down?" I couldn't deliver the whole line with a straight face. There was just enough light for me to see Kalif glaring at me as I fell back onto the bed in giggles. It was probably inappropriate, what with my parents being kidnapped, and his being traitors, and mine being accused of murder, but once I got going, I couldn't stop, like all the stress crawled up inside my ribs and wriggled every time I tried to breathe.

Kalif tried valiantly not to smile. He stood over me for a moment, and then tackled me, rolling me over. We landed with his arms tangled around me, his body spooning me from behind.

"For the record," he said in my ear, "I don't want you to be anyone but you."

I laughed until my sides ached and my eyes filled with tears. Kalif shook his head at me, but he didn't let go. And as my giggles finally died down, I realized what he'd last said to me was more romantic than anything we could have done in the dark.

SEVENTEEN

I wasn't sure how long we lay on the bed in the dark, but eventually my brain began to clear. Incubated in the cozy warmth of Kalif's arms, I started to think about our plan.

I rolled over, nuzzling Kalif's throat with my nose.

"Mmm," he said.

"Are you awake?"

He sighed. "Yeah. Barely."

"Do you want to sleep?" I asked. "Or work?"

The way his arms ran down my body told me that he wanted to do something else entirely, but then he sat up, rubbing his face. "Work. I've got another hour in me, at least."

I was pretty sure that he didn't, but I wasn't in a position to argue. If Mom and Dad were going to be executed, we needed to find them as quickly as we could.

Kalif set up the laptop on the tiny table in the corner, and opened it. "Can you get online from here?" I asked.

"The hotel connection is terrible," Kalif said. "But I brought the portable hub."

I stiffened. "Will your parents be able to track that?"

"No," he said. "But if I need to get into the server—which I probably will—they could hire someone to track that. After they dig their way back into the system, that is. I changed everyone's passwords before I left."

I smiled. "You weren't kidding about bringing them down with you."

Kalif shrugged. "They'll get back in. Eventually."

While Kalif got to work on the trace, I sifted through the stack of papers about the murders, spreading them out on the bed. I divided the papers into piles, one for each murder. There were seven cases in all, ranging from Ruben Ferreira twenty-six years ago to that CEO who died last month. The rest were spread between the intervening years, so far apart that it seemed improbable that they could be related. The police hadn't linked the crimes together. The victims had all been shot to death, but that wasn't exactly an unusual means of murder.

I worked through the Ferreira file first, which was where I found the damning evidence. The images came from a security feed, complete with a time and date stamp from ten years before I was born. Two men stood over a woman unconscious on the floor. Her hair spilled over the carpet. The next page showed an enlargement of the woman's face.

I stared down at the photo. It was my mother. That much younger, she looked almost identical to my home body. That figured, since I'd made it in her image.

I shook it at Kalif. "This can't be real," I said. "There's no way."

Kalif left the table and sat next to me on the bed. He took the image out of my hands, looked it over, and swore.

I found the copy of the police report on the incident. "She got knocked out," I said. "A second assailant attacked the two men, and when they came to, she was gone."

"This looks bad," Kalif said. "It happened after one of the murders?"

I scanned over the papers, piecing together the story. "The Ruben Ferreira killing. Several witnesses said they saw him with his two body guards, but the guards both turned up later with alibis. Ruben was killed in a hotel, and another guest said they saw one of the guards fleeing the scene after the gunshots. Hotel security followed him, knocked him out, and they claimed he turned into her."

Kalif cringed. "What'd the police think of that?"

184

"They thought hotel security was in on it, but they couldn't make anything stick." I slumped over. "Do you think it was them?"

Kalif scrutinized the photo. "Could be doctored."

I rubbed my forehead. "By who? Your parents?"

He looked at the picture of Mom again. "Or some cop at the time? One who knew about shifters?"

I covered my eyes with my hand. "Or some other shifter could have been impersonating my mom, pretending to be knocked out." There were so many possibilities, and trying to eliminate each one would take time, and probably a trip to Chicago.

Kalif leafed through the other files. "Do you want help looking through the rest of these? I can look through them if you want, and show you what I find."

I shook my head. That wasn't the right way to work. I shouldn't believe anything I didn't see with my own eyes, even if it came from Kalif.

Besides, his trace was my best hope for finding my parents. I gestured toward his computer. "How long is that going to take?"

He looked regretful. "A while," he said. "This is good work— better than I've seen before." He smiled. "And this time it isn't *mine*."

That made a sad sort of sense. If we were dealing with another group of shifters, they'd be as paranoid as we were, or maybe even more so. I just hoped we weren't dealing with a tech who was better than Kalif. If *he'd* decided to betray us, my parents and I were screwed.

As Kalif returned to his computer, I sat paralyzed on the bed, bending forward as my previous doubts returned to sock me in the stomach.

Kalif had come with me to help me, which was exactly what he would have done if his parents were using him to watch me. He'd even suggested that they *wanted* him to do exactly that, so that I would take his admission as evidence that he was trustworthy.

185

But it wasn't. Words weren't evidence of anything. Aida and Mel proved that. Kalif had left with me so easily, without me needing to convince him.

But if Kalif was lying to me, what was his goal? Certainly not to help me find my parents. To delay me, then? Until it was too late?

Kalif glanced up at me. "Jory?"

"Yeah?" I must have looked as terrified as I felt. I hadn't had my guard up with him. I hadn't thought that I needed to. Kalif had a way of disarming me.

Was that purposeful? How long had I known him, really? Just a handful of months. Maybe it was all an act, right down to his ineptitude at shifting.

Kalif leaned across the table. "Maybe you should get some rest, and look at the files in the morning."

That sounded like a delay tactic to me, though at the same time it made perfect sense. That was exactly the sort of thwarting Kalif would be doing if he didn't want me to find my parents at all. It was also what a concerned boyfriend would say.

I rubbed my temples. My thoughts spun through the loop a few more times, until I was certain I must be literally losing my mind.

"Hey," Kalif said. "Talk to me."

I shook my head, trying to snap out of my funk. But it was too late; I was running on stress fumes and no sleep. I reached for the smart, capable actress version of myself, but she wasn't there. "I'm just thinking."

"About what?"

I waved a hand in the air, failing to look nonchalant. "About how I don't know who to trust anymore."

Kalif nodded slowly. "But you know you can trust me, right?"

It took me too long to respond. He shut his laptop.

"Jory," he said. "I'm just trying to help you."

I shut my eyes. I had to get used to using my training against the people close to me. That's what everyone else had been doing. "Isn't that what you would say if you were working with your parents?"

Kalif looked at me in disbelief. "You mean if I helped them kidnap your mom and dad?"

"No," I said. "If you'd done that, why would you have helped me find them?"

The words sounded like hollow reasoning, even to me. I knew better than to believe them. The two-man con was one of the oldest tricks in the book. One party would pretend to be the enemy, and the other would be the friend, while they were really working together all along.

"Jory," Kalif said, "I swear to you, I am not working against you. My parents are going to be livid when I go home. I can't even imagine what they're going to do to me."

I closed my eyes and lay back on the bed. "I think I'm going crazy."

I lay quietly, eyes closed, and after a bit I heard Kalif turn back to his work. He didn't come over to comfort me, and I wondered if it was because he thought I needed space, or because he was offended that I'd even suggest that he'd betray me. It was a terrible thing to think.

It would be even more terrible if it were true.

I focused on breathing slowly. In and out. In and out. If Kalif was out to get me, I would really be all alone in the world. I had to trust him.

For now.

I didn't intend to fall asleep, but the next thing I remembered was waking to daylight creeping under the heavy curtains. The papers I'd been searching still lay scattered about the bed. Kalif was stretched out on the floor, asleep with his head on his balled-up hoodie. I wondered how late he'd worked. I wanted to wake him up to figure out what he'd found, but the harsh cold of last night's doubts still haunted me.

I moved quietly to the table, stepping carefully so as not to

187

wake him. Kalif's phone sat next to his computer. He'd brought a disposable, so Aida and Mel couldn't use the phone to track us down. I picked it up. Trusting Kalif would be easier if I allowed myself some verification.

I looked at his text messages and his call records, but all of his recent communication was with me. I checked the phone's features. One could erase the entire history, but not the individual entries. He hadn't been using his phone to contact his parents, then.

I flipped through the other open tabs on Kalif's computer. There were the files Kalif had been searching—the server files already open.

These all looked like the sorts of things I expected him to have open—his parents' emails, that deleted mission report. I opened his web browser and paged through his history. Halfway down the page, I found the link for his email.

My cursor hovered over it. Searching his email was crossing a line—one we crossed every day in our work. But if we were together, did that make it different?

No one else seemed to think so.

I clicked.

My heart stopped. There, on the top, was an email with his mother's name on it. Proof that he was corresponding with her. Once I read it, I'd know for certain that there was no one to help me. Kalif lay still on the floor, his head resting on his arms. It wasn't too late to slip away.

I opened the email.

Kalif, it said. *We understand that you want to help Jory, but please help her by bringing her home. The people who have her parents will not hesitate to kill her, and you, if you interfere. If you care about Jory, you can show it by keeping her safe. Your father and I love you, and want you to be safe. Please come home.*

I read it once, and then again. Resting my head in my hands, I took long, slow breaths. Aida hadn't sent it from her email that was hosted from Kalif's server. She must still be locked out of her account. I could decide that this email, too, was part of the setup. But the fact was, it was impossible to know the true motivations of another person. This was what we did with our lives; we fooled people. But not each other. We weren't supposed to do this to each other. Mel and Aida made that mistake—they spied on their own son, they betrayed my parents. From what Kalif said about their past, they didn't even trust each other. Maybe my parents were the same. But I didn't want to be like that. Kalif had to be innocent until proven guilty, or whatever relationship was growing between us was going to die a cold, lonely death. And it would all be my fault.

I closed the email, and then the computer. I knelt beside Kalif on the floor and put a hand on his shoulder. He stretched and opened his eyes. Then he reached for my hand.

Our palms fit together like they'd been made for each other, and I wondered if we were subconsciously shifting them to be so. If I was, I could no longer tell—the shift had become part of my home body. I could already tell that in the last few days, my subconscious projection of myself had become older, more mature, more conventionally attractive. I wasn't trying, or stretching. Kalif was changing me.

I had to trust in that change, or I couldn't trust in anything. Kalif sat up, and I leaned close to him, whispering in his ear. "I looked through your email to see if you were conspiring with your parents. Just thought you should know."

Kalif rubbed his eyes and turned so his cheek brushed mine. "And am I?"

"You have an email from your mother. She says if you love me you'll bring me back home where we'll both be safe."

"Sounds like her. She always goes for the guilt trip."

I pressed our foreheads together. "I'm sorry for doubting you."

"Yeah, well," Kalif said. "It would have been a really good con, if I were a total asshole."

"Forgive me?"

And instead of answering, he cupped my chin in his hand,

brought my lips to his, and kissed me deeply.

An ache spread through me. Instead of the need to rush and forget, I felt a deep longing, a wish that couldn't be granted. When I found my parents, Kalif would have to go home. He couldn't come with me; my parents wouldn't believe that he was on our side, even if I did. They'd never allow me to contact him again, not after what his parents had done. I wanted to slow down these moments, to savor them as long as I could.

But every moment I did, my parents were at risk.

I drew back, and we held each other, catching our breath. "Did you trace the ISP yet?" I asked.

Kalif sat back on his hands. "Still working on it. I quit when my eyes started closing. Did you sleep okay?"

I stretched. "Surprisingly. Though I wish I hadn't slept in my jeans."

Kalif nodded. "I thought about waking you. But I figured we both needed to get some sleep." He smiled. "Plus I had to write that email from my mom, to make sure that when you woke up and looked for evidence against me . . ."

I punched him in the arm. "Shut up."

"Come on. That one was funny."

"Maybe," I said. "I'll let you know if I ever recover my sense of humor."

"Seriously, though, there *is* something I need to tell you."

A chill ran through me. That wasn't the follow up I was looking for. "What?"

Kalif played with the ends of my hair. "You should know, my parents didn't find your family by accident. They're always looking for shifters—that's why we'd worked with Helene's family in the past. The people at Megaware did follow your dad. My dad had done jobs for them before, and they called him to try to track your dad down."

I leaned hard against the bed. "You were working for Megaware?"

"No." He spoke quickly, rushing to explain. "Dad took the tip and refused the job once he figured out it was another shifter.

Then he and Mom followed Megaware to track you down. It wasn't easy, since you guys had moved, but they did it."

They found us. And then they acted like it was an accident. They'd been liars from the very beginning. "Why?"

"I always thought it was because they don't want to work alone. But I guess I was wrong."

I closed my eyes. They were hunting us. Maybe they already knew about the murders, even then. Or maybe they fabricated them after the fact, to convince Asylum to take my parents out of the picture.

If they'd followed my family even after we shifted and moved, that meant they were very, very good. It seemed such a shame to waste such talent and resources on destroying other people's lives.

My heart sank. Of course, that's what my parents did, wasn't it? I'd always thought it was a weakness that I empathized with the victims. But maybe it wasn't.

Maybe that was the only thing keeping me from becoming like them.

"Thank you for telling me," I said.

He shifted uncomfortably. "I didn't tell you before because it seemed harmless," he said, "but obviously it wasn't."

He should have told me when we were investigating Megaware. But he was no doubt used to keeping his parents' secrets. I hoped that was all there was to it.

I stood. "We need to move," I said. "You can keep searching from another hotel."

"I did some looking last night." He handed me a notepad with an address written on it. "The only hotel within walking distance is a nicer one, but I called ahead, and they'll take cash with a deposit. We have enough."

"Let's be older," I said. "Teenagers paying cash look like trouble."

"All we have is our jeans. What's our angle?"

I walked over to the mirror over the sink. "Give me a minute. I'll figure something out."

191

I stood in front of the mirror for five minutes, experimenting, before I settled on an impersonation of a tourist. A tall woman with well-kept blonde hair and flawless skin would appear responsible even in casual clothing.

"Here," I said, spinning around for Kalif. "Make yourself something to match."

I had to coach him a bit, but we left the hotel looking like a pair of newlyweds bumming around the Bay Area. We were old enough to be trusted with a hotel room on a cash deposit, but young enough not to look out of place in the clothing we had on hand. It was perfect, if I did say so myself.

When we reached the new hotel, I went into the office with Kalif, because these personas went together as a package. I perused the brochures in the lobby while Kalif paid the clerk, even picking up a couple brochures for some shops in Carmel and flashing them at Kalif with a carefree smile. "We should go there."

Kalif rolled his eyes. "Sure. More window shopping."

I smacked him in the arm with the pamphlet, and we both grinned. The clerk finished checking us in, and handed Kalif a pair of room cards. "Fourth floor," he said. "With a view of the city." Kalif handed me one of the cards, and we held hands into the elevator. I rested my head against his arm, wishing we really were these two people, instead of ourselves.

Shifting was a dangerous game. Sometimes, you didn't want to shift back.

When we got upstairs, I put the bag with Kalif's equipment down on the double bed. I pulled the curtains closed so we could change into ourselves, but not before admiring the balcony view from the sliding glass door. It was perfectly focused on the skyline of San Jose, the shiny buildings rising together, like blocks on a bar graph.

My newlywed persona, I was sure, would have come up with a more romantic metaphor. But there was no use stabbing at romance now. Kalif was too worried about my mental state, and more importantly, we had work to do.

Kalif set up his computer on the end of the dresser, while I laid out the papers again, to consider the cases with a fresh mind.

The reports were mostly unsolved murders, though in a few cases someone had been convicted for the killing—a brother-in-law in one, a downstairs neighbor in another. But in every case I found hints that shifters were involved. Some bystander swore they saw the killer somewhere else that night. The murderer inexplicably left clothes behind at the scene. Nothing the cops couldn't explain away, but enough that I could recognize the signs.

None of the other reports had clues that it was Mom or Dad who committed the murders. I studied the picture of Mom. It was possible for Aida and Mel to have guessed what Mom looked like when she was younger, especially since the picture made her look so much like me.

I was reading through the details of the final murder—the one Mel claimed to have seen. The victim was a white-collar guy, the CEO of Graphasoft. He had an established cocaine addiction, and the murder looked like a back-alley shooting. But it turned out after the fact that he'd been inflating his company stock to cut and run, which wasn't illegal, but was the kind of thing that would ruffle the feathers of people around him who might want the business to stay afloat.

In short, it looked like exactly the sort of job my parents would take, if they were inclined to kill people.

I flipped through the papers again. What if my parents did do it? What if Kalif and I were working to free murderers instead of innocents?

I shook my head. They were still my parents, and they clearly weren't receiving anything like a fair trial. They'd been snatched in the night. That wasn't the work of justice. This had to be a setup.

Combing over the report, I found it: a tiny footnote, a piece of information the police had gleaned from talking to the victim's wife.

She'd been having an affair, the report said. And she'd told her lover exactly where her husband would be and when, so she could convince him it was safe to meet up.

Then her husband wound up dead. And she never saw her lover again.

My stomach turned, and Kalif's words repeated in my head. *He's seducing someone, okay? It's his preferred method.* If Mel had a calling card, this was it.

I glanced over at Kalif. He leaned intently over his computer, the screen casting white light over his face. I couldn't falsely accuse his father of murder. I had to be sure. But if it had been Mel who killed this guy, I didn't know how I'd ever know for certain.

And then I looked down at the date.

"Kalif," I said. "Do you have that mission file your parents deleted from the server?" He'd been so upset about the lost data, but we'd never pieced together why his parents would remove that file, out of all the mission reports my parents had logged.

"Yeah." He clicked on something, and then tilted his screen in my direction. "It's right here."

I glanced back at the report on the CEO's murder. "The date. It was January seventh?"

He squinted at the screen. "Yeah. What of it?"

I got up from the bed, newspaper clipping in hand, and stood behind his chair to see the date for myself.

The murder took place the same night as the deleted mission.

I handed Kalif the paper. "They erased my parents' alibi."

We both stared at the screen. I leaned over, wrapping my arms around Kalif's shoulders. The muscles in his back stretched tight. "Your parents thought they'd be home that night," I said. "But my parents went out without telling them first and yours came home and discovered the people they'd framed had to be in two places at once."

Kalif leaned his head back against me, and let out a long, slow breath. I expected him to be angry, but his voice sounded

194

resigned. "Dad thinks we're descended from assassins. Maybe it's not that far a stretch to become one."

I squeezed him tighter.

He looked at the report again. "Do you really think this was him?"

"We need to find proof," I said. If we could gather enough evidence, we might be able to talk my parents out.

EIGHTEEN

A few hours later, I stood outside a Los Altos mansion, smart phone in hand. The police report listed this as the residence of Sylvia Stoddard, widow of CEO Will Stoddard—the CEO who was shot to death in the alley following a drug deal.

I'd dressed as a woman in her mid-forties for this job; a woman knocking on the door unexpectedly would draw a lot less suspicion than a man. I'd bought these clothes on the way over, but I'd had to hike ten blocks through the winding, tree-lined streets, because busses didn't travel through neighborhoods this rich. The last three streets hadn't even had sidewalks. I guessed the rich didn't walk, either. Or maybe they walked on their estates; I couldn't even see most of the houses from the road.

If I'd realized how long a walk this would be, I might have just called Sylvia on the phone. But talking in person would give me a chance to read her body language, to know if there were things she wasn't sharing, and also to disarm her a bit. People were accustomed to scam phone calls. Going in person gave me the chance to seem nice and harmless. And, to her, that's exactly what I was.

I double-checked the address on the mailbox with the one on my phone, and then tucked the phone into the pocket of my pants suit. The path to the door wound through several weeping willows, to a set of tall steps leading up to a pair of oak double doors.

Here went nothing.

196

I climbed the steps up to the door and rang the doorbell. I couldn't hear whether or not it rang through the door, but a moment later, a voice spoke to me through the intercom above the doorbell. The voice sounded like a woman in her mid-fifties, so this could very well be Sylvia.

"Hello?"

"I'm here to talk to Sylvia Stoddard," I said. "I'm a private investigator looking into her husband's death."

There was a pause. "I already have an investigator."

I nodded. If she'd hired one, she must not have been satisfied with the police work. "Of course. But I was hired by friends on the board of directors of your husband's company. They were concerned that the police hadn't done enough."

"Don hired you, then."

I remembered a Donald from the list of members of the board, but I couldn't remember his last name. It was a gamble, but I had to take the chance. "Yes."

Another pause. "And I suppose you'll want to come in to speak with me."

I smiled. "That would be very helpful, ma'am."

A moment later, the door swung open. I recognized Sylvia Stoddard from a photo I'd seen online of her and her late husband at a charity banquet. In that photo, her hair had been blonde, but she'd dyed it darker now, and I could see flecks of gray at the roots.

"Hello," I said, holding out my hand. "I'm Anne Temple. Pleased to meet you."

Sylvia shook my hand. Her grip was light, and she looked me up and down, appraising me. She didn't look at all pleased to meet me. "So you've come to interrogate me about my late husband's death, hmm?"

"No," I said quickly. "I just wanted to hear your side of things. That's all."

She narrowed her eyes at me. "Well, you may as well come in." She led me through her entryway and into what I supposed one would call a living room, if it hadn't looked so very un-lived in. The white furniture was immaculate; as I walked in, my shoes left footprints in the orderly vacuum lines on the carpet.

Did CEOs of tech companies make this much? It probably depended on their stock options, but I found it more likely that one or the other of them came from money, as well.

Sylvia motioned me to a loveseat, and then sat down herself, resting her elbows on the wooden arms of her chair. "I suppose," she said, "that you're here to ask me about Brian."

I nodded. According to the police report, Brian was the name of her lover. "The police didn't seem to think that he was involved. But it seems suspicious that—"

"You're damned right it's suspicious," Sylvia said. "I've had a man looking for him, but he's turned up nothing. How does a man just disappear?"

I swallowed. I knew *exactly* how. And if her investigator didn't, he wasn't going to turn up a thing. "He's found nothing?"

Sylvia nodded. "I suppose I know how to pick them. William was proof of that."

I nodded. All the reports, except the medical reports from the coroner, had referred to her husband as Will. I wondered if she'd always called him by his full name, or if this was something that she did to give herself distance after his death.

"And your husband," I said. "Did he know about the affair?"

Sylvia waved a hand dismissively. "I'm sure he suspected."

There was another explanation for why the man might have disappeared. If her husband had discovered the affair immediately before his death, he might have done something about it. The death might even be tied up in that struggle—which would make it much less likely that Mel had been involved.

"Do you think," I said, "that your husband might have contacted Brian, before he died?"

Sylvia actually looked amused about the idea. "I don't know why he would have," she said. "He never contacted any of the others."

My cheeks reddened, and I suppressed them so she wouldn't

notice. A seasoned private investigator wouldn't blush at infidelity, would she? But I suddenly became very aware that I had invaded the home of a much older woman to ask her about the intimate details of her love life. I couldn't believe that Mel *preferred* to work that way. I was absolutely certain that this conversation would not have been easier if Sylvia had her clothes off.

I lightened my cheeks even more.

"So you had . . . many affairs?"

Sylvia gave me a wry smile. "Don't look so scandalized. My husband and I had an arrangement."

I blinked. They both knew, and didn't care? That was even more screwed up than Aida and Mel. "Do you mind . . . may I ask . . ."

Sylvia laughed. "You want to know why we were still married?"

I nodded.

"Because divorce is for the young and the foolish," she said. "It's financial suicide. William and I had been together so long that trying to disentangle our finances would have left us both with a mess to clean up, just a few years before we wanted to retire. It was obviously in our best interest to stay together."

That made sense. It was basically the same situation that Aida and Kalif were in. It was clearly in their best interest to keep their family and business together—even if they were uncomfortable with Mel's methods. "But that couldn't have been easy, could it? Staying married to someone you didn't love?"

Sylvia leaned toward me. "If I didn't know better, I'd think you were accusing *me* of wanting to kill William."

I froze. That *did* sound like where I was going. And it was plausible, wasn't it? I'd been assuming that the people who hired Mel would have been his business associates, but infidelity was a powerful motivator for murder, especially in a situation where divorce wasn't a viable option.

But sitting in a widow's parlor and accusing her of murder? Not the smartest plan, especially since I was working alone.

Sylvia sighed. "Not that it's any of your business, but I *did* love William. I loved him the day he died, and I love him still. I never would have wished this on him. Never. I told him drugs were a young man's folly. I begged him to get professional treatment. It wasn't as if we couldn't afford it. But he was sure going to a facility would be the end of his career." She huffed. "His death was the end of it anyway, just like I always knew it would be."

I sat back in my chair. She sounded sincere. My parents might have been able to pick up on little signs better than I could, but for my part, I believed her.

Sylvia sighed. "If you find Brian, I'll be impressed. You've seen the police report, yes? Don acquired that for me with his own connections, and I gave a copy to my personal investigator."

"Your investigator," I said. "Would he know more?"

She shrugged. "Perhaps. You can ask him when he arrives."

The hairs on the back of my neck stood up. "Are you expecting him?"

Sylvia looked surprised. "Didn't I say that? He asked me to inform him whenever I receive inquiries about my husband's case. He wants to make sure that he has all the information. I sent him a text message while we were at the door, and he said he'd come right over."

I narrowed my eyes. "And he makes house calls? On a moment's notice?"

Sylvia smiled. "He's very attentive. Should be, for what I'm paying him."

My pulse quickened, and it was all I could do not to claw at the upholstery. This could just be an investigator who was so well paid that he jumped at the chance to feel useful.

But if Aida and Mel were trying to pin their murders on my parents, it only made sense to keep a persona in the picture, to watch their backs. It was a perfect con. Sleep with a woman to get the details of her husband's habits, then turn around and present yourself as her investigator, to be sure she doesn't get any closer to the truth, and get on her payroll on the side. Very clever. Also, completely disgusting.

Sylvia's hall clock chimed on the hour. I smiled, and looked at the exits of the room. There was only the door we'd come through, and the bay windows, covered in sheers. I wasn't going to climb out one of *those* right in front of her.

But I had to get out of here. *Now.*

"How long will he be?" I asked.

Sylvia looked down at her watch. "Only a few more minutes, I should think."

I gave her what I hoped was an easy smile. "Do you mind if I use your bathroom while we wait?" Inwardly, I cringed. That excuse was so overused that it bordered on suspicious. But Sylvia just smiled graciously, and stood. "This way."

Sylvia's house was enormous, but it wasn't exactly a fortress; it wasn't hard to pop the screen out of her bathroom window once I'd opened it from the inside. I moved across her yard, keeping bushes and lawn swings between me and the house. When I reached the stone wall at the back of her property, I used her stone birdbath as a step, and hoisted myself up onto it.

I crouched on top of the wall, surveying the neighbors' yards. And on the far side of the backyard neighbor's swimming pool, I found what I was looking for—a pair of children's swimsuits, laid out to dry in the sun.

I sat down on the wall and jumped down, my legs aching even more from this impact than from the last. I watched the house as I approached the clothes, but none of the blinds stirred.

Beyond the swimsuits, in the side yard, I saw a child's bicycle, lying on its side with a pedal jammed into the dirt. I picked up the larger of the two swimsuits—a girl's Little Mermaid one piece—and moved to the bicycle, picking it up out of the dirt as well.

At times like this, I wished I could shift invisible. Instead, I stepped behind a large lilac bush and stripped down, leaving my business suit and shoes jammed inside the bush, and stepping into the swimsuit. I paid particular attention to my curves, reducing them, softening my frame into a chubby little girl with a round belly and soft legs. I moved from shrub to shrub, trying to stay out of view of the house until I was safely out of the side gate and out to the street. And then I hopped on the bike and pedaled furiously down the street.

The block that Sylvia lived on was so large that I was afraid her investigator would be gone by the time I rode by her house.

But there, parked on the street, was Aida and Mel's black SUV. If they'd had more time, they might have brought a vehicle I wouldn't recognize. But this was a quick house call. To get here this fast, they couldn't have come from San Jose. Whichever of them had been closest must have bee-lined it here.

They'd prioritized this over whatever else they were doing.

That meant they knew it was me.

My palms sweated against the rubber handlebar grips. I continued to ride around the block in my stolen swimsuit. I'd clearly made my persona a little bigger than the girl who owned it, because the shoulder straps were starting to cut into my skin. When I completed my circle around the block, I rode just past the house where I'd taken the bike, and then took my shrub-hidden path back into the side yard. I listened, carefully, but heard nothing, so I returned the bike, and then stepped back behind the lilac bush to change back into my clothes and a fresh new persona for the walk home.

I'd have to wear the same business suit, though. What if Mel or Aida came looking for me? What if Sylvia identified my outfit? That was the information they'd try to get out of her. That's what they'd be looking for.

I needed something to distract them. I pulled the smart phone from my pocket, and took note again of Sylvia's address. Then I dialed 911.

An operator answered. "What is your emergency?"

"I'm calling to report a domestic dispute," I said. "I hate to be that neighbor, but her boyfriend is threatening her, and I'm worried."

I smiled as the operator took Sylvia's address. Aida and Mel would be able to slide out of this, but it would distract them for a bit.

It would also send a message. If they thought they were going to catch me that easily, they'd totally underestimated who they were dealing with.

When I got back to the hotel, Kalif was still working on the trace.

"Bad news," I said. "That lover was definitely your father. Your parents are keeping tabs on the widow, and they came after me."

Kalif looked up at me in alarm. "You're okay?"

"Yeah," I said. "I called the police on them, to keep them busy."

Kalif rubbed his forehead. "I thought knowing they were involved was *good* news."

I shook my head. "No. Finding out your parents are murderers is never good news."

Kalif nodded. "Touché."

I walked over and rubbed his shoulders. "You can't be okay with this," I said. "So don't even pretend."

Kalif looked down at his computer. I didn't understand everything on the screen, but he was clearly still working on the trace.

"Do you want to take a break?" I asked. "Get food?"

Kalif shook his head, half in disagreement, half, it seemed, to clear it. "I'm so sorry," Kalif said. "I can't believe that I didn't catch on to this."

I bent over further, burying my face in his neck. "It's going to be okay," I said. "Because now you and I are going to set it right."

NINETEEN

Kalif kept working on the trace for the rest of the day, while I tried not to hover. He barely looked up at me, his eyes glued to the screen, but his jaw set in the same angry way that Mel's had when we confronted him with the truth.

I didn't tell Kalif he looked like his dad. No need to add insult to injury.

By evening, we'd eaten nothing but chips from the vending machine and little packets of complementary saltines. I didn't like leaving Kalif alone to go get food, but we both needed to eat, and he probably needed space. It wasn't easy finding out your parents were probably murderers.

I should know.

I found a burger joint down the street, and hurried there and back. When I returned to the room, Kalif's chair was empty. I moved frantically through the room, searching for him, for a note, for any sign that he hadn't run off on me. The bathroom door was open, and the bed and table were empty. The room was small; there were few places to hide.

I took deep breaths, looking over Kalif's laptop and hard drives. He'd left all his equipment, so I told myself he couldn't have gone far. If he was leaving me forever, he'd have taken the computer.

I leaned over the screen, and found the computer processing some data.

He'll be back, I told myself. *He probably just went to get some air.*

And good for him. I was sure he needed it.

I was pulling the food out of the bag when I felt the draft from the balcony door. The curtains were still drawn, but there was a one inch crack between the door and the frame.

When I pulled the door open, I found Kalif sitting cross-legged against the wall, looking out at the lights from the city. He wore his home body, but the shadows concealed him from passers-by. He had his arms tucked around his waist and his shoulders hunched forward, like a pill bug rolling himself up to shut out the world. His face looked younger, and his cheeks more filled out, more like Aida's.

"Hey," I said. "They should really put some furniture out here."

He smiled at me. "This'll do."

I hesitated in the doorway. "Do you want company?"

He unwrapped one arm, gesturing to the space beside him. "Please."

I retrieved the food, we checked hands, and I sat down beside him. I spread the burger wrappers on the concrete in front of us. The cold seeped through my jeans when I sat down next to him, so I moved blood through them, warming myself.

We sat shoulder to shoulder, staring down at our food. "You okay?" I asked.

"I don't know," Kalif said, "and I'm annoyed about it."

I nudged him. "It's understandable if you aren't."

Kalif glared angrily at the sky. "Is it? It's not like I didn't already know my dad was a douche."

"Yeah, well. Douche and murderer are separate things."

Kalif didn't look convinced. "So once I get this trace to work, what are we going to do?"

"Find my parents," I said. "Maybe we could show these other shifters what we found, make them see that my parents didn't do it."

Kalif gave me a doubtful look. "They're vigilantes. You'd be taking a huge risk trying to make them see reason."

Since I didn't know anything about them, it was an even bigger risk than trying to talk to Aida and Mel had been. "Then we'll have to break them out."

He sighed. "Going up against shifters will be a whole different game."

My stomach clenched. He was right, of course. The path ahead was dangerous. It was one thing to worry about tech used to trap shifters, and another thing to know you'd be dealing with a fortress used to contain them. "I have to do this," I said. "But you don't. If you want to just find the trace for me and go home, I understand."

Kalif settled his arm over my shoulders. "I'm not going anywhere. I just want to be sure that we're considering what we're up against."

The more I considered it, the more saving my parents felt impossible. Even if we did track them, Mel and Aida had probably already warned these other shifters that we were coming.

Kalif cleared his throat. "So what about after we free your parents? What then?"

I tried to stay still, but my body stiffened, and from the way he shifted against me, I could tell Kalif noticed. I knew what happened. I'd always known. I thought Kalif knew, too, and we were intentionally not talking about it.

Why bring it up now?

It wouldn't do any good to lie to him. "My parents will want to run. Fast and far."

Kalif sat as still and stiff as I did. "And you're going to leave with them."

I sighed. "I don't want to. But what choice do I have? Our families hate each other. How would we ever survive that?"

Kalif leaned into me. "It's all very Romeo and Juliet, isn't it?"

I groaned. "And look what happened to them."

"Here's the thing," Kalif said. "You know what I always thought their mistake was? It wasn't falling in love or getting married. It was that they did all that, and then they went home afterward. It's the need for their families' approval. That's what they couldn't survive."

My breath caught. "You don't want to go home anymore?"

Kalif tilted his head against mine. "How can I?" he asked. "It's not like I can take you back there."

The thought that I could keep him was too good to be true. "It wouldn't be dangerous for you, though, because you're their son."

"Maybe I'd be safe," he said. "Maybe not."

A chill ran over me. Would Mel be willing to kill his own son to protect his secret? For Kalif's sake, I hoped not. "You can't come with my parents. They'll never trust you."

"I know," he said. "I wouldn't, in their shoes."

"So what are our other options?"

Kalif was quiet for a long moment. And as I looked out at the city lights, I was sure he was going to admit defeat. We were a problem without a solution.

Then he turned, speaking words into my ear that sent tingles down my spine. "We could run off together."

I sat, stunned. Could we do that?

I wouldn't leave my parents now, not when they were about to be executed. But once they were free, what then? I couldn't go back to being their trainee daughter, hoping for safe missions so I could help out. Kalif and I were young, sure, but not children. Especially not after all we'd accomplished together.

I tucked my face against Kalif's neck, breathing him in. I knew what I wanted. I just hadn't dared hope for it. "Is that what you want?"

He spoke into my hair, like he was trying to muffle the words. "Yes. Is that crazy?"

"Completely insane," I said. I sat up and looked Kalif in the eye, to make sure he wasn't joking, but he looked dead serious.

"I can't believe we're actually talking about this," he said.

"Me, neither." This was not at all where I'd expected this conversation to go. I closed my eyes and kissed him, letting my lips linger on his. And for the first time, I considered the idea that he and I could be a permanent thing. We could live together, work together. Build a life together the way my parents had.

I wanted that life—the partnership. And I couldn't imagine anyone kinder to have that with than Kalif.

The kiss deepened, turning serious. I ran a hand through his hair and held on.

When we broke apart, we stared at each other, each bowing under the weight of the decision. I tried to imagine how my parents would react when I broke them out and then ran off. It made sense tactically. Kalif's parents would almost certainly chase them, and him as well. The last place we should all be was together.

That's how I'd explain it to them. They'd hate it, but what could they do? They wouldn't be able to stop me for fear that I'd shift and disappear.

I breathed in the night air. "What will we do?" I asked. This was the first time I'd envisioned a future where I didn't join the family business. I'd lied and stolen because my parents did, but given the mess it had landed them in, I couldn't help but think that maybe my hesitation to hurt people wasn't a weakness I had to get over.

Maybe it was the strength that would keep me from being like them. It seemed obvious now, but it had never occurred to me to think that I might want that.

"I don't love the idea of screwing people over for a living," I said. "The fruits of that are all around us, and I hate them."

Kalif considered that. "So, what? You want to live like regular people? Get normal jobs? I've got skills I could use for that."

He did. But giving up on using our powers sounded just as distasteful as the crimes we'd committed.

"No," I said. "I love running jobs with you. But it seems like there's got to be some use for our talents besides stealing things and spying on people."

He raised his eyebrows. "What did you have in mind?"

I didn't realize how much I meant the words until I said them. "I just think it's a waste, the way your parents track down other shifters and then turn them over to be killed. Maybe . . . maybe we could find other people like us, and help them. My mom talks about Dad finding her like he saved her from the pits of hell. There are probably a lot of scared shifters who feel that way."

Kalif smiled. "It's not like I love crime." He paused. "That's what's annoying me, I think. We screw people over, and don't think twice about it. The way I've been living, I *am* destined to turn into my father. And then I'll lose you, and it'll be my own stupid fault. Or worse, you *won't* leave me, and you'll be miserable."

Like his mother. "You're not him."

"I know," he said. "That's what's so annoying. I shouldn't be afraid of turning into him, but I am."

I folded my hand into his. "Maybe the fear is what's going to stop you," I said. "Maybe it's there so you can see what you want."

His arm tightened around me. "I want to be with you," he said. "Shifter saviors or normal jobs, or whatever."

"Good," I said. "Then it's a plan." One that sounded wonderful, if only we could survive long enough to free my parents first.

It took me half an hour to convince Kalif not to sleep on the floor that night. He stood near the bathroom door, wringing his hands. "Look," he said, "I know you think it's stupid, but I still feel like if we do anything while your parents are still in that place, that I'm taking advantage of you while you're upset, and that makes me a bastard."

"Like your father."

"Like my father." Kalif looked at the mirror. "I look like him just thinking about it."

He did. It must have been hard, being able to look in the mirror and see the way your father has shaped you, all the while trying not to be like him.

I collapsed onto the bed. "I'm not trying to pick on you," I said. "I just think it's lame for you to practically propose to me and then sleep on the floor."

Kalif stared at me. My body shrank a little. I probably shouldn't have used that word, but I was pretty sure that's what we were talking about. My parents said they were married, but basically they'd just run off together. Most shifter marriages were common law, since we didn't exist in a legal way.

Kalif gave me a pleading look. "You have a point," he said. "Can I just admit that and then sleep on the floor?"

I sighed. "I'll sleep in my clothes, for goodness' sake. Just lie down in the actual bed and get some actual sleep."

In the end, he did, even though it meant that we both slept in our jeans again. I curled up against him with my head on his sleeve and his arm running under my neck, and he rolled into me, wrapping his other arm around my waist. I fell asleep to the rhythm of his breathing, and I let myself be happy to curl against him, tasting the idea that we could do this every night. Forever.

I woke up when he moved away. I looked at the clock. It was four AM. We'd only been asleep for a few hours. Kalif sat on the edge of the bed, rubbing his eyes.

"You okay?" I asked.

"I can't sleep," he said. "So I might as well get to work."

I sat up and stretched.

"You should get some more rest," he said.

"So should you. But I don't want you to be alone."

"I'm not," he said. "But you're going to need to do fieldwork as soon as I find a lead, and I don't want you doing that on half a night's sleep."

I lay back down. "Fine," I said. "But it's cold here without you."

Kalif pulled the laptop off the table and brought it over to the bed, propping himself up with some pillows. I curled up at his side, facing away from the screen. Even through our jeans, his body warmed mine.

"Much better," I said.

Kalif ran a hand through my hair, and then started typing. When I woke up, Kalif had fallen asleep leaning back against the pillows, the laptop still on his thighs. I reached up and touched the keyboard, waking it up from hibernation. The window showed a map of an office park in Sunnyvale, which was probably ten miles away. I sat up straight. He'd found something.

Something close.

I kissed Kalif on the cheek. As he stretched, I lifted his laptop to keep him from accidentally tipping it off the bed.

"Hey," he said. "Sorry. I didn't mean to fall asleep." He ran a hand through his hair, squinting at the laptop screen. "I traced them to Fiji, and the Cayman Islands, and Nigeria," he said. "And then guess where?"

"An address in Sunnyvale."

"Right. It's in a business complex. I was thinking we could check it out."

"Did you look into the company it came from?" I asked. "We'll want to have something to go on."

He clicked to a search engine. "These are the things I don't think of at six AM."

I took his computer from him. "Please. You haven't had a proper night's sleep in a week."

As I searched, Kalif spooned against me, his arm draped over my waist.

Focus, I told myself. But I couldn't bring myself to move away.

The email originated from a company called Systems Development Limited. I scrutinized their website. This was exactly the sort of name shifters would give to their company. It didn't draw attention to itself. Their website was full of non-information about what a great tech company they were, without any clear description of exactly what kind of work they did.

Eventually I found an explanation on a former employee's blog, whining that he had tons of experience, but couldn't find a job. According to him, Systems Development designed microchips for lots and lots of money and no recognition. *I've designed tech for every major company you've heard of, but you won't find my name in the by-line.*

"This sounds like a great front," I said. "It's a good way to get rich and make connections."

"Tell me about it. Their network security is insane. Took me a long time to verify that this was the right place, and not just another mask."

I'd expected that, but it still felt like bad news. "No doubt their physical security will be insane as well. They're protecting other people's secrets as well as their own. Plus, they'll know we're coming. They'll have shifter deterrent tech." Even Mom and Dad probably hadn't ever encountered such a place.

Except this one. And they obviously hadn't been able to escape from it.

"How many shifters do you think we're dealing with? Can't be that many, can there?"

I pointed to the blog. "This guy won't be one," I said. "He's far too candid." I poked around the company website, looking for employee information. Systems Development was privately owned, so it was more difficult to get information about their business structure, but eventually I found biographies of the CEO and CFO, a husband and wife team.

"Wendy and Oliver Carmine," I said. "Could be them, or could be one of their employees who just happens to be a shifter. Or a shifter who disguised himself as one of their employees, to send emails from their server." I sighed. Tracking shifters was layer upon layer more complicated than tracing regular people.

Kalif squinted at the screen. "Carmine. That sounds familiar."

"Really?"

"Yeah. Let me see that." He took the laptop from me and started typing. After a few searches, he pulled up one of his conspiracy forums. A look of recognition spread over his face. He tilted the screen to me. "Take a look."

I laid my head on his chest. He'd pulled up a three-month-old thread on one of his conspiracy forums. A man who called himself Hunter had profiled Wendy and Oliver Carmine, claiming they were shifters.

I sat straight up. "Does he have actual evidence?"

Kalif scrolled down. Hunter was apparently stalking these people, which made me wonder if the Carmines were aware of the situation. The real kicker came far down the thread. It was a photo from a night vision camera—two people asleep in bed with a green tint cast over them. Hunter claimed to have broken into Wendy and Oliver's hotel room when they were in Seattle for a business trip. Kalif clicked on the photo to enlarge it.

I grabbed Kalif's arm. Those people didn't look anything like the Wendy and Oliver seen in their official company headshots.

But they both looked quite a bit like Aida.

Kalif's face paled looking at the screen. His eyes widened, and he looked more like Aida than I'd ever seen him.

"No way," I said. "If you saw this before, why didn't you—"

"I wasn't paying attention," he said. "I didn't think it was real."

I shook my head at the screen.

It was possible that these were shifters posing as sleeping people, but if that was the case, I wasn't sure what Hunter's motive would be for posting them in a forum. I scrutinized their faces. The likeness to Aida was subtle—too much so to be an actual impersonation—but it was there. The man had a blanket tucked up to his chin, but his forehead and hairline were mirror images of Aida's, and the woman had Aida's chin and lips. Each feature was only present on one of them. These were more likely to be parents than children.

When Kalif finally spoke, his voice was quiet. "It actually makes sense, if you think about it. There aren't that many shifters in the world. And my mom was willing to do whatever these people wanted."

"She's scared of them," I said. And for the first time, I wondered what kind of life Aida must have had before she met Mel, if she thought living with him was a preferable arrangement. "Have you ever met your grandparents?"

"Never," Kalif said. "On either side. You?"

"No," I said. I knew that Mom's parents were normal people, but Dad's were shifter spies. They taught him everything they knew, and he taught Mom. The job just seemed suited to our abilities. I wondered if it was passed down for generations, or if the fit was so obvious that many shifters arrived at it independently.

Kalif shook his head at the screen. "My grandparents were all shifters. I assumed my parents didn't know where they were. They never talk about them, and we move around so much, it would be easy to lose track."

These shifters looked pretty settled to me. "What happened to Hunter?" I asked.

Kalif scrolled down again. Other people posted for pages and pages, discussing the veracity of Hunter's claims, asking him questions.

But Hunter never posted in the forum again.

My pulse picked up. "If that's real, why is it still there? Couldn't the Carmines have gotten it taken down?"

"It's hard to remove an image once it's been online," Kalif said. "There'd always be a cached version, at least. Plus, making a fuss would lend legitimacy to Hunter's claim. The harder they fought, the more attention they'd draw."

I looked at the pictures of Wendy and Oliver again, both in their personas, and asleep. The resemblance to Aida was undeniable.

My voice shook as I spoke. "They've set up permanently like this, with well-known work personas, and they think *we're* the security threat?"

Kalif stared at their photos. "Tell me about it."

I shook myself. Here I was focused on me, when he just found out he had grandparents who were also murderers. I put a hand on his arm. "I'm sorry," I said. "Are you okay?"

Kalif's voice was clipped. "Fine."

"Really. If you want to talk about it—"

He snapped the laptop shut. "I don't. We need to get to your parents, before it's too late."

And while I wanted to talk him through this, I couldn't deny that he was right.

TWENTY

While Kalif showered, I pulled up a light rail map and plotted a course that would take us to Systems Development. The overhead photos of the business complex showed a wooded area, with wide buildings spanning the spaces between the trees. Today was Sunday, so hopefully the complex wouldn't be too busy. The light rail would take us within a few blocks of it, by way of a strip mall where we could buy some cheap clothes.

Kalif came out of the bathroom smelling like lemons. He was already dressed, but had a towel tossed over his shoulders.

I wrapped my arms around him.

"Hey," he said.

I nuzzled my face into his neck. "Sorry about your family," I said.

"Yeah, well," he said. "Thanks for not kicking me out with the lot of them."

I ran my hands through his still-wet hair. "I guess they're just making it easier for you not to go home, yeah?"

He rolled his eyes. "Easier by the minute."

I held up my light rail directions. "We better get changed, so we can go."

Kalif nodded. "What should we wear?"

"We could go to the big and tall store, and go as those fat men. Or we could get you a bra."

Kalif smiled. "I'd probably hit on you either way. Don't get me too far out of my element."

"Loiterers in love again, then? You're good at it."

He rolled his eyes. "That's a backhanded compliment, if I've ever heard one."

I held up my palms. "Hey, I was cool with the fat guys."

Kalif kissed me, pushing me toward the door. "Fine. Teenagers it is. Different kids this time, though."

"Of course." I faced the mirror and changed my face and hair so I looked thinner and prettier than I normally did. I darkened my hair, and let it hang down my back in brown clumps, like it badly needed brushing. Mom always said that was a secret to good shifting. Plastic, magazine-cover people were always gorgeous and well-groomed, but real people were full of contradictions.

Kalif chose an unkempt haircut that hung into his eyes.

I flipped it with the back of my hand. "Won't that drive you crazy?"

"Nah," he said. "Why, does it look wrong?"

"It's fine," I said. "As long as you can manage not to fiddle with it constantly." On the other hand, he looked about sixteen, so maybe fidgeting would be appropriate. "What about me?"

His eyes slid up and down my body. "You need to put on some weight," he said. "Otherwise you're going to turn heads."

I puffed out my stomach and thighs a little, making sure I could still fit into my jeans, and added some padding to my cheeks and jaw line. I always felt bad for normal girls when I did that to go unnoticed. I didn't make the fat-phobic culture, but I still felt dirty when I used it to my advantage.

We packed everything into our bags to haul with us, and left the hotel without checking out to catch the light rail into Sunnyvale. When we got to the discount clothing store, I picked us out some new t-shirts and jeans, plus a blazer-skirt combo and some white collared shirts and slacks. We'd need extras for Mom and Dad, plus changes of clothes so we could slip away without being recognized as the same people who came in. I

217

intentionally bought the clothes a few sizes bigger than we all normally were, so we could look tall and imposing, if we needed to, or overweight and unthreatening if we didn't. I also bought us four pairs of practical shoes. There was a very real possibility we were going to have to run in these, so I didn't waste time with fashion.

We paid cash for the clothes and a backpack to carry them in, and then Kalif and I both changed into different shirts and jeans in the bathroom.

We walked the last few blocks past a park, where manicured grass gave way to marshy reeds, and ducks congregated near picnic benches, waiting to be fed. On the far side of the park, marked only by a low curb, the public land ended and the industrial buildings began. We followed a trail that wound through enormous weepy trees, passing the occasional building hidden between the branches. The buildings had both numbers and addresses, but we had to wander past most of the park before we found Systems Development Limited—a sprawling building with four stories staggered over each other like they wished they'd been designed by Frank Lloyd Wright.

We cuddled up on a bench thirty yards away from the building and studied it. The architecture was trying hard to look casual, even haphazard, but every window to the building was mirrored. The landscaper had planted juniper shrubs under every window on the main floor, so anyone who wanted to get to the windows would have to climb through a web of sticky branches. Around the side was a loading dock entrance. The door was recessed under the overhang of the second floor, so there was no way to get close without walking by rows of those shrub-guarded first floor windows and a mess of security cameras.

I ran my lips over Kalif's earlobe, then whispered to him. "It doesn't exactly look like a prison."

Kalif shivered, which was probably only half an act. "It seems like this has a lot of what I'd be looking for if I wanted to hold people."

He was right. The building was secluded visually, but not in a way that would arouse suspicion, since it was part of a legitimate business community. They had a vehicle entrance, so they wouldn't have to haul prisoners in from the parking lot. "So where would they be keeping my parents, then? Do you think there's a basement?"

Kalif flipped his hair out of his eyes and looked back toward the park, where the bay lands crept into the city. "With the water table so high? If they do, then they've got some very good water pumps."

I nodded. "That's something we can look for." I took Kalif's hand and we walked around the back of the building, branches of a particularly large tree spanning overhead. And there, near the base of the tree, was a pipe sticking out of the ground. No water came from it at this moment, but the ground around it was wet, like it had discharged recently.

"Sump pump," I said, turning away from the building so cameras wouldn't catch me mouthing the words. "That means basement."

Kalif scanned the building again. "Let's keep walking. Their security is probably watching us already."

The next building over held the complex offices, a bank branch, and a little sandwich shop with booths and tables and a sign boasting free internet. "Let's get some lunch," Kalif said. We walked in and he sat down at a booth in the far corner and opened his laptop while I ordered for us both. Kalif didn't want to eat—he wanted to check out the local network security.

When I got back to Kalif, I offered him the sandwiches. "Tuna on white, or turkey on wheat?"

"I'll take the tuna," Kalif said. He unwrapped the sandwich with one hand while staring at his screen. I sat down across from him.

"What did you find?"

"I can see their wireless network from here," Kalif said. "They have a couple networks, actually. But they're encrypted, of course."

"Of course," I said. "So you can't hack in?"

"No, I can," Kalif said. "But I'm going to have to go all out on it. I can set up a DDOS attack so their security people will be busy worrying about that, and then work on the problem while they're distracted."

"And once you're in?"

"I'll get into their security workstations and see what it looks like in there."

"Perfect," I said. "And you can do that from here?"

Kalif frowned. "I'd rather be on the other side of the country, but it'll be easier from here."

I looked around the sandwich place. There were two men in suits eating in the opposite corner booth, and a woman in slacks eating a sandwich in front of her laptop. No one was paying a bit of attention to us.

"We better eat slowly," Kalif said. "This won't take forever, but I'll need an hour or two."

I still finished my sandwich long before Kalif was done. There was only so much staring at the back of his laptop I could do without interrupting him or being conspicuous. I started to fold a napkin, but I didn't want the cashier to remember me as the girl who did napkin origami. I didn't want her to remember me at all.

"I'm going to take a walk," I said. "Call if you need me."

Kalif gave me a look. "You're not going to do anything dangerous, are you?"

"No. I won't get any closer than we already did."

"Just be careful."

I squeezed his shoulder. "I will."

I got up from the table and walked out of the shop and back toward the Systems Development building. I traced the path back where Kalif and I had come, and then went past the building toward a little creek that ran under the walkway and toward the city park.

There in the side of the creek bed I found more drain

pipes—one of them spitting out water this very minute. I was at least thirty yards from the building now, which meant that there was more area underground here than just a direct basement. I wondered how big the complex was; if Kalif couldn't find the floor plans on their network, maybe we could check with the city planning commission, or the fire department. Whatever was under there couldn't be too secret. It still had to be inspected, and it still had to be up to code.

Unless the Carmines were powerful or rich enough to avoid inspections.

As I walked back past the building, I watched my feet. Mom and Dad might be held somewhere else, or they might be dead. But I also might be walking over their heads right now, so close that if I dug down ten feet, I could reach them.

But if that was true, they were being held in a shifter facility, and clearly a well-funded one. The guards here might be checking palms, and I had no way to secure the palm codes of any of these shifters—at least not without kidnapping and torturing them, which, while not technically against the rules, was not something I was prepared to do.

I wandered farther through the complex, winding around other buildings. I found thick bushes on one end of the complex where I left some of our changes of clothes, and more bushes in the park on the other end, where I left others. The landscaping would offer us a place to change, if we could only get my parents out this far. Then we'd be able to become anyone, and slip away.

I kept more clothes tucked away in Kalif's messenger bag. Mom and Dad would need to change immediately, or they wouldn't make it out of the building unrecognized.

When I finally wandered back to Kalif, he was still staring intently at his laptop.

"Any luck?" I asked.

Kalif didn't even look up at me, he just closed the window where he was working and turned the computer so I could see. This was a security camera image, complete with timestamp at the bottom. The time was the same as the one on Kalif's laptop. This was live.

There, lying on a cot in the center of a closet-sized room, her back to the camera, was my mother. She wore a t-shirt and a pair of sweats, but no shoes.

I gripped Kalif's hand across the table. "She's there."

Kalif nodded eagerly. "She is. That's a room in the basement."

I studied the image. "That's her home body."

Kalif nodded. "She'd have fallen asleep long ago. No need to keep up the façade after that, I suppose."

"What about Dad?"

"Hang on." Kalif turned the screen away again, so that the other people in the shop couldn't see it. Not that anyone was looking. The two men in suits had left, and the woman a few tables away was still typing. He toggled through a few more images before finding Dad sitting against the wall of a room similar to Mom's, wearing identical clothes.

"Do you think they're decoys?" With the other missions, we'd thought we had a safety net in Aida and Mel. If I messed up this infiltration, we had no one to call to bail us out.

"Could be," Kalif said, "if they have enough shifters handy that they can spare two to sit around all day on the off chance someone comes to break your parents out."

"They know we're coming," I said. "Your mom will have alerted them. Do you think they can detect you in the system?"

Kalif shrugged. "I don't think so, but it's hard to tell from here."

I looked over his shoulder at the entrance to the shop. If they knew he was in the system, how long before they found us here?

"Can you check the security footage and see how long they've been there?"

"Yeah," Kalif said. "Give me a minute."

"Work fast," I said.

Kalif pulled up the feed to that room—but they were only keeping tape six hours back. That made sense if they were trying to operate in secret; they'd need enough footage to view themselves if something went wrong, but not so much that they'd leave long tracks for someone like us to follow.

Kalif put the tape on fast forward. Dad flew through the hours before our eyes. Even in the hours of the early morning, the lights in his cell stayed on, so he would lose track of the day and the night. At first he slept, his home face showing to the camera. He'd woken just an hour before we arrived, which made me wonder if they'd been interrogating him into the night.

"That looks real," I said. Now we just needed to check for recent anomalies, to make sure it was still him.

When Dad woke up, he paced the room. Shortly after, a pair of men came in, wearing the same identical faces. They came at him, one of them holding cuffs, the other wielding a Taser. They were taller than average—maybe six-four or six-five. They bound him to a chair and paced around and around him, mouths moving.

"Is there sound?" I asked.

Kalif shook his head.

I couldn't read lips, but I could tell that Dad was refusing and denying whatever they were saying, shaking his head vigorously and snapping at them. I physically jolted when one of them cuffed him across the back of his head.

Kalif turned the screen away from me. "I'll check it," he said. "You don't need to watch."

I did need to. If I was going in, I needed to know what was waiting for me in there. I turned the computer back. Kalif watched me more than the footage, probably trying to decide if he needed to insist. I made my body relax, so he wouldn't have any evidence that he did.

The tape ended where we began, with Dad sitting on the cot, staring at the wall. It didn't appear that they'd tortured him.

Yet.

"He didn't leave the room," I said. "It's him. Can you check my mother?"

Kalif pulled up the extent of her tape—also only six hours. She lay on the cot facing away from the camera, her breath even. The men didn't come into her room, and she never stirred.

Though my arms were shaking, I hugged Kalif around the waist. "Thank you."

He gave an exhausted sigh. "Don't thank me yet. That's just the good news."

"And the bad news?"

"The security in this place." He whistled.

I put my elbows on the table, leaning in. "It can't be worse than we expected."

"Whoever designed this was obviously a shifter. And he really knew what he was doing, too."

"All right," I said. "Spill. What are we up against?"

"The main floors have pretty standard enterprise class security. Palm scanners, eye scanners, card readers, point detection alarms. The usual."

"Okay," I said.

"But you were right about the basement. They've got most of the same devices down there—no card readers, but some biometric scanners, plus some deterrent devices, like fast-setting foam and fog barriers."

I raised my eyebrows. Most security was all about detecting and recording incidents, so that human guards could respond personally, or so there would be evidence for the police. But alarms could be set to trigger deluge water systems to flood areas, or guns to encase invaders in foam so they couldn't leave before the guards got there to cut them out.

I'd studied invasive deterrent technology, but I'd never been in a facility that used it—Mom and Dad would never send me into a situation that dangerous. "That's pretty intense."

Kalif's words came out in an eager rush. "But that's not even the genius part. The biometric scanners—they're obviously set up for shifters." He pointed to a line of data on the screen. "See this?"

"Yes," I said. "What is it?"

"This scanner is set up to respond only to these three particular scans, and only if they're given one at a time, in order."

A horrible sinking feeling settled over me. "It's a code."

Kalif's eyes shone with awe. "A door code. Using retinal scans. It's genius."

I glared. "Maybe it runs in the family."

He bit his lip sheepishly. "That's not what I meant."

I smacked him on the arm. "I'm just saying, you don't have to be so excited about it."

I could tell he was trying to rein it in, but he wasn't succeeding. "I'm just thinking about the applications. Think about the kind of security we could build with technology like this."

I was used to thinking about breaking through tech, not building things with it. "You're right. But that doesn't make me happy to find it *here*."

This was terrible news. Retinal scans were even worse than iris scans—they used the complex pattern of blood vessels in the retina of the eye, instead of the color patterns in the iris. They were almost perfectly accurate on normal people, and a nasty trick to fool for us. It had been a while since I'd practiced retinas. Dad had suggested I master irises first, because they were both easier and more common.

"The good news is I'm already in the system," Kalif said.

I shook my head warily. "I fail to see how that's going to make me capable of doing this."

Kalif took my hand. "Hear me out. I have an idea."

TWENTY-ONE

wo hours later, I walked through the business complex in my blazer and skirt, dressed as a forty-something woman with bobbed brown hair that didn't at all suit her square face and pear-shaped body. I had to make her shorter than I was, so a camera doing weight analysis wouldn't detect an anomaly. As a result, the skirt dipped to mid-calf, and the blazer hung unfashionably at mid-thigh. I was careful not to cut my height so short that I'd look like a child in grown-up clothing, though. Nothing screamed amateur shifter like the appearance of a kid playing dress up.

I'd changed in the park bushes, but now I walked all the way around on the street side to approach Systems Development from the other direction. This should make it a little harder for their security team when they tried to put together the breach later. Much later. When we were all safe and gone.

As I passed the first building, I put on my cell phone headset and called Kalif, then pocketed my phone.

Kalif answered. "Are you headed in?"

"Walking now," I said, as quietly as I could. "I'll be there in a minute."

"Hang back. I'm watching the door, but there are two women talking in the hallway."

"Will do." I walked slower.

Kalif was still set up in the sandwich shop. I'd wanted to move him farther away, but he said security might find the breach and

226

kick him out of the system any minute now. And I needed him in; I couldn't do this on my own.

According to the schematics Kalif found in their system, the basement was accessible by hallway from the south side entrance to the building, and I looped around slowly, giving Kalif time to announce the all-clear. Through the phone speaker, I could hear the clicks of Kalif typing, and the hum of voices in the sandwich shop, but neither of us spoke.

"Okay," he said finally. "Go."

I picked up my pace. I approached from the west, where the bathrooms were located, because there were no windows along that wall through which I might be noticed. When I arrived at the door, I whispered "code," into my headset, and Kalif listed off a set of numbers which I typed into the key pad.

"I've looped the camera inside," Kalif said. "Let me know when you reach the basement stairs."

I slipped through the door and found a clear hallway, just like Kalif said I would. I ducked under the window on the first door to my right, and then reached the door that was supposed to go to the stairway down.

"I'm here," I said. I heard the click of the electric lock—one that Kalif could trigger remotely. I scanned the crack between the door and the doorframe. At the top of the door, I could see a dark patch on the inside of the frame—the magnetic alarm sensor. Before I opened the door, I readied a magnet on my fingertips. It was smaller than I would have liked, but the only magnets I'd been able to find nearby were attached to cell phone dashboard clips. They would have to do.

I slid it along the doorframe and onto the sensor at the top as I pulled the door open. Now as I opened the door fully and slipped through, the sensor—and the attached alarm—believed it was closed. I shut the door behind me, safely inside the first man-trap.

"How'd I do?"

"Perfect," he said. "No alerts."

"Did I trip any alarms upstairs?"

"Two," Kalif said. "Motion sensor and floor plate. I disabled them. No one should find the alert until they go digging. I've restored the camera upstairs, so tell me before you go back up."

"Will do." I hurried down the stairs, and at the bottom, found the eye scanner.

I steeled myself. I could do this.

"I have the intercept up and running," Kalif said. "So I can bypass the alarms and give you a couple practice tries. Do you have the diagrams?"

I pulled my phone out of my pocket. "Got it," I said. A retinal image appeared on the screen. This was Kalif's idea—if I had an image of the scans I was trying to match, I might be able to form them more accurately. The image wouldn't work under most normal circumstances, of course. I wouldn't have looked much like Emmeline if I was bringing a reference along to match her eyes. But in this case, if anyone saw me, I was already screwed.

"Okay," I said. "Here goes nothing." I stepped up to the eye scanner. I went over the lines of the blood vessels on the screen, shaping each one as I glanced over it. Kalif's program printed a ruler down the side of the page, so I could double check the sizes as I went. I mentally locked each section of my eye as I left it, so I wouldn't lose the pattern before I got to the scanner.

"Ready," I said.

"Go," Kalif said.

I pressed my forehead against the rest on the front of the scanner. The scanner beeped once, but nothing happened.

I steadied myself on the scanner, making sure to hold on to my persona, even though what I really wanted to do was curl up in a ball.

If I didn't get through this, my parents were dead, and Kalif and I were going with them.

"Okay, second vessel on the upper right," he said. "It's quadrant A7 on the diagram, you see it?"

The diagram swam before my eyes. Why did I always screw

this up? "Okay."

Kalif must have heard the loathing in my voice. "You're doing fine. A7. Tighter on the curve. That's the only part that's off."

I steeled myself, trying to adopt his confidence. "Okay. Trying again."

I tightened the curve, trying to interpret my eye into the precise shape of the diagram. Then I pressed my face to the scanner again.

The scanner beeped once more, at a higher pitch.

"Great!" Kalif said. "One down. That only took thirty seconds."

It felt like five minutes. I had to push a button on my phone to keep the backlight on. This pattern was entirely different from the last one. They really made their shifters stretch to enter these codes. More evidence that there probably weren't many of them; even Mom or Dad would have a hard time with this.

When I thought I had it locked, I turned back to the scanner. "Ready," I said.

"Hold it there." He paused. "You got it. Two down."

I squeezed my phone in my hand and went about rearranging again.

"Check me," I said, facing into the scanner.

"B8," Kalif said. "You're missing a branch on the third vein over."

Rush jobs. Never a good idea. "Sorry. That was sloppy."

"You're doing fine. Tell me when you're ready."

I focused closely on those particular veins, making sure I got the diameter right.

"Okay," I said. "Hit me."

The machine beeped, and the door lock clicked ahead. "Good to go," Kalif said.

I hopped up and down on my toes—a decidedly unprofessional move. "It's open."

"Don't forget the magnet."

I opened the door the same way I had the one upstairs, sliding the magnet onto the frame as I opened the door gradually so the sensor wouldn't trigger.

Kalif swore, and a rush of fog spurted into the hallway ahead of me. I froze in the hallway. I'd messed this up, too.

"It's okay," Kalif said. "The tape is looping, so the security upstairs won't see the fog. But if anyone comes down—"

I wanted to collapse. "They'll notice something's wrong right away."

Kalif should have practiced voices more. He couldn't mask his worry. "Yes."

I could feel my muscles hardening, my body lengthening, ready to bolt. I tried to rein it in. At least with the fog, any cameras Kalif missed wouldn't detect my shifting. If they were using fog as a deterrent, the guards probably had access to infrared goggles. They'd be able to see me, but I wouldn't be able to see them.

"I need to move fast," I said. "What'd I do wrong?"

Kalif's fingers clicked on the keys. "I'm guessing the magnet didn't hit the sensor quite right."

I blew breath out into the fog, which rippled around my face in little eddies. "Okay," I said. If we'd had time, I would have bought one of these sensors and tried different magnets on it until I found the kind that worked best. At least we had the means to control the damage.

I could still do this.

I ran a hand down the wall and moved ahead, my other hand in front of me to make sure I didn't run into anything. My fingers brushed something solid, and I stopped.

"I've reached another door," I said. "After this, Mom is down the left hall?"

"And your dad is down the other hall on the right. But don't mess this door up, because that alarm triggers the roll-down doors and the foam."

At least this one didn't have an eye scanner.

I checked the door ahead for the alarm sensor, and found it half an inch from where the first one had been. That must have been what went wrong with the last door—I hadn't checked to see if they were installed differently, which was a sloppy mistake. I slid this magnet over the frame at the top, clapping it onto the space where the door opened as quickly as I could.

"I'm through," I said.

"You're in. Who first?"

"Dad," I said. He'd be upset to see me, but he was the more likely of the two of them to see the necessity of going along now, and yelling at me later.

"Three doors down to your right."

I could almost breathe. "Thank you."

"Don't thank me yet. We still have to get you back out."

I edged along the wall to my right. The lights down here were probably automatic and wired to the doors, because the hallways were dark except for the emergency lighting along the floor. Between the darkness and the fog, I couldn't see, so I counted doorframes with my fingertips. One, two, three. I felt my way along the wall until my hand bumped the eye scanner on the far side of the third door—Dad's door.

I pulled the phone back out, squinting at the lit screen through the fog. Since I'd recently done them, I could get the general shape without much trouble. Then I went over each part of it, holding it close to my face to see through the fog, making sure I hadn't missed anything.

"I'm ready at the sensor," I whispered.

"Okay," Kalif said. "Take your time."

I took deep breaths, resisting the urge to push through. Dad was just beyond this door, but I was no use to him if I got caught now.

The machine beeped for my first scan, and then for my second.

"Nice," Kalif said.

I went over the last diagram, making sure not to miss that tiny branch Kalif had pointed out to me before. Then I took the last scan.

The door clicked, and I turned the doorknob and pulled the door outward.

Dad looked up at me as I came in, billows of fog following after us. He jumped to his feet and I offered him my hand. After I gave him our signal, he grabbed me by the shoulders. It was all I could do not to collapse against him. This was my dad. *Alive.*

But I stayed on my feet. We still had a job to do. There could be no celebrating until we all got out of here in one piece.

"Jory," he said. "How did you get in here?"

"I'm sorry," I said. "I know I shouldn't be here."

"None of us should be here," Dad said, "and it's been so long, I was beginning to think you wouldn't find us."

I froze in place. "You wanted me to find you?"

Dad's grip on my shoulders tightened. "I wanted your mother to live. And I wouldn't mind living myself. Did you find her?"

"She's in a cell down the hall. Mel and Aida framed you for a bunch of murders. But it was them. They're the killers. They set you up."

Something about the sharp way Dad sucked in his breath made me pause.

"Dad?" I said. "Did you know?"

"I suspected as much," he said. "The way it went down during that job. They were the only ones who knew we were there."

I cringed. It had taken me a lot longer to figure that out. "Do you know where we are?"

Dad shook his head. "Not exactly. But there are two new shifters here. They work for a tech company called Systems Development."

I raised my eyebrows. I knew Dad was good, but to figure all that out from inside a cell was impressive. I guessed I shouldn't have been, though. He was experienced at this, and it was his job to know all the higher ups in Silicon Valley. "We're in the basement of the Systems Development building now."

Dad looked surprised at that. "In their basement. That's bold."

I nodded. "How did you know it was the Carmines?"

"I knocked out one of the men who questioned me. He

turned into a woman I didn't recognize, though she looked suspiciously like Aida."

"I think it's her mother," I said.

Dad nodded. "When she came to she was disoriented, and she turned into Wendy Carmine."

I wished the cameras had saved footage farther back. I would like to have seen that. "Did you know they were shifters before they took you?"

"No," Dad said. "It's a longterm cover, and obviously a good one." The fog grew thick in the room, and Dad moved into the doorway, peering into the hall. He waved it away from his face. "Nice cover, yourself."

Yeah. We'd totally pretend that I did *that* on purpose. And that I hadn't ruined our chances of hiding down here if anyone noticed the fog.

Kalif's voice in my ear made me jump. "I've lost visual of the room. Where are you?"

I stepped up to the doorway with Dad. "We're moving back into the hall now."

"Good," Kalif said. "Tape is still looping, and so far no one's come downstairs."

Dad's hand latched down on my arm. "Who are you talking to?"

My heart thudded. Oh, crap. I hadn't thought about how I was going to explain *that*. "Kalif. He helped me get in here—"

Dad's grip tightened and he reached for my earpiece. I dodged. "No," I said. "He's on our side. He's disabled all the alarms for us and—"

Dad's voice was low and patronizing, like he was trying to talk a knife away from a toddler. "Jory. You know the Johnsons betrayed us. I know you like him, but you can't trust him. It's probably a setup."

I tried to shake Dad off, but he held on. My relationship with Kalif was more than the stupid crush it had been a few days ago. I *trusted* Kalif. I *did*. But suddenly the fog felt tight around me.

"If it's a setup," I said, "then we're already inside the trap."

I expected Kalif to question that, to say something to defend himself, but the line was silent. Dad and I stood perfectly still, breathing, listening. This was obviously the ominous moment. The time Kalif would disconnect the phone, turn on the alarms, and bring our captors down on us.

The fog muffled all sound; I heard nothing but silence, and my own breathing.

Finally Kalif said, "Jory? You there?"

I swallowed, hard. "I'm here. You?"

"Of course. But you need to get moving. The halls are clear, but I don't know how much longer we have."

We. Because we were working together.

I stood up straighter. This was *my* mission. *I* was the one who'd gotten his door open, not Dad. I twisted out of Dad's grip and then grabbed his arm with my own hand.

"Come on," I said. "Let's go." And then I stalked down the hall in the direction of Mom's cell—on the opposite side of the basement from Dad's room. Dad hesitated for a moment, but then his feet padded along behind me as I pushed through the fog, eddies swirling in my wake.

I paused in front of the door that led to the man trap. Now that there were two of us, we should use that asset, instead of blundering around together in the dark. "You wait here," I said. "If anyone comes after us, they'll probably come through here." I paused. "And they'll probably have infrared."

Dad was already feeling around the hallway. "No doubt."

"The door's unlocked," I said. "With a magnet over the sensor." I smiled. "And the make is Allegion, in case you were wondering."

"Noted," Dad said. And he must have decided I wasn't a total fool, because he let me move down the hall after Mom without further argument.

When I got to Mom's door, I paused. "Sorry about that," I said to Kalif.

"Yeah, well," Kalif said back. "It's not like we didn't see it coming. Maybe I should hang up before you talk to your Mom."

"No. We need your help to get out. We work together, and they're just going to have to deal with it."

"Okay," Kalif said. I could hear his smile, too.

Rolling back my shoulders, I stepped up to the final eye scanner. "I'm unlocking Mom's door now."

"'Kay. I've got you covered."

I smiled. Of course he did. I'd get Mom out, and he'd help us sneak back upstairs. Nothing to worry about here. And to prove it, I entered each of the eye codes perfectly, without a single hitch.

"Beautiful," Kalif said. "Now get your mom and get out before the Carmines realize what I've done to their security."

I hauled her door open. Mom scrambled to her feet in the corner, still wearing her home face. She stared at me in alarm, eyes wide, obviously not knowing who I was. "Mom," I said. "It's me." I held my hand out to her, and she hesitated, and then took it. I shifted my palm softer—the first part of our signal. But her hand clamped down hard on mine, as if to hold me in place.

And the other part of the signal didn't come.

Panic clawed at my throat. Was this not Mom? I jerked my hand away, but she held on tight, tugging the door closed behind us to keep too much fog from rolling in. I realized only after the door closed that I should have called out for Dad. He might have heard me, even though the fog dampened sound. But these rooms were probably sound-proof.

He wouldn't hear me now.

I closed my mouth. If I wanted to keep my line open with Kalif, I'd better not alert this shifter to him, either.

"Jory," Mom said, her voice sneering. "Good to see you. I was hoping you'd come along."

Blood rushed to my head. That tone. I'd heard it before. This could be one of the Carmines—a total stranger—or . . . .

I shifted my hand rougher instead, tightening the skin across my palm the way I did in the first part of my signal with Mel.

Mom smiled, and returned the signal. I wished I could melt back into the fog. *Mel.* How had he gotten here first? Hadn't we checked the video feed for continuity?

Yes. We'd thought Mom had been asleep, but it must have been Mel. Or had he found a way to pause the camera, looping the tape like Kalif was doing now?

I gasped for air.

"Jory?" Kalif said. "Are you okay? I'm looking at the visual and it looks like—"

"Very good," Mel said, continuing to crush my hand in his grip. "What gave me away?"

My voice came out as a croak. "It was the sneer," I said. "You should trademark it."

"Jory?" Kalif said over the earpiece. "What's going on?"

Mel's eyes flicked to my earpiece. He must have been able to hear Kalif's voice. He reached out his hand for it.

I pulled away, leaning as far from it as I could. "It's your dad," I said.

Kalif swore, and began to say something else, but Mel snatched the earpiece off my ear, and I didn't catch what it was. Before I could stop him, Mel snapped the earpiece in half and dropped it on the floor, then backed me against the wall, frisking my pockets until he came up with my phone. "Bye, son," he said into the receiver.

And then he hung up.

TWENTY-TWO

Mel jammed my cell phone into his pocket. I pressed harder against the wall, trying to get away from him, but he leaned into me, flattening me against the wall in a way that made every hair on my body stand on end. He may have looked like Mom, but he didn't smell like her. He smelled a little like Kalif, if he'd been bathing in a pool of anxiety and danger. This wasn't just my boyfriend's father—he was a murderer, and a traitor, and a guy who slept with every mark around just because he could. My skin washed cold. What was he going to do to *me*?

Think. I couldn't worm away from him. Even if I did manage to slip away—which was unlikely since he had me so literally cornered—he could bring all the security in the place down on me.

Dad was in the hall. If I could maneuver Mel out there, Dad would be able to help me. I'd just have to make sure Mel made it obvious that he wasn't Mom.

That's what I needed to do. It would work, but only if Mel didn't know Dad was there. "Where's my dad?" I asked. "What have you done with him?"

Mel smiled. "You got all this way, and you still couldn't get to either of your parents. Not so smart now, are you?"

Right. That was exactly what this was about: which of us was smarter. Leave it to Mel to get a kick out of proving himself better at the shifter game than a couple of teenagers.

Except he wasn't, not quite. I still had Dad, and that meant

I had an edge that he didn't.

I needed to figure out what his plan was and steer it toward my father. "So what now?" I asked. "You turn me over to Aida's parents? Tell them I'm an accessory to murder?"

Mel rewarded me with a look of surprise. *Yes*, I thought. *I do know more than you expected me to.*

But he recovered quickly. "You're going to come with me," he said. "Quietly, if you want to live."

My joints locked up. *Focus.* I did want to live, so the most important thing I could do was take control of the situation.

He wanted me to be quiet. That meant he was trying to hide from someone, and that someone could only be the Carmines. They had to know he was here—he'd done something with my mother, after all. But if he got me in the same room as them— "You're afraid I'll tell them the truth," I said. "That you killed all those people." They might know he was here, but he couldn't risk them knowing that he had me, lest they question me.

Hell, they didn't have to ask. I'd *shout* it at them.

Mel's sneer was back.

I forced myself to smile. "They're going to know," I said. "Kalif is in the system. He can reverse whatever tricks you had set up to cover your escape. He's recording it right now—everything you do to me."

I flashed my eyes meaningfully at the corner of the room where the camera would be, but it was well hidden. I couldn't see it from here.

I doubted Mel could either, but he followed my gaze, just for a second. I felt a surge of confidence. This was working. I had him worried.

Then Mel grabbed my arm and twisted it hard against the wall. I tried not to wince, but I couldn't help it. Mel yanked my phone from his pocket and pressed it against my face. "You're going to call him back," he said. "He's going to cover our exit. He'll make it look like I was sitting here all along. Like you were never here and I never left. Got it? Otherwise, you die."

Mel pressed his hip against me, and I felt a metal object dig into my side. I looked down, and I could see it: the outline of a gun in a holster under his shirt.

My heart pounded. I looked up at the invisible camera again, the images of the shooting victims flashing through my mind. If Mel was trying to hide from the Carmines, he couldn't kill me here. He wouldn't want to leave a mess.

No doubt Kalif was having a panic attack, watching this. At least I'd laid to rest the idea that he and Mel might be working together. Mel wouldn't have wasted an opportunity to rub that in my face, now that he had me. His ego wouldn't allow for it.

But what was Mel planning to do to me, if not kill me? No doubt Aida was waiting on the outside with transport, to take me out of here. And then? They couldn't hold me forever, and I was dangerous, now that I knew the truth.

I had to get away from him.

"I'll call Kalif," I said. "Once we're outside. He already has the hallways masked. We can get that far without getting caught."

Mel breathed in my ear, and I craned my neck away. "Not a chance," he said. "I'm not giving him the opportunity to do anything stupid."

I closed my eyes. Stupid, like bring the Carmines down on us. The very thing he ought to be doing. I didn't need to get all the way outside—just out the door, where Dad would have the upper hand when he came after us. "Fine," I said. "From the hallway, then."

Mel grunted. "Don't get any ideas," he said. "The others won't think anything of it if I put a bullet into your head. If I tell them you brought a gun in to break out your parents, they'll be glad you're dead."

I nodded, though I had a hard time imagining that people who wanted to torture information out of my parents would be glad that Mel shot me in the head after I was already disarmed. He was just trying to scare me into doing what he wanted.

Mel pushed the door open and hauled me out into the hall.

The fog was still thick around us, and I was relieved not to have to look at Mel's cruel version of my mother's face. I held still, listening, but I didn't hear Dad.

"Fine," I said, a little louder than I needed to. "Give me the phone. I'll make the call." I couldn't see Mel's face to know if he was suspicious, but he held tight to both my arms, pushing me against the wall so he could feel my every move.

Now that we were in the hall, Kalif couldn't see us anymore. "He won't believe it's me," I said. "We should just get out of here while we still have cover."

I felt Mel shrug. "We can go back to the cameras. Or you can convince him."

The gun dug into my side, and I forced myself to breathe evenly. I heard the beep of my phone dialing, and then he pressed the receiver against my ear.

It rang once, twice, three times. And then Kalif picked up. "Dad?" he said.

"No, it's me," I said. "Your dad wants you to cover our exit." Mel leaned in tighter, pushing the gun further into my hip. If he didn't have the safety on, he was risking his own flesh as much as mine. "He has a gun."

Kalif breathed for a moment, and then I heard a loud tap, like he'd put something down on a table. He sounded farther away, like he was talking to someone else. I was near certain that Mel couldn't hear.

"Like I said, they're in your basement," he said. "I have all the evidence you need. But if she dies, I'm going to send everything I have to the NSA. I have pictures of all of you. Proof they can't ignore."

I bit down hard on my lip to keep from yelling into the phone. What was Kalif *doing*? Sure, calling the Carmines made sense, but threatening them? He was setting himself up as their enemy, when we needed to earn their trust.

But at this moment, what I needed most was for Mel to move down the hall where Dad could save me. "Okay, great," I said into the phone. And then to Mel, "He's got it."

Mel banged my head against the wall. My teeth dug into my lip, and I felt blood run down my chin. I cried out, hopefully loud enough that Dad would hear.

"Right," Mel said. "I'm sure he agreed that easily."

If I hadn't been trying to work under threat of death, I might have made a better show of it. Mel jerked the phone away, and turned it onto speaker.

Fortunately, Kalif was back. "Jory?" he said. "Are you okay? I can't see you anymore."

"Your dad is right here," I said, hopefully signaling to Kalif not to let Mel onto what he'd done. "We're in the hall, getting ready to go back up through the man traps. Cover us, okay?"

Kalif was silent for a moment.

"Kalif?" I said. "Do it for me?"

"Okay." I cringed at how uncertain he sounded. He almost certainly thought this was Mel instead of me.

"What are you going to do?" I asked Mel. "If you don't have any way to check up on him, you'll just have to trust him, right?"

Mel grunted again. I was fairly certain that he didn't love that plan, but he was the one who'd decided to corner me down here in the basement. It was clever to use the same cover that got me in as a means to get back out—but like most clever plans, it had serious drawbacks.

Like that it relied on Kalif, and Kalif was most definitely on my side.

Mel hesitated just a moment longer, then hauled me toward the exit. I listened through the fog, straining with every step for the slightest footfall that would mean Dad was near.

But I didn't hear anything. Mel brought me up to the doorway where I'd left Dad to stand watch, but he didn't appear.

Where was he? He was supposed to attack Mel. Didn't he know he was supposed to be saving me?

Then I heard the voice booming down the hall, in a direction

I'd never been.

"Our people are already looking for you," the man said. "We'll find you in a matter of minutes."

My throat constricted. That sounded like the other half of Kalif's conversation, but this guy—probably Oliver—didn't sound cooperative.

Mel pulled us both against the wall, clamping a hand over my mouth to keep me from crying out. There was one more door ahead of us, and then the man trap, and then the stairs to the hallway up.

I licked the back of my teeth. I could bite Mel, and make him let go. Then I could yell out and get Oliver's attention. But if Oliver had immediate access to me, would that weaken Kalif's position?

The man continued, his voice rising in anger. "Why would the NSA believe a punk like you? Who do you think you are?"

My stomach dropped. This had to be Oliver Carmine. He must have been down in the basement all along, in a room without cameras so Kalif couldn't see him. Did he have Mom down here? If so, where the hell was Dad?

Mel held me tighter. I hoped that he didn't realize that Oliver was talking to Kalif. Kalif's gambit would work better if Mel wasn't expecting it.

Oliver was silent for a moment. "You expect me to believe that? I think I'd know if I had a grandson."

My heart sank. I'd announced to Mel that these were Aida's parents, but what if we were wrong? We'd based that assumption on one photo. Dad had thought he saw the same thing, but if we'd guessed wrong Kalif might have weakened his own position by making an assertion that wasn't true.

But even as I thought that, every muscle in Mel's body tightened. His hand pushed harder over my mouth, pressing my bloody lip against my teeth. It was all I could do not to cry out.

The comment about Oliver knowing if he had a grandson meant something to Mel. Had they been hiding Kalif from his grandparents, just like they'd been hiding them from him?

"I don't respond well to threats," Oliver said. "When we talk face to face, you might want to pick another tactic."

I could taste blood from the cut on my lip. Mel's hand grew sticky against my face, and I resisted the urge to claw at it. I wanted to kick Kalif for putting himself at risk like this. I hoped he was at least fleeing the complex while we spoke, because a big tech firm like this probably *was* capable of tracking him down in a matter of minutes.

I leaned back against Mel. If Oliver wasn't willing to help us against Mel, I was better off trying to get away from Mel on my own than I was trying to use the Carmines as allies. I shifted my feet, trying to get Mel to lighten his grasp, but I felt his muscles bulge as he increased their density to hold me still.

His whole body was tense. And for the first time, I thought I detected fear in his stance.

My hands broke out in sweats. Who were these people that even *Mel* was afraid of them?

A woman's voice shouted from farther down the hall, her voice dampened by the fog. "Oliver," she yelled. "The prisoners are loose!"

Mel twitched and leaned in the direction of the door.

That had to be Wendy. No one who wasn't a shifter could have come down through those security measures. They must have been in a room without cameras; Kalif hadn't seen them on the security feed, but if they'd come down the doors and into the fog, Dad would have gotten the jump on them. She must have encountered Dad. He probably heard them and went to investigate. He hadn't been expecting me to run into danger when I went to break out Mom, particularly if he was watching Wendy and Oliver at the time.

Mel hesitated for a second and then body-checked me forward, one hand still on my mouth and the other arm locked around my shoulders. He shoved me through the door at the bottom of the stairs.

I let him push me along, my mind racing. My main task had to be to get away from Mel. Mom and Dad were professionals. If they were loose, then they'd be able to get the upper hand. Wouldn't they?

I could have collapsed to the floor and made him drag me, but Mel could more than overpower me. I could adjust my muscles to be denser and stronger, but he was heavier than me; his body would always have more mass to manipulate, and he was far more experienced. I needed something more than physical resistance to get away from him.

I didn't have much time to think about it. Mel forced me toward the door to the first man trap. But it opened even before we reached it, and Mel shoved me against the wall.

Before the fog funneled in, we both caught a look at the person in the doorway—a shifter wearing Aida's face.

Mel's hand shot out, grabbing hers, and I gathered that they exchanged signals. Through the door, where the fog was thinner, I saw Aida giving both of us a look of surprise, and then she took my hand as well, confirming her identity.

My heart hammered. Now there were two of them and one of me. Maybe I would have been better off with Oliver Carmine. These two definitely wanted me dead because of what I knew. He didn't respond well to threats, sure, but what about pleas for help?

Before I could speak, though, Mel hauled me through the doorway and into the man trap, where the fog was still thin in the air. The door closed heavily behind us. Even if I screamed, Oliver probably wouldn't hear me now.

But instead of helping us up the stairs, Aida narrowed her eyes at Mel. "What the hell are you doing?" she asked.

Mel tossed me against the wall and I caught myself with my hands.

"Saving her," Mel said. "Now we all need to get out of here before your parents find her. Kalif is covering my trail."

My palms stung. *Saving* me? I turned around to face them.

"Right," I snapped. "My hero."

Aida narrowed her eyes, first at me, and then at Mel. "If you were going to pull something like this, you could have let me in on it. I could have distracted my parents. Where are they?"

I blinked. So Wendy and Oliver *were* her parents. But Aida wasn't in on Mel's plan? She and Mel always worked together, just like my parents did. And she'd have just as much interest in covering up the murders as Mel would.

Wouldn't she?

Mel recovered quickly. "I didn't want you to give it away," he said. "You're terrible at lying to them."

Aida paused. She wasn't putting up much of a front for Mel, either, and for a moment, I felt justified for not being a master of lying to people who were supposed to be close to me.

This was my opening, though. If Aida didn't know Mel had been trying to intercept me, what else didn't she know? "You didn't really think you were going to get away with it," I said to her. "Framing my parents for your murders."

Mel made a move toward me, but Aida grabbed him by the arm, holding him back. She looked at him uncertainly, but she spoke to me. "I'm sorry about what your parents did. But they're the killers, not us."

I edged along the wall away from Mel. Did she really believe that? I was tired of dealing with trained liars—it was always so hard to tell when they were telling the truth. "They couldn't be," I said. "We found files where you deleted their alibi. Did you think we were stupid?" I pointed at Mel. "He even seduced the wife of the victim. How obvious can you get?"

Mel wrenched out of Aida's grasp and closed his hand over my throat. But Aida's wide eyes told me everything I wanted to know. She'd had no idea. She wasn't in on it.

Mel softened his face and glanced over his shoulder at her, but it couldn't have been very convincing when he had me pinned to the wall by the neck. "She's lying," Mel said. "They fabricated some story to prove her parents' innocence, but it's just denial."

Mel's hand shook at my throat. He was losing control of this situation, and fast. He sounded desperate, like a man who already knew he was caught. And despite the sharp pain of Mel's tightening hands, I couldn't help but smile a little.

Mel must have seen, because he moved his hand up to my mouth. He pulled me from the wall with the other arm, twisting me in front of him.

There was no time to gloat. If I could play Aida against Mel, I'd have one more person on my side. If she could get her parents to listen to reason, it would be seven shifters against one.

This time I peeled my lips apart beneath Mel's fingers and bit him, hard. He muffled his own yell, but withdrew his hand, shaking it. As he did, I looked up at Aida, forcing a look of sympathy onto my face. She deserved my pity, after everything Mel had dragged her through, and if she hadn't dragged me and my parents through the mess, I might have been able to feel it instead of just act it. "I'm sorry he did this to you, but you have to help me fix it. You can talk to your parents. You can tell them the truth. He set us all up."

Mel recovered, and twisted my arms behind my back so hard that jolts of pain shot down my spine. I doubled over.

"You can't *believe* her," he said. His voice was pleading, but Aida didn't cave.

She spoke quietly. "That's why you wanted to work with them for so long. It wasn't to gather evidence. It was to pin the rest of your murders on them." She glared at him, betrayal in her eyes. "And I *helped* you."

"Honey," Mel said. "Think about it. She's desperate." The softness in his voice was so convincing, I wondered if he'd talked himself into his own lies, or if he was just that strong an actor.

I twisted my face toward Aida. "He has a gun," I said. And in the brief glimpse I caught of her, a look of fear crossed her face. I recognized that look—I'd seen it in the park, when she'd stood in front of me, insisting that I didn't want to mess with Asylum.

Guess what, Aida. Your husband is worse.

My vision started to darken, but even in the dim light, I saw Aida's shoes step forward. "Let her go," she said.

Yes. I had her. I squirmed against Mel's grip, but he held me tight. I kept pushing against his grasp, because if he felt he had to hold onto me with both hands, he wouldn't be able to reach around for his gun.

"Mel," Aida said. Her voice control skills shone. She held her tone perfectly even, almost robotic. I guessed that underneath it, she wanted to scream. And at that moment, I actually did feel sorry for her. It wasn't her fault that she married a monster.

"Let go of her," she said. "It's over."

"No," Mel said. His voice was ice. "You're going to let me up the stairs."

My heart pounded in my throat. He'd given up pleading. Now he was just going to force his way out, with me as his leverage.

I blinked hard, fighting to keep alert despite the shooting pain in my back and arms. What should I do now? Stall them here until the Carmines came up the stairs? But if my parents won that fight, they might be the ones to come this way. How would Aida react to them?

I needed her good and firmly allied with all of us. Me. My parents. Kalif.

I choked words out. "It's too late. Kalif has the proof of what you did. He's negotiating right now to deliver it to the Carmines." Mel twisted my arms further, and I fell to my knees. My face hit the floor, and pain radiated into my jaw.

Mel's hand slid around my neck, locking down on my throat. I felt his fingers grasp for my windpipe, for the pressure points that would knock me unconscious.

For half a heartbeat, I waited for Aida to stop him. And she did step closer, her feet shuffling on the ground near my face.

When she spoke, her careful, collected tone was gone. Instead, she broke into hysterics. "Kalif's talking to my parents?" she said. "He's here? They know that he *exists*?"

I twisted my neck, trying to keep Mel from getting a good grip. His knee hit my back as he fought to hold me still.

And as my vision turned into a bleary cloud of white lights, I heard her say one last thing: "We can't let them get to him." And she pushed past Mel and me, yanked open the door, and ran down the stairs and into the fog.

TWENTY-THREE

My pulse pounded in my ears as Mel's hands tightened around my throat, bearing down on my windpipe. My head swam, but two thoughts were clear to me. One: Aida had abandoned me to the non-existent mercy of her murderer husband. All sympathy I might have had for her disappeared with her. And two: Mel was absolutely going to kill me. If not right here in the hall, then somewhere else, somewhere he was certain my body would never be found.

My mouth opened, but no sound came out. I buffed up the muscles in my neck until they bulged, trying to keep Mel from cutting off the blood flow at the pressure points, but he just enlarged the muscles in his hands, clamping down tighter. I couldn't scream for help, and even if I could, who was going to help me? Everyone else was dealing with the threat downstairs. A threat so compelling that Aida left me for dead.

Mel's knee sunk further into my back, and my brain fuzzed, my thoughts flowing together into a slippery ooze. My pulse banged in my head; I gagged on my own saliva. Mel pinched off my windpipe, cutting off air as well as blood, and my lungs sucked frantically, trying to draw breath.

And at that moment, eyes dark and lungs starved, I remembered my training. I focused all my energy on shrinking, so my body collapsed out from underneath Mel, growing smaller inside my clothes.

Mel kept his grip on my throat, but when my muscles stopped

bracing against his, he lost his balance, crashing on one knee to the floor next to me. And with all the strength I had left in my oxygen starved body, I pushed against him, twisting and rolling away.

But I was disoriented while Mel was fully alert. He caught me as I rolled onto my back, slamming my shoulders to the ground with his forearm. My lungs gasped for air and my vision began to return—spotty, as if I were seeing through an old black and white television. It was enough, though, to see Mel's hand as it struck toward my throat, as if to crush my windpipe.

I jerked my head to the side, taking the blow to the side of the neck. I expanded my knee again so it was larger than normal and brought it up to strike him in the groin, but he had both his knees on one side of me, to prevent me from doing exactly that.

My knee slammed against his hip instead and knocked against the gun under his shirt. I brought it up again, this time hitting the gun just below the holster. I felt it slide down his side, dislodged by the blow. Mel went to reach for it and I twisted away from him, forcing him to grab me by the shoulders or lose his grip. He slammed me back to the ground. The back of my head knocked against the hard floor, and I winced.

The whole room seemed to spin around me, but I heard the clank as the gun hit the floor. Mel shifted his hips toward it; he'd heard it, too. But his hands were occupied and mine were free. I reached toward it, enlarging my hand just a bit to close my fingers comfortably around the handle.

Mel's hand clamped down on my wrist, jerking hard on my arm, but in doing so he let go of my shoulders, losing his leverage. I pushed away from him, scrambling backward, and brought the gun up to point it at his face.

I'd never shot a weapon before, but my dad had given me some basic instruction in case I ever found myself at gunpoint. Most importantly, I knew how to turn the safety off, which I did, immediately. Holding the gun in two shaking hands, I braced myself against the wall. I was only a few feet from Mel.

If he moved to disarm me, I could shoot him, and even with my inexperience, I was pretty sure I could handle point blank.

"Don't move," I said. "I'll kill you." And I was surprised to find that I meant it.

My dad always said there was no such thing as self-defense for a shifter. We were in the business of deceit—if those lies found us on the wrong end of a gun barrel, we had no business killing to cover for ourselves. But I hadn't deceived Mel. I hadn't influenced him to kill those people, or to cause my parents to take the fall for it, or to corner me down here in the dark.

Mel made those choices, not me. And I wasn't willing to die for them, or to leave my parents to that fate.

He crouched on the ground, arms at the ready to fend me off, though I didn't want to be one inch closer to him. I had my back to the door downstairs, which meant both that I could protect my parents from Mel if they came up the stairs, but also that the Carmines and Aida would be at my back if they did. Mel's sneer reappeared on his face as he looked at how I was holding the gun.

"You have no idea what you're doing with that thing," he said. "Put it down and I'll let you live."

Right. He sounded so sure of himself, like he had the upper hand. And maybe he did. We were less than two yards apart. Maybe he could disarm me before I pulled the trigger.

My best odds of surviving to help my parents and Kalif were to hang on to the advantage I had. "Go confess now," I said. "And I'll let *you* live."

Mel wavered for a moment, as if trying to decide what to do. I squared my shoulders, steadying my aim. If he thought he could disarm me safely, he'd have done it by now.

A thud came through the door to the downstairs, like the one my body might have made when Mel forced me to the floor. Mel flinched. It took all my willpower not to turn around. His fingers flexed as he stared over my shoulder at the closed door.

"Fine," he said. "You win."

I wasn't stupid; I didn't lower my gun one inch. But Mel still took me by surprise, and did the last thing I expected his ego to allow of him.

He spun around and ran up the hallway in the direction Aida had come. I pushed off the wall, following him for several steps. He was going up the stairs, and as far as I knew, both my parents were still downstairs. If he was running away, should I let him go? My head spun. Shooting a running man in the back wasn't self-defense by any standards.

I took a few steps toward him, and my foot kicked something loose on the floor. I bent down to grab it—my cell phone had fallen out of Mel's pocket during the scuffle, probably at the same time I dislodged the gun. I clutched it. I could let Mel go and call Kalif, so he could talk me through whatever was going on downstairs.

But as Mel arrived at the doorway ahead, he reached for the eye scanner. He grabbed it with both hands and yanked, and I heard the crunch as it detached from the drywall. Then he moved through the door and shut it behind him.

I blinked. We had to use the eye scanners to get out as well as to get in; even with the door codes on the cells, the Carmines were wisely paranoid about prisoners escaping. Without the scanner on this side, Mel would be able to lock the door on the other side, and my parents and I wouldn't be able to reopen it to get out.

This place was a fire marshal's nightmare, and it was about to become my prison as well as my parents'. Mel's pride wouldn't let him just run. He was going to seal us in behind him, maybe because he was afraid we would follow, but no doubt also to be sure that my parents and I couldn't escape from whatever Aida had run toward.

We can't let them get to him, she'd said. They were her parents—Kalif's grandparents. Why would she be afraid of them? Why keep him a secret?

I heard a thump near where the scanner would be on the

other side. Mel was going to enter the eye codes to lock it. And once the door was locked, I was finished.

I ran to the door. I jammed on the handle, but Mel had it stuck tight. It was metal core; it would take quite a bullet to go through that.

I held the gun out in front of me, aiming it at the wall, a few feet from the door, where the scanner would be. Don't hide behind drywall, Dad had told me. Bullets go right through. How long would it take Mel to enter the eye codes? Could he have done it already? I couldn't let Mel lock us down here. I couldn't. My father would understand, wouldn't he?

With shaking fingers, I pulled the trigger. I jumped at the noise. A dark hole appeared in the paint, cutting right through the drywall and into the other side. I heard a shout on the other side of the wall. My body seized up, but my hand kept squeezing, as if detached from my body, until the gun gave a sickening, empty click.

No more noise came through the wall. My stomach turned. The floor seemed to sway, and I swallowed saliva and bit my lip to keep from vomiting. Had I *killed* him?

I didn't want to look; I didn't want to see. But I had to know. I had to confront what I'd done. When I jerked the door open, I expected to see Mel dead on the floor. Instead I found a streak of blood splattered across the thin carpet, and I saw Mel's back as he hobbled up the stairs and out onto the main floor of the building, dragging one leg, his pants bloody through the knee.

I swallowed, hard, my limbs shaking. The gun in my hand was empty. There was nothing more I could do. Someone with experience might have saved some bullets, but I hadn't thought about that until now.

And though I couldn't be glad he was getting away, I also couldn't help the feeling of satisfaction that followed as I watched Mel Johnson run away from *me*. His face was turned away from me, but I was certain he wasn't sneering, now.

I gave myself a moment to smile. I couldn't take longer than that, though. I still had a job to do. My parents were still locked in a secure facility, with shifters of unknown allegiance.

I checked the gun barrel to verify that it was empty, then jammed it into my pocket. No need to leave it lying around for someone else to find and use against us. Even an unloaded gun could be used as a threat.

Another thud came from downstairs, followed by the sound of a door slamming. No doubt they'd heard the gunshots down there, and possibly upstairs as well. Did Aida think I was dead? With how quickly she'd left me here, I wasn't sure she would care. I braced against the wall, waiting for an invasion from either direction.

None came, so I pulled out my cell phone and dialed Kalif.

He answered on the first ring. "Jory?" he said. "Are you with my dad?"

"No," I said. "I got away from him."

Kalif was quiet for a second.

I wiped blood from my chin. He knew his father might have my phone. Now I had to prove to him that this was really me. "Ask me anything," I said. "But do it fast."

Kalif paused. "Our first kiss."

I smiled, and my lip stung. "In Andrea's car, leaning against the gear shift. Very sexy despite my horrific timing."

Kalif laughed. "Good enough for me."

I wasn't sure if he was talking about the kiss or the evidence of my identity, but I agreed either way.

I took a deep breath. There was so much to tell him, and so little time. I stuck to business. "My parents are down in the basement with both the Carmines. I need to go after them. We can use the fog for cover, but our position might be better if there were witnesses. Could you shut off the fog and trigger the alarms to bring down security?"

"No," Kalif said. "Their security people kicked me out of the system, and it wasn't safe to stay put. And witnesses will be hard to come by. The Carmines set off their company active shooter protocols. The building was pretty empty anyway, but everyone who's here today is hunkered down in their offices."

I closed my eyes. That meant they'd be expecting gunshots. I wondered if the Carmines set up this protocol on purpose, in case they had to pull guns on prisoners.

If so, that meant they were prepared to.

"How do you know that?" I asked. "You should have gotten out of here before you called them."

Kalif sighed. "I'm hiding in the bushes. A couple of employees ducked out and ran for their cars. I heard them talking about it."

I grit my teeth. "Go! Can't they, like, triangulate your cell phone or something?"

He didn't answer the question. "I'm not leaving you here."

"Thank you," I said. "But you're an idiot."

"Tell me," Kalif said. "If it were me inside, would you leave?"

I chewed on my lip, and winced at the blood.

Of course I wouldn't.

I heard a beep on Kalif's end. "What was that?"

Kalif was quiet for a moment. "Text from my mom." He swore. "She's down in the basement with you."

"Yeah," I said. "I know."

"She says she wasn't in on the murders. Like I'll believe her."

"No, it's true," I said. "You should have seen her face when she realized your dad was kidnapping me."

There was another beep.

My lip ached from the permanent indents I was gnawing into it. "Jeez," I said. "Silence your phones. All of them."

"Will do," Kalif said. "My mom wants me to get out of here, too."

"Your mother and I agree on exactly one thing."

Kalif didn't respond to that either, but at least I didn't hear any more beeping. "She says the Carmines want to pose as your parents and come after me, as if they're trading me them for my information. If she's on our side, maybe you should—"

"She's not," I said flatly. "When she heard you were in trouble she left me for dead. Your dad had his hands around my neck and she ran off to keep your grandparents away from you."

Kalif sputtered. "My dad had his—"

"He's gone now," I said. "But if you see someone limping away with a bullet in his knee, you might want to steer clear."

A stunned silence followed.

"I'm sorry," I said. "I'll fill you in later, but right now I need you to get out of here so I can deal with my parents."

It took him a second to swallow that. "You need me. If I don't distract them, they'll come after you."

"No," I said.

"Think. It's the best plan."

I waited for a better one to come to me, but it didn't. Still, the danger to Kalif was too great. "Your mother said it's dangerous for your grandparents to get their hands on you. They didn't know you existed, she's that afraid of them. Think about it. You know too much. We can't let them use you against us."

Kalif's voice was low. "And if they aren't focused on me, we know any one of them would kill you. She'll be with them. She'll protect me."

I balled my fist. Aida didn't sound confident of that the last time I saw her. She sounded terrified. "If she's so afraid of them, why is she playing along with them at all?"

He drew a sharp breath. "I don't know. Maybe she has a plan?"

"She told you to go. If she had a plan, that's it."

Kalif sighed. "Fine. I'll tell her to meet me one place and hide in another, okay? That way they won't even see me."

Oliver had threatened that he could find Kalif in minutes, but it might have been a bluff. Plus, if Kalif didn't distract the Carmines, I didn't see how I was going to get my parents out. "Fine," I said. "But don't trust your mom. Don't tell her anything."

"Okay," Kalif said. "Be careful."

"Yeah," I said. "You, too." I dug my nails into my scalp. What he was about to do was the opposite of careful. It was foolish and reckless.

And possibly the only chance my parents and I had of escaping alive.

We hesitated there, and in the space that followed, I realized what I wanted to say. *I love you. I couldn't stand it if anything happened to you, so get out of here, would you?* But before I could get the words out of my mouth, Kalif beat me to it. "Go," he said. "I don't want you down there any longer than you need to be."

I set my feet wide apart to steady me. My throat ached where Mel's fingers had dug into it. "Okay," I said. And then I hung up the phone. I moved down into the foggy part of the facility as quickly as I could. At least if the Carmines were posing as my parents, they wouldn't be simultaneously looking at the readouts from their infrared cameras. That should give me the chance to hide, and wait for them to go find Kalif. Then I could find my real parents and we could all get out of here.

I crouched down in a doorway around the corner from the hall where I'd heard Oliver talking; if anyone did come around the corner with infrared goggles and a gun, there was no reason to give them a large target.

My mind played at the ghosts of noises in the silence, but when I heard the last security door opening, the noise was unmistakable.

Oliver Carmine's voice cut through the fog. "You kept him a secret for sixteen years. So I know you're a good liar."

Aida chattered back, like she was trying to prove him wrong with her lack of control over her own voice. "I'll deal with him," she said. "You don't have to hurt him."

They moved farther up the stairs, but I heard Wendy's voice growing fainter. "We'll consider that," she said.

And then they were gone.

I pulled out my phone, holding it close to my face and texting Kalif. *They're on their way, and they're talking about hurting you.*

I held my breath, hoping that would be enough to finally send him away.

No luck.

Okay, Kalif texted back. *I've told Mom to meet me on one side of the compound, but I'm on the other. The chase will give you a few minutes, and if they come back too soon, I'll intercept them.*

My heart pounded, and my head swam. If he was watching to know when we left the building, then he was close. Too close. For a second, I thought I might black out. I knelt down on the floor and touched my forehead to it. What was I doing letting Kalif walk into a situation that dangerous? I might trust his loyalty, but I could still doubt his judgment.

But if he split, how would I get my parents out?

I planted my hands on the floor. I had to get my parents up there so I could help him, in case things went wrong.

More wrong.

I heard a click through the fog. It sounded like a door, but the dampened sound meant I had no way to know how far away it had been. I climbed to my feet and pressed down the hall in the direction Wendy and Oliver had been. The fog remained thick. Kalif was right. Unless they had a flush system, it would last for a while longer.

There ought to be a second exit to this place, but without Kalif to check the schematics for me, I didn't know where it was. Besides, I was no Mike Menendez, but what with the total lack of emergency exit signage, this place didn't seem up to code to me.

There were three doors down this hallway branch. Two had eye scanners, like the ones on the doors to my parents' cells. The third one couldn't be a cell—unlike the others it had the hinges mounted to the inside.

I stepped up to one of the eye scanners, and jumped at the thump that came from the next door over. I moved closer, my ear to the wall, listening. The thud came again, like someone banging on the inside of the door, but with something sharper than their fist.

Another thump came, and then a ka-chunk noise as the door

handle fell to the ground. I flattened myself to the wall just outside the door and watched as the door swung open.

Dad stepped through the doorway, an axe in his hand. The room behind him was already thick with mist; this door must have been opened earlier—probably when they caught Dad and locked him up.

I reached my arm toward him faster than I should have, and had to jerk back to avoid the downswing of his blade. "Um, Dad?" I said. I stepped into the doorway with him, so we could see each other's faces clearly.

His eyes widened and he reached for my hand. Now, standing this close, I could see that the side of his head was swelling, like he'd been punched in the face. He limped slightly as he moved out of the doorway and into the hall, and I could see that the back of his pant leg was torn and bloodstained. We swapped signals, and he let the axe drop to his side.

"Where," I asked, "How did you . . ."

He smiled, slapping the handle of the axe with his palm. "It's a fire precaution," he said. "I found it earlier when I was hiding, and used the fog cover to sneak it into the nearest cell, so that if they caught me—"

"You'd have a way out." I smiled back. A fire axe. Maybe the building was up to code after all. "And pulling it out didn't set off an alarm?"

Dad shook his head. "I think the auditory alarms are suppressed. Was that your doing?"

"Kalif's," I said. "Thank him."

Dad frowned. Clearly he didn't want to be thanking Kalif for anything, even though he should.

I'd save the argument until I had both my parents together. I didn't have time to make it twice. "Where's Mom?"

Dad's head jerked farther down the hall. "This way." He strode in that direction, holding the handle of the axe in one hand, and resting the back of it in the other. He took the axe to the door handle on the other cell. Then he slipped the axe handle through his belt, put his fingers in the hole where the handle had been, and yanked the door toward him.

I got a clear look at Mom before the room filled with fog. I wasn't prepared for what I saw. Mom lay on her back on a metal-framed cot, blood matting her hair. A precise set of thin red lines stretched across her face from her nose to her ear, and she was missing a notch out of her earlobe.

My throat closed up. They'd been cutting her face; the worst thing you could do to a shifter. We could change our flesh to look like anyone, but scars weren't natural. Neither were open wounds. We couldn't hide them; we couldn't shift them.

Even if Mom got laser treatment, she wouldn't be able to look like anyone else for a long, long time. Maybe ever.

If they were willing to use methods like this, no wonder Aida didn't want the Carmines getting their hands on Kalif.

I grabbed Dad by the hand. "Why didn't they do this to you?"

His voice was low. "They wanted one of us they could still threaten," he said. "One of us they could still use. They tortured her and made me watch, unless I'd give them the information they wanted to get to you."

She turned and looked at us, still lying on the cot. At first, I was afraid that she couldn't get up, but then she sat up, as if trying to orient herself. As she did, her whole body shook.

I took a step back. "To *me?* I thought this was all about the murders."

Dad nodded. "It was. But Mel and Aida ratted you out as well."

I stepped back, stunned. That couldn't be right. I'd been living in their house. If they'd wanted to turn me over, they could have done it. "I don't think so," I said. The words tasted bad in my mouth, but I spit them out anyway. "I think they were protecting me."

Dad looked taken aback, and I couldn't blame him. I hadn't believed a word of Aida's speech about how much they wanted to keep me away from Asylum. I thought that had just been an excuse to keep me from pursuing my parents.

I set my jaw. Mel had tried to kill me and Aida had left me for dead. Even the realization that they'd once cared about my safety didn't earn them any good will after *that*.

"What do they want with me?" I asked. "I'm not a murderer."

Dad shook his head. "It's not just about rogue shifters for these people. It's about subduing *any* shifters who aren't under their control."

My heart lodged in my throat. So *that's* why Aida was hiding Kalif. With his knowledge of their missions and technical expertise, he'd be useful to them.

But she was *working* with these people. Shouldn't she *want* to help them out?

Mom seemed to come to her senses, then. "Jory?" she said. "They got to you?" Her hands clawed at the cot frame, and she scooted back on it, as if trying to find a safe corner to hide.

Dad rushed toward her and steadied her in his arms. I stepped forward, and we all exchanged signals.

"It's okay," Dad said. "Jory broke in to find us. We're safe for now but we need to move quickly."

"Let's go," I said. "Now, before it's too late."

Dad moved to scoop my mom up into his arms, but she pushed him away. "I can walk, Dale," she said. "I'm not an invalid." Her limbs shook as she pushed herself to her feet, but she got there, and stood before us, straightening herself up in what I was sure was a show of proof. She wasn't helpless.

But in her eyes, I saw fear, not just of the Carmines, but of the future.

Even if we escaped, how were we going to hide now?

I shook myself and stepped toward the door. There would be time to worry about that later. I'd gotten away from Mel, but this was no time to get reckless. We still had an escape to execute.

As we all moved out into the hallway, I looked at my phone. I didn't have any texts from Kalif. I hoped that meant that things were going well, not that they'd already gone horribly wrong. An image flashed through my mind of Wendy Carmine, holding a razor blade to Kalif's face.

I reached for the nearest wall for support. We needed to get up there, now. There still might be a direct exit—one that wouldn't require us to walk through the lobby to get out. In the hallway, I paused in front of the third door. "Dad," I said. "What's in here?"

I jumped as Dad brushed up against my arm. He was closer than I thought he'd been.

He put a hand on the handle, listening at the door. "I don't know."

I wished that I could safely call Kalif, but without the schematics in front of him, he probably wouldn't be much help. "Open it," I said. "Maybe it's another way out."

Dad took his axe to the door handle and kicked the door in. Then he fumbled on the inside for a light switch.

What appeared before us wasn't an exit, but the next best thing. It was a closet filled with changes of clothes of all sorts and in all sizes. The Carmine's costume wardrobe. Of course they'd have one of those in their basement facility.

Dad clapped me on the back. "Well done," he said. And he grabbed the edge of one wardrobe rack and rifled through it.

Dad tossed us each a set of gender-neutral business casual pants and shirts. That was smart—it would allow for the greatest flexibility as we left the building and got away. I'd drilled fast changes, but my parents had twenty years of field experience on me. They both whipped on their new outfits before I could finish mine.

As we climbed the stairs out of the fog, Mom put a hand on my shoulder. I didn't turn; I couldn't look her in the face without wincing, and I didn't want her to see me react to her like that.

"Where are they?" she asked. "How did you distract them?"

My stomach dropped. I couldn't avoid it any longer. "Kalif is distracting them."

Mom's fingers dug into my bone. "No," she said. "They betrayed us."

"Not *Kalif*," I said. "His parents."

Dad's voice was kind. "You keep saying that," he said. "But you can't be sure—"

I spun around on him, standing a step above so I could look Dad directly in the eye. "Do you see the Carmines swooping down on us?" I asked. "Because Kalif knows what we're doing right now, and if he'd betrayed us, do you think they'd be letting us out of the basement? What possible way could that benefit them?"

Dad hesitated. I was right, and he knew it. When we stepped out of this hallway and onto the main floor of their building, we introduced all kinds of variables to the equation. Down here, they had us cornered. Up there we'd have witnesses, new forms to take, spaces to run, open areas to escape.

So unless Kalif was keeping my confidences, it made no sense for them to let us escape this way. Aida thought Mel had dragged me off, maybe killed me. She wouldn't know that I was down here to come after my parents. They thought we were already contained.

"I'll make you a deal," I said. "If they're waiting for us at the top of the stairs, I'll admit you're right. Maybe Kalif betrayed us and maybe he didn't, but at the very least, we can't trust him. But if I'm right, and the Carmines are really distracted somewhere else, then you have to help me save him."

"Dale," Mom said. She turned toward him, like she'd already decided I was too deluded to convince. "No."

But Dad looked at me intently, like he was actually considering my proposal. Finally, he nodded. "Okay. It's a deal."

Though I still couldn't bring myself to look directly at Mom's face, I could see her out of the corner of my eye, glaring at Dad.

"He really is on our side," I said to Mom. "And he has the proof that you didn't commit any of those murders."

Dad's eyes flicked to Mom, just for an instant.

A sinking sensation settled over me, and I glanced at her, locking down my face, forbidding it to react to the cuts. I was glad that I looked, because otherwise I would have missed the expression that passed over her face. Her cheeks seemed to sink, and her face grew thin. She looked . . . guilty. "Mom?" I said. "I tracked Mel back to the murder of that CEO. You weren't involved . . . right?"

Her whole body seemed to deflate.

I grabbed her by the arm. These murders had taken place years—years that she hadn't even known Mel existed. "But Mel as good as admitted to it," I said. "You couldn't have worked with him."

Dad pulled me away, turning me and marching me up the stairs. "It was a long time ago," he said in a low voice. "It was just once. That's how I met your mother. I was trying to stop her."

For a second, I saw the papers in my hands—the ones with the pictures of Mom's face. The things Mom had told me about the way she met Dad flashed through my mind. She'd been on a job. She'd behaved like an amateur. He'd caught her, and revealed to her that he knew what she was.

The first murder. That *had* been them. Or at least, it had been Mom.

All this time I'd been fighting against Mel, and my own *mother* was a murderer. "You were right," I said quietly. "Maybe I can't trust anyone."

Dad's hands rested heavily on my shoulders. "No," he said to me. "If you believe that, you'll go insane. We're the same people we've been your whole life. Things happened in the past, but that doesn't change the present."

But it *did*, didn't it? I was releasing a murderer into the world.

I took a deep breath, trying to calm myself. Someone who killed a long time ago. Before Dad, Mom had never even met another shifter. He'd changed everything for her; that's what she said.

And when she did, I hadn't even begun to imagine her full meaning.

We stopped in front of the door that led to the first floor of the Systems Development building. Mom stood just behind us. I waited for her to say something to defend herself, but she didn't. She still addressed Dad: "What's the plan?"

Dad handed Mom a set of keys over his shoulders. "I got them in the scuffle. They wouldn't get me through the scanners, but one of them will work in their car."

I felt a pang of guilt for what I'd said. This was exactly why we worked in teams. Why we *had* to trust each other. Because Dad was right—working alone, able to be anyone, was enough to drive a person insane.

Maybe even drive them to murder.

I could work out what that meant for my opinion of Mom later. I was sure it wasn't enough for me to leave her with people who would torture her. For now, that was enough.

"And you?" Mom asked.

Dad's voice was firm. "If we're not caught going through these doors, Jory and I are going to find Kalif."

I gave a sharp nod.

Mom sighed, and Dad reached out to rub her shoulder. He had to keep his promise now. If he didn't, he'd be illustrating my point that I couldn't trust anybody. "Thank you," I said. And I put my hand on the door in front of me, and pushed it open.

TWENTY-FOUR

As I looked into the empty hallway, my heart pounded. The building looked deserted. The lights had all been turned off, so the only illumination came from the upstairs emergency lighting and the sun shining through the glass on the far end of the complex. I'd been in the basement so long that my eyes took a second to adjust to the glare.

Behind me, I could feel Mom and Dad pressing into me, all of us standing at the ready, waiting for the attack.

All seemed quiet. The blinds were drawn in the office windows; all the lights behind them were out. Any employees who were around today must have believed in the active shooter scenario. My gunshots would only have convinced them further.

Sunlight shone through the branches of the surrounding trees, pouring through the glass doors and ceiling-high windows. I looked out the doors, searching for guards, and that's when I saw them.

Kalif had backed himself all the way into the courtyard area just outside the door. Relief flooded over me, but only for a moment. Two people wearing my parents' faces stood in front of him, facing us, pinning him in place.

I stood in the doorway, resisting the urge to hide back in the hall. But the sun was at their backs, and those were mirrored windows. From the outside, they were reflective and opaque. We could see them, but they couldn't see us. They'd backed him into a corner, and stood close enough that if he tried to open the door, they'd be on him in seconds.

Next to Kalif stood an enormous, broad-shouldered man. He stood square on both his legs, so I knew that he couldn't be Mel, who would still be limping, at least, even if he'd managed to clean up his knee.

I recognized the face the man wore from the headshots of Oliver Carmine I'd seen online. I might not have known who he really was if it hadn't been for his trembling posture; the shock and fear on his face was a mirror image of the look that Aida had given me when she told me about Asylum.

I'd never seen her this afraid, though. Her whole body quaked, which, when it had taken a form as tall and broad-shouldered as Oliver Carmine's, made for a combination that would have been comical under happier circumstances.

Aida stood right next to the pane of glass next to the door. She said something to Kalif that was muffled by the glass, but everything in her posture was pleading. She was trying to get him to cooperate, to save his life.

No doubt to switch sides and bring my parents and me down.

I was right. It wasn't a trap. I wondered if Kalif had been forced to intercept them to keep them from coming back into the building and finding us. He must have done this on purpose—chosen a corner of the building where I would find him, but they wouldn't be able to see me.

I couldn't help but be proud of him for that.

Mom craned her neck over my shoulder to get a look at the group of them. She pushed past me out the door, and took a step in the opposite direction. "There has to be an exit this way," she said.

I grabbed Dad by the arm, holding him in the doorway. "You promised," I said. "It's not a trap, and they have him cornered."

Dad paused, assessing the situation. We all held our breath. The Carmines' attention remained fixed on Kalif, and Kalif and Aida's attention were likewise on them.

Then Dad turned to Mom and pointed down the hallway.

"Go out the opposite side and find their car," he said. He turned to me. "Where's the parking lot?"

"North side," I said. I looked over my shoulder at Mom. "We'll meet you there."

Mom didn't look happy, and I couldn't blame her. In the sunlight her cuts didn't look *as* bad, though the Carmines would still recognize her in an instant, and she wouldn't be able to take on any persona without having to give some horrifyingly memorable excuse. She stepped back into the hallway and shifted her hair to be longer and stringier, combing it with her fingers to hang in her face. Then she moved down the hall away from us, to find a way out of the building on the opposite side.

Outside, Kalif extended his hand, angling it toward the door and away from the Carmines. He had something in it—something small and rectangular.

His phone. No doubt that's how he convinced them he was going to send the files to the NSA. He had his finger on the button—one touch away from spilling their secret. At least, he claimed he did. And if anyone could pull that sort of thing together in a rush, it was Kalif.

Dad leaned against the doorway.

"So," he said. "Do you have a plan?"

My pulse picked up. This was my dad. He made plans; I followed them.

And now he was asking *me*?

Dad waited, quietly, and I was afraid that if I didn't come up with something, he'd force me to admit that anything I could do was too dangerous.

I had to think of something.

Aida's shoulder—dressed in one of Oliver's suits—brushed the glass. The pane she stood by stretched to the same height as the doorframe; if the glass was broken, I could step right through it. My fingers brushed the gun in my pocket. Empty, but still a threat to anyone who didn't know that.

I checked Aida's hands and the hands of my fake parents. No

one had a weapon.

"Jory?" Dad said.

I held up a hand for him to wait. I wasn't going to just spout off a plan without thinking it through first.

He was the one who taught me that.

If I put the gun to Aida's head, if I tried to use her as leverage, what would the Carmines do? I might be able to use Aida as a hostage to drag Kalif away. She was their daughter; she worked with them. Even if they didn't care about Aida's life, they wouldn't want to startle the maniac with the gun.

I needed a persona, one they would believe was both competent and dangerous. And I knew of one competent, dangerous person they all ought to be at least a little bit afraid of. A maniac who might be motivated to drag his family out of a dangerous situation, and would be willing to put a gun to his own wife's head to do it.

I shifted my face and body to look like Mel. "Is this convincing?" I asked, turning my profile to Dad.

He raised his new eyebrows at me. "Good," he said. "Nice sneer. But what are you going to do?"

I pulled the gun out of my pocket and into my hand.

Dad looked down at it with alarm.

"It's not loaded," I whispered. "But I'm going to use it to threaten Aida and get Kalif out. Can you break the window with the axe? And cover my back?"

While he still eyed the gun nervously, Dad nodded in approval. "That could work," he said.

My breath left me. "Really?" I said.

Dad put a hand on my shoulder. "You do good work," he said. "I'm proud of you."

And even though Kalif was still in danger, I couldn't help but smile. For a split second, I let myself enjoy the squeeze of Dad's hand on my shoulder. He was proud of me. And impressed enough to follow my lead.

I shook myself. Focus now; preen later. When I peeked out

at them again, I saw my fake father's foot crunch down on something small and black. Bits of plastic shot out from under his shoe.

Kalif's phone. His *leverage*.

The Carmines had gotten it away from him. Now he didn't have anything to bargain with. There were three of them and one of him; he'd be trapped here. I couldn't let that happen. We were leaving here, together. All of us.

I twisted Mel's mouth into a cruel smile. It might not fool them, but it was only for effect. The gun was the ticket. I couldn't shoot anyone with it, but I could put on a show.

And I was a shifter. Shows were what we did best.

Dad tightened his hands around the axe. I readied the pistol in my palm. We left the doorway and moved up to the mirrored glass. The sun still shone at the Carmines' backs, increasing the glare. They wouldn't be able to see us until we touched the glass.

Dad shifted his face into a persona I'd never seen—a Hispanic man with a thick brow ridge. He stepped to the side of the windows, hiding in the corner of the building at an angle where he could break the glass, but keep himself hidden.

I could get a good look at my fake parents' faces now. They looked angry—a sign that things weren't going as planned. They both held their hands at their sides, tense and at the ready.

"Now," I said.

Dad nodded, pulled the axe back over his shoulder, and brought the flat butt of it down on the glass with all of his might.

Aida jumped about a foot as the glass rained down into the courtyard. That gave me the opening I needed, and I counted one second, making sure to follow the falling glass, instead of stepping under it.

I stepped through the empty pane, my feet crunching on puzzle-shaped pieces of glass as sunlight danced off them and reflected up onto Aida's face.

And then I wrapped a thick arm around her shoulders, one

hand at her throat, the other bringing the pistol up to her head. I turned my voice into Mel's. "No one moves," I shouted. "Or I'll kill her."

Behind me, I heard Dad swear. A quick glance behind me told me he was watching the reflection of the scene in a broken shard of glass that leaned against the frame of the door. My eyes darted up, looking for what caused him to react.

I saw it immediately. In the seconds it took me to step through the glass, both of the Carmines had drawn guns, and were pointing them squarely at Aida and me.

My throat closed up. We weren't supposed to kill people. Why were *all* of the other shifters carrying guns? Were these people just as sociopathic as Mel?

Was everyone who was not me a murderer?

I knew I should be talking now, but I couldn't so much as squeak. I stood behind Aida, at the wrong end of not one but two pistols. They were smaller and darker than the one in my hand, but no doubt these two were loaded.

All the blood drained from my face. I dragged my eyes away from the guns long enough to see the hardened looks on my fake parents' faces.

They were going to kill us—all four of us—and sort out their cover up later.

TWENTY-FIVE

I recovered from the sight of the weapons as quickly as I could, but I was sure my look of surprise had been obvious. I was giving away my fear, when I should have been presenting a cool, calm front.

I tried to talk myself down now. Just because the Carmines *could* shoot us didn't mean they *would*. They were supposed to be interested in justice, right? Not killing.

I didn't believe myself, but at least I kept my gun hand from shaking.

Over the Carmines' shoulders, I saw movement between two buildings. Mom had made her way from the parking lot. She was behind them, but too far away to reach us in a hurry. Her eyes widened as she looked over my shoulder at Dad.

I knew what she had to be thinking. What the hell had we done?

I swallowed, hard. This could still work. It depended on my performance, now. It depended on Kalif, and on Aida.

I tightened my hand at her neck, the way that Mel had done to me. "I'm taking my son," I growled in Mel's voice. "You people are crazy. You've always been crazy, and we're not working with any of you anymore." I jabbed the tip of the pistol into Aida's temple, hoping to influence her to plead my case, but she didn't. She just let out a pitiful mewling noise, like a frightened kitten, and her knees buckled from underneath her.

I tightened Mel's arm around Aida's shoulders, and prayed

that it was me she was afraid of.

But what happened next made me certain that it wasn't.

The Carmines held their weapons steady, and started shooting. Later, I would realize that Dad must have already been moving. I don't know what he'd seen that I hadn't—some subtle twitch of her arm muscles, some near-imperceptible shift of his stance. Some indication that the Carmines were ready to shoot that motivated even my pacifist father to violence. Dad flew around me with his axe raised, his feet sliding on the bits of glass as he careened toward them.

A crack deafened me. The next thing I knew, Dad fell backward, and I shoved Aida aside, putting my arms out instinctively to catch him.

Afterward, I would try to count the gun shots, but I'd never be sure if there was one or many. All I felt was his weight bearing down on me. I stumbled back, dropping my father on top of a squirming Aida, whose massive frame seemed to shrink under his weight. I blinked as wet droplets flew into my face, and I stared down at the red, sticky mess that speckled my shirt, Dad's neck. Shards of metal had lodged themselves in his jaw, tearing away the flesh from the bone.

The bullets might as well have hit me, because I could feel them tearing my own heart to shreds, leaving a bloody mess where my family should have been.

When I looked up at the spot where I'd seen Mom, she was moving toward the car. I could see her mouthing something, but silence rang in my ears. It was only when the Carmines turned toward her that I realized she must have been shouting. She must have been telling me what to do.

Over the tide of panic that welled up inside me, I knew what she wanted.

She was telling me to run.

As my hearing returned, I became aware of Kalif shouting at me as well, though I couldn't tear my eyes away from Dad's face. His eyes didn't so much close as shrink, pulling back into his head. His nose retracted, cartilage flattening. His lips shriveled together, leaving nothing but twisted flesh where they had once been, ending in a bloody torn hole where one half of his chin should have been.

"Dad!" I shouted.

Then I felt a tug on my arm as Kalif ripped the gun from my hand and pointed it at the Carmines. I looked up in time to see their guns point at him, their faces hardened, ready to shoot again. I scrambled toward him, trying to block their shot to him the way Dad had done for me.

But Aida got there first. Her body had shrunk to her normal size, her face shifted into a bizarre mix of her own and Oliver's. Soaked in my father's blood, she threw herself bodily at my fake mother, clawing at her gun. The impact knocked them both into my fake father, throwing him off balance.

Kalif grabbed me by the arm, pulling me physically from Dad. His hand found mine, and we exchanged signals faster than I ever had before in my life. "Run," he said in my ear. "Just run."

My real Mom ran toward the parking lot, pointing furiously at me to show me where to meet her. I could feel the wave of anguish drawing up to its peak, ready to crash down on me, pulling me under into oblivion.

I couldn't let it. I had to keep moving. I stood on shaking knees, and forced my body to move.

Fake mom buffed up her arm and threw Aida to the concrete behind her. Kalif and I turned toward the parking lot just as the copy of my father regained his footing and brought his gun up to shoot us. My shoes pounded the pavement, leaving behind a trail of Dad's blood. Shots rang out behind us.

Behind me, I heard Aida scream: "Stop it! Leave him alone!"

A sickening smacking sound followed, but not a gunshot. They might have been willing to kill her to get to me, but now they were going to beat her. Why ruin a perfectly good tool, I supposed, when they could keep her to use another day.

274

We left him there. Everything in me wanted to go back for my father. His face might be gone, but it was still his body. We couldn't *leave* him there.

I forced myself not to turn back.

If I went back for him, I'd join him. That wasn't what he would have wanted.

As we reached the curb, Kalif looked back over his shoulder, and I was afraid that he would turn back for his mother—I could tell from her cries that she was still very much alive. But instead, he wove across the parking lot in a zigzag pattern as more gunshots followed behind us.

My training came back to me—the things Dad had told me about how to avoid getting shot. I could hear his voice in my head, steadying me, rehearsing the things I'd been taught: Hand guns aren't that accurate. Don't run in a straight line. Get behind obstacles, preferably the kind you can't shoot through. Above all, *keep moving.*

So we did. I waited for the pain in my back, for the force that would sprawl me out onto the pavement, for the bullets that would rip through the flesh of my back and leave me as empty and blank as my father's dead face.

My stomach twisted and my mouth watered. I was going to be sick.

Ahead of us, I saw Mom climbing into the driver's seat of an SUV that was parked along a curb. Mom leaned far forward in her seat, scanning for us. When I turned to look over my shoulder, I could see the fake version of my father following, gun raised.

Mom didn't wait to check our hands. She just threw open the rear passenger door as we raced for the car. Kalif and I leapt across the bench seat in the back, and Mom wheeled down off the curb and across the parking lot before we managed to get the door shut.

My hands felt sticky. I looked down to find them smeared with blood. The whole front of my shirt was splattered with it.

As I sat there, I became aware of the droplets clinging to my face, my hair, my eyelashes.

Dad's blood.

If I washed it off, what would be left of him?

I had nothing, not a picture, not a sentimental gift. We couldn't afford attachments like that.

But that meant all I had left of my father was the way he stained me.

I shivered.

The whole car reeked of copper, with the extra burning edge of gunpowder. As Mom peeled out of the parking lot, I became aware of the blood on Kalif's arms, probably from when he pulled me away. Wind rushed through the missing driver's side window, and Kalif rolled his down, creating a cross-breeze, clearing the air.

Kalif took my hand, not even reacting to the blood.

After she hit the main road, Mom extended her hand back and we all exchanged signals. She opened the glove box and came up with a packet of Kleenex. "Try to get clean," she said to me.

I had to. Trying to hold onto his blood would be seriously warped. I stripped down to my tank top, spitting on the tissues and trying to get rid of the blood. "Stop that," Kalif said. "You're just smearing it."

I twisted around in my seat, scanning behind us. But no more cars tore out of the parking lot.

My heart began to slow. We'd done it.

"They'll be following us," Mom said.

I searched the road again, but the cars following us had all come from farther up the road. We turned one corner, and then another.

"I don't think so," I said. "We took their car. It probably took them a moment to find another one."

"We need to keep moving," Mom said. Her voice raced, as if trying to outrun the truth along with the Carmines. "They won't stop that easily."

"Mom," I said. "I think we've lost them for now. We should slow down. Make a plan."

Mom shook her head so hard that her hair tossed over her shoulders. "They said no one escapes. They said—"

I turned back around in my seat, and put a hand on her shoulder. The bottom of our lives had dropped out from under us and we were in free fall.

Mom would be feeling it even more than I was. "Mom," I said. "I'm sorry about Dad."

In the rearview mirror, I saw Mom's lip quiver. That's what this was about. She wanted to stay in crisis, to use the adrenaline to push through, to numb the pain. We both knew that as soon as we stopped, we were going to feel it.

But we had to think through this situation clearly, just like always.

That's what Dad would have done.

I glanced over my shoulder one last time. "They may not be following, but they'll be able to track the car. We need to park it somewhere."

"The train station," Kalif said. "We can leave the car and go anywhere from there."

Mom shook her head. "No good. The train goes in a straight line. We need someplace bigger. Someplace with crowds. Someplace we can get clothes."

"The water park," I said. It had just opened a few weeks ago. "Crowds and locker rooms. Clothes left lying around."

Dad and I had gone there last fall, right before they closed for the season. We'd tubed down the tallest water slides until we weren't certain our SPF fifty waterproof sunscreen was working anymore. Neither of us could afford a sunburn—we wouldn't be able to shift it—and I remembered scrutinizing Dad's nose for signs that it was time to stop. His nose, that withdrew into his face and left him entirely blank.

I shivered. Kalif ran his fingers over my shoulders.

And then, for the second time that day, one of my parents accepted my plan as the best course of action. Mom pulled onto the freeway, headed in the direction of the water park.

I looked down at my hands. "We need to find a gas station first," I said. "One with a bathroom outside."

"In the meantime," Kalif said. "You better stay down." I let him guide me down, resting my head on his knees, looking up at the tops of the trees as they passed by outside the windows. I was aware of Kalif watching behind us, and Mom stopping for red lights and changing lanes without weaving. I hoped that meant she was calming down. I could feel tears building under the surface. I needed Mom to help me, to do the good spy thing and hold it together with me, because I wasn't going to be able to keep them at bay forever.

If Dad were here, he would be the strong one. He'd hold things together for both of us. If I hadn't insisted that we save Kalif, he would be. But in that situation, likely as not, Kalif would be the one who was dead, instead. And did I really wish I'd made *that* trade?

I traced a slow circle with one finger around Kalif's knee, following the way the car seemed to spin around me. It was a terrible question—the kind with no answer. What I wanted was never to have had cause to ask it.

I looked at Mom's hands, her nails etching grooves into the sides of the steering wheel. If it wasn't for me, they'd both be dead. Kalif and I were a team. Of course I went back for him— that's what Mom would have done, if Dad were the one who was trapped.

And in the end, Dad approved of that. In the end, he stood by me. He had my back. In that situation, he trusted me to handle whatever was going to come our way.

Now, that had to include handling his death. I closed my eyes, listening to the hum of the wheels against the road. And then I realized what Dad must have seen in me, standing there in the hall.

If I could run a successful job against four experienced shifters, I could handle anything.

Even this.

We drove in silence down the highway until the twisting waterslides came into view. Mom found a gas station down the block with a drive-thru car wash. She pulled the car into the tunnel, out of sight of the street and the storefront.

I climbed out of the car and stood, letting the water wash away the blood. The spray was so strong, I felt like it might take my skin with it. I took advantage of the moment out of sight to shift into someone younger, a child who could pass by unnoticed. The form felt unnatural, though, and I had to focus to hold on to it. After everything that had happened in the last few days, it was hard to even pretend to be a child.

I climbed back into the car before the soap started, and when the wash was done Mom pulled around behind the car wash. In the trunk, she unearthed several changes of clothes. I should have known they'd be there. This was a shifter car. We kept changes in ours, always.

We all ducked down into the car, changing faces and clothes. We left the car with the keys still in the ignition and snuck around the back to walk up the block to the amusement park. Water dripped from my hair, but the sun beat down on me, drying it. A sopping wet girl was less conspicuous than a bloody one.

Kalif led us straight up to the gates and bought tickets with cash. We probably could have snuck in, but there was no need to risk it when we could just pay. Once we walked through the gates and became part of the crowd, Mom slipped into the coin-op locker rooms to pick locks and fish through unattended bags to come up with enough clothes for us all to change again.

I pulled Kalif into one of the family changing rooms—the one room kind with a locking door. Here, away from eyes and cameras, we shifted our faces into ourselves and rested them together.

Kalif kissed my forehead and whispered, "I'm so sorry about your dad."

"We saved my mother," I said. She might be scarred and unable to do her job, possibly forever, but at least she was alive.

My eyes were still dry, though we were safe enough now to cry. If they'd managed to follow close behind us, they'd have caught us by now. We'd change clothes and then faces again and then disappear, which was what we were born to do.

"That's true," Kalif said. "But I didn't think it would happen like this."

A knot hardened in my stomach. This wasn't how things were supposed to go at all. We were going to free my parents, and then we'd run off. They'd be together; we'd be together. But now instead of four, we were three.

And that meant the plan had to change. "I can't leave my mom now," I said. "Not with her face the way it is, not after she just lost my dad."

Kalif nodded. "Of course. We can talk about that later."

"No," I said. "We have to talk about it now."

"Can't we do this after you're settled somewhere?" His voice was pleading.

And that's when I knew he knew. We weren't going to run away together like we'd planned. The truth of that sat in my stomach like a stone.

Dad had believed me about trusting Kalif, but Mom hadn't liked it. And now, that very thing had gotten him killed. Kalif couldn't come with Mom, and I couldn't leave her.

And that meant we had to split up.

"What are you going to do?" I asked.

He sighed, his arms circling my waist. "I have to go back for my mother," he said.

I pushed away from him. "You can't go back into that mess. They'll *kill* you."

He shook his head. "She won't let them find me. She and I have an arrangement—a place to meet that even Dad doesn't know about."

I shivered. "Really? Do you think she knew then, what your dad was capable of?"

Kalif shuddered. "She lived with him for two decades. I don't think she was willing to admit what she knew, even to herself."

I shook my head. "I don't like it. I don't want you putting yourself in danger without me to watch your back. Your mom could be dead. Or they might have locked her up like my parents. You're not thinking of breaking back in there."

Kalif looked down at the floor. "No. Not on my own, at least. I'll just go check to see if she shows. If she doesn't, I'll contact you, okay? And I'm not leaving yet. I'll help you and your mom first."

Even I couldn't believe what I was about to say. "No," I said. "Mom doesn't trust you. She's probably already planning how we're going to get rid of you."

Kalif gave me a pleading look. "I don't want to leave you like this."

I leaned against his chest, and his arms tightened around me. "Just tell me how it works out," I said. "Just tell me a story with a happy ending."

He paused, and for a horrifying moment, I thought maybe he couldn't think of one. But then he leaned down and spoke in my ear. "You'll take care of your mom. You'll do that until she's okay. I'll find my mom, and make sure she's the same. And when we're done, we'll meet up. It isn't forever. It's just a delay."

Trapped tears burned behind my eyes. I buried them in his sleeve. It wasn't fair of me to cry while I was asking him to walk away. "But I won't be able to contact you. Even if I email you, the Carmines might track it. They know you exist now. They'll be watching." I didn't add that Aida was just as likely to turn me over. The bruises at my throat proved her desire to protect Kalif didn't extend as far as protecting me.

Kalif pulled a pen from his pocket, found a torn bit of a receipt on the ground, and scribbled something on it. "This is an email address I've never accessed from home. Send an email to it when you need me. Let me know where you are, or how to reach you."

I stared at the paper. Getting separated hadn't been part of the plan. "When did you make that?" I asked. "Didn't you mean to leave with me?"

Kalif's eyes burned into mine. "I did. But the longer I thought about it, the more I thought lots of things could happen that might separate us, once we got your parents. Not this, though. I never thought about this."

That's the way we'd worked, him and me. We just kept charging forward like things would always go our way. And even now, after facing the consequences, I didn't know what else to do but continue that way.

I looked at the paper, memorizing the address in case I had to leave it behind. Then I squeezed his shoulder. "Okay," I said. "I'll send you an email as soon as we land somewhere. Be watching."

We were both quiet, then. Both waiting for the other one to say that this was a bad idea. That we should forget about everyone else and just run off together like we planned. But I didn't want Kalif to always regret not going back for his mother. And I couldn't leave mine, not when she'd just lost Dad.

"I love you," I said.

Kalif smiled. "You, too."

The idea of carrying on without him or my dad, just Mom and me trying to find a new kind of normal, was enough to break my heart like he was already gone. How long would it be, before it would be right for me to contact him, and for him to answer?

Kalif must have sensed that I was wavering, because he turned my chin so he could look me in the eyes. "We will always find each other. I know it seems like you can't count on anything right now, but you can count on that."

And in that moment, I believed him. What else could I do?

Kalif kissed me, long and slow, and I tried to memorize the sound of his breathing, the warmth of his body. I stored up the feeling of his hands on my back, his mouth against mine.

I was going to need these memories—the reminders of something true and good. The reality of my father's death hadn't hit me yet, not fully. I knew already that it was going to seep into my soul slowly, like a drafty chill. Kalif couldn't be there to help me through it. He couldn't be there for me like he had been for the last few days. The memory of this wasn't going to be enough to take the pain away.

But I already knew holding onto it was going to help.

When we left the changing room, I could see Mom watching us, a bag of clothes tucked up under her arm. She wasn't close enough to eavesdrop at the door, but she'd be learning things just by watching us now.

"Don't come back after you change," I whispered to him. "That's your chance to get away." He squeezed my hand in response, and I did the brave thing. I pulled away and led him over to Mom.

Mom distributed some clothes, all the while watching Kalif. The way she eyed him, I knew we were making the right choice. I couldn't risk letting him stay.

Not for any of our sakes.

Kalif took a step away, headed for the men's locker room. "Let's meet by the front gates," Mom said. And Kalif nodded, not giving Mom any indication that he had no intention of showing up. He looked down at the clothes in my hands: shorts and a fresh tank top, as if noting them. Then he squeezed my hand, and I turned around, watching him go.

If Mom sensed that we were saying goodbye, she didn't comment. She just pulled me into the girl's locker room and toward the largest stall. When the tall door was closed behind us, she turned me to look at her. The cuts on her face looked redder and angrier now. We'd need to stop by a pharmacy for supplies—she couldn't afford an infection.

"I want to see your face," she said.

No one could see us in here. I faded into myself, and she did the same. Mom ran a hand under my chin. "You look older," she said. Then she pulled me into a hug.

Older though I might look, I could feel the little girl part of me bubble up, and my eyes filled with tears. "You were gone so long," I said. "I thought you were dead."

And even though I knew that Mom was hurting even worse than I was, her voice was calm and comforting, like the way she spoke to me when I was a little girl. "I would have been, if you hadn't come for us."

And there it was. We did it, Kalif and me. We found Mom and Dad. We got them both out. If it weren't for us, they'd both be dead, or worse.

But somehow, I still ended up with only one of the people that I loved.

Mom's hands gripped my shoulders. "How did you *do* that?" she asked. "That facility was secure. How did you even know where to look?"

I staggered. The story was too complex to tell here, or maybe ever. "I just did what you taught me to do," I said.

And as Mom nodded, I realized that I stood an inch taller than her. I wasn't just older; I'd grown taller, too.

The edges of her mouth turned up at the corners, in the closest thing she could muster to a smile.

And that's when I knew, even though she didn't say.

It wasn't just Dad I'd impressed. Mom was proud of me, too.

When she pulled away, she fidgeted with her stolen clothes. "I know you and Kalif are involved, but we still can't trust him."

"It's okay," I said. "He's not going to meet us. He's going back for his mother."

Mom sighed. "That's for the best."

She sounded relieved, like I was finally taking the advice she'd given me, and stepping away from Kalif for good. I knew she was right—this was for the best—but not for the reasons she was thinking.

Mom and I turned away from each other, shedding our clothing and sizing our bodies to match the new sets. The shorts and tank top were much smaller than my usual—this persona was going to have to be young again, if I didn't want her to look like her clothes had shrunk in the wash.

I sighed as I put them on. People would be coming back for these clothes—real people who needed them. This was the opposite of what I wanted to be doing—more stealing, more hurting other people. I'd never felt that way about stolen clothes before—obviously my parents and I had done much worse.

This wasn't how I wanted things to be. But for today, we had to survive.

When we walked out of the room, I couldn't help looking around for Kalif. He might not have worn the clothes that Mom picked for him, choosing instead to procure his own. He could have been anyone, anywhere. As we pushed into the crowd, an overweight man in a wife-beater passed me, and for a split second, his fingers brushed mine. I looked over my shoulder at him as he disappeared toward the entrance to the park.

He turned around and looked at me, too. And, for a moment, I saw him smile.

I got the message. This wasn't goodbye. Aida said no one escaped from the Carmines. But *we* escaped. We saved my mother. We held on to each other when everyone else wanted to drive us apart with doubts.

We'd keep escaping. We'd keep holding on. Against the odds, I felt more sure of that than I ever had before.

Kalif and I would be together again.

I could count on that.

ACKNOWLEDGMENTS

First thanks on this book are due to Brandon Sanderson, who went far out of his way to support this book. I am forever in his debt, and there's no nicer person to be indebted to. Thank you, as always, for your friendship.

Thanks always to Isaac Stewart, for his advice, his expertise, and his friendship.

Thanks to Eddie Schneider for his tireless championing of my work, and especially of this book.

My writing group—the Seizure Ninjas—read several different endings to this book, and never complained. Thank you for your excellent feedback. This book would not exist in its final form without you.

My beta readers, including Kathy Cowley and Megan Grey, gave excellent feedback on this book. I know there were more of you. Thank you.

As always, I am grateful to my amazing editor and incredible cover designer—Kristina Kugler and Melody Fender. You girls make me look far better at this than I am. Thank you.

And last of all, thank you to my husband and daughter, whose patience for my craziness seems to be without limit. Love you.

Janci Patterson is the author of two contemporary young adult novels: *Everything's Fine* and *Giftchild*. This is her first science fiction novel. For more about Janci, visit her online at jancipatterson.com.

Also by Janci Patterson

Everything's Fine
Giftchild

CPSIA information can be obtained
at www.ICGtesting.com
Printed in the USA
FSHW04n1055260218
45030FS

9 781516 999422